RUNNING
SCARED
LCR ELITE

BY CHRISTY REECE

Running Scared

An LCR Elite Novel

Published by Christy Reece

Cover Art by Patricia Schmitt/Pickyme

Copyright 2016 by Christy Reece

ISBN: 978-0-9967666-1-6

To obtain permission to excerpt portions of the text, please contact the author at Christy@christyreece.com.

PROLOGUE

Eight years ago

She was free!

She had told herself this day would come. Over and over again, she had repeated the mantra that had given her hope, the will to survive. She had told herself that she would one day escape. That there would be one moment of inattention. One moment when *he* wouldn't be around, the servants would be distracted, an opening would present itself, and she would be able to find her way out. She had almost given up, almost believed it would never happen.

Had there been other opportunities, and she had missed them? It shamed her that this might be true. She had been drifting in a state of despair and pain for so long, she had stopped looking for an opening. But after his declaration tonight, she'd had three choices. Accept that she would be tied to a monster forever, kill herself and end her misery, or find a way to get the hell out of there. In her mind, there had been only one acceptable choice. If she died in her attempt, then so be it. At least she would not have died a coward.

The click of her heels against the asphalt had her looking down at her clothing. A floral patterned dress and three-inch heels weren't exactly travel wear, but she didn't care. She counted herself fortunate that her opportunity had come when she was wearing something decent. There had been too many times that she had—

No, she wouldn't think about that now. She was free, and that was all that mattered.

A different kind of fear hit her as she abruptly took in her surroundings. She had been so focused on getting away that she hadn't given thought to where she was going. Where was she? All around her were tall buildings—skyscrapers. And people. So many people. For so long she had existed in silence. All the noises together, the traffic rushing by, people chattering on their cellphones or with each other, horns blowing, machinery grinding. The cacophony of sounds was deafening.

She wanted to ask someone the location but feared what might happen if she did. What if they thought she was crazy for not knowing where she was? What if they took her to the police? Her heart beat faster as panic threatened. Maybe they knew him. Maybe they would call him and he'd come for her. What would he do to her this time? The one and only time she had tried to leave, he had...

No. No, she couldn't take the risk. She drew in a deep, calming breath to settle herself down. She would just walk around until something looked familiar. It was as simple as that.

As if she were just another person and knew exactly where she was and had a destination in mind, she blended with a crowd waiting at a traffic light. When they went, she went. When they stopped, she stopped. It wasn't until she'd walked several blocks that she realized that none of the conversations taking place around her were in English. How was that possible? Everyone at the mansion had spoken English. Although he'd had an accent, he had always spoken English. She had thought she was in the US.

Skidding to a stop, she ignored the irritated grumbles coming from the people who bumped into her, almost ran over her. She assumed they cursed her. Raising her head, she looked at signs above businesses. She recognized a few of the letters. An old saying popped into her head: It's all Greek to me. And it was true. The signs above her were written in Greek. Did that mean she was in Greece? If so, what city? She didn't speak the language. How was she going to find someone she could communicate with? Someone who wouldn't turn her in?

The blare of a ship horn startled her. She glanced to her left and realized she was close to the docks. Giant cargo ships, small boats, and cruise ships were lined up in a neat row. At the very end, a ferry was slowly shuttling away from the dock.

Disappointment swamped her. That would have been her best bet to escape. Even though she had no money, she might've been able to sneak onto the ferry and hide in one of the cars. It would probably return in a few hours, but she couldn't wait around. She had to find a place to hide.

Another loud blare came, this one from a giant vessel at the end of the dock. A cruise ship. It was large, at least ten stories high, and would hold hundreds, if not thousands, of people. Could she sneak onto the ship? It was so big she could stay hidden until they reached another port of call. She didn't care where it took her. As long as it was far away from *him*, that was all she cared about. She had to try!

Her mind made up, she headed toward the ship. For the first time in her life, she made a decision for herself. It didn't matter where she was going, and a part of her didn't care if she lived through the adventure. She only knew that she was at last free. If freedom meant death, then she would accept her fate. She had no fear of death, not if the alternative was to be returned to him.

Going back to that monster was something she would never do.

CHAPTER ONE

Sinjar, Iraq
Nineveh Province

Shots whizzed by, dimpling the crusty dry ground, pinging the rusted abandoned cars around them. Riley Ingram forced herself to stay focused. She was tempted, oh so tempted, to turn around and look. Even more tempted to turn around and return fire.

Breath rasped from her aching lungs. Bruised ribs from a training exercise last week throbbed with an unceasing ache. They hadn't expected this kind of action. What should've been a low-risk op to gather intel had turned inside out in seconds.

"Dammit, Ingram. Move it!" her partner, Justin Kelly, roared. "I'm going to be very pissed off if you get shot today. Haul ass! And I mean…now!"

Too busy trying to save said ass to be offended, Riley ground her teeth and kept running. Justin was several feet behind her, firing random shots. Killing any of the scum-suckers chasing them wasn't in their plan, but neither was getting shot at in the first place. Dammit, she should have figured out another way.

"Head north," Justin shouted. "Fox and Thorne are waiting."

Without a break in her stride, she veered north. If either she or Justin were injured, the chances of them surviving were slim to none. These thugs were out for blood, and thanks to her screw-up, something even worse than a bullet awaited her if she was caught.

She'd already made a mess of this op. She was absolutely not going to get her partner killed, too.

Gritting her teeth, Riley gave it all she had.

Justin was breathing down her neck, almost even with her. She spared a glance back. In an instant, Riley comprehended his thoughts, his body language. She'd seen that fierce, protective look in his eyes too often not to recognize it. He was considering doing something stupid, like hauling her over his shoulder. Which would slow him down. No!

Reaching for her last ounce of adrenaline, she surged forward.

Didn't matter. Her partner was stronger, faster, with an indomitable will that wouldn't back down. He would do what he felt was right, one hundred percent of the time. Without any seeming extra effort, he reached out and pulled her off her feet. Half carrying her, half dragging her, he raced toward the black SUV on the other side of a rusted fence.

Stopping abruptly, Justin released his hold on her and yanked out his wire clippers. Riley whirled around and fired shots in the direction of the men running toward them. The bullets struck the ground just short of their feet, right where she wanted them to.

"Let's go," Justin growled.

Getting off one last round, Riley went through the opening her partner had created. The instant she was on the other side, she resumed shooting. Justin slipped through behind her, then pulled her with him toward their rescue vehicle barreling toward them.

The SUV squealed to a stop, and the doors popped open. Aidan Thorne grabbed Riley's hand and dragged her into the back with him. Justin leaped into the front seat. Sabrina Fox was behind the wheel. The instant they were inside, she tore down the road.

"Everybody okay?" Sabrina asked.

His heart still thundering in his chest, Justin Kelly twisted round to check on his partner. That had been too close for comfort. Riley's face was a stark-white mask. This should have been an easy op of intel gathering and nothing more. That kick to her ribs a week or so ago wasn't healed yet. Even though they'd expected no trouble, he should've suggested she sit this one out. He knew better than anyone that unexpected shit happens.

Knowing she would resent being babied, Justin growled, "Ingram, you want to answer the question?"

"I'm fine," Riley gasped out. "Just a few twinges in my side."

Justin didn't even bother to argue. He knew she was in pain, but until they could get to safety, none of them could do anything about it.

"I'm sorry, Justin. I overreacted, and it blew up in our face."

He noted three distinct things. First, she had called him Justin, something so rare he could count on one hand the number of times it had occurred. Second, she had apologized to him in front of other operatives. Riley Ingram didn't show vulnerability. Ever. And third, she had *apologized*.

The last was the thing that pissed him off.

"What are you apologizing for?" he snarled. "Fighting for your life or fighting to keep from being raped?"

"If I hadn't slugged that guy, none of this—"

Justin held up a hand, stopping more idiotic words from coming. "Let me get this straight. You think I'm upset that you didn't allow those bastards to attack you while I stood by and watched?"

"Well…no. I just—"

He leaned over the back of his seat and got in her face, more furious than he'd ever been in his life. "Listen and listen good, Ingram. The day I stand back and let my partner get attacked just to save my ass is the day I walk away from this job for good. You got that? You did the right thing."

As if realizing their conversation had gotten a little more intense than she'd planned, she nodded and clamped her mouth shut.

Breaking the tension, Thorne asked, "So, you guys want to tell us what *did* happen?"

Justin gave a frustrated one-shouldered shrug. "Got blindsided on our way to the meet. Five dirtbags thought they'd get their kicks by harassing two strangers. When they realized Ingram was female, they got other ideas."

"I should've kept my mouth shut."

Justin glared at her and then cursed himself for doing so. She didn't need any more blame put on her. She was doing a damn good job of that all by herself. Ever since she'd been injured last year, her confidence level had dipped. And lately…lately he didn't know what the hell was going on with her.

"Dressing like a guy was your best defense, Riley," Sabrina said. "Don't beat yourself up. It should've worked."

As small and slight as Riley was, they'd had no choice but to dress her as a young boy. The bullies had seen someone smaller. While two of them had tried to distract Justin, the other three had gone after Riley. Their intent had been to harass and intimidate, probably to rob. When they'd looked closer, saw the delicacy of her features and realized she was female, their intent had taken on a darker tone.

Facing the front again, he pulled out his cellphone. "We need to let Malak know what happened."

"Already done," Thorne said. "He texted that you hadn't shown up. We figured there was trouble, so we made the appointment across town." He checked his watch. "In about twenty minutes."

"Good," Riley said. "We'll keep the same plan as before."

A tense silence filled the vehicle. Justin knew that both Sabrina and Thorne were waiting for him to object. He should. Not only was his partner hurting physically, she'd lost even more confidence. And that was exactly why he wasn't going to object. Even though he'd always known much of Riley's tough attitude was a self-defense mechanism, she needed to regain her equilibrium. Coddling her would further erode her confidence.

And bottom line, he trusted his partner. If she believed she was up to the task, then he damn well believed it, too.

"Sounds good," Justin said.

He dared a look behind him. The relief on Riley's face reinforced his thoughts. Now to get the information they'd come for and get out without bloodshed.

Riley allowed herself to relax back against the seat. The car weaved in and out of traffic with an ease she admired. Sabrina navigated the narrow streets as if she'd been born here. Riley kept her eyes open for possible threats, grateful to be in the company of some of the most competent LCR operatives she knew.

LCR leader Noah McCall had chosen each operative on the Elite team for his or her talents and skills. She was only one of a handful without military or covert experience. The biggest reason she was even a member of the Elite team was sitting in the front seat—two hundred twenty pounds of aggravated male. Though he wasn't known for his easygoing attitude or friendly expression at any time, today Justin Kelly's granite-like expression would rival even the fiercest of ancient warlords. He was worried about her, and when he worried, he had a tendency to act like a hungry bear with a bee up his butt.

She and Justin became LCR partners before the Elite team was formed. He was former special ops and by rights should have had a partner with the same level of experience. But from the moment of their first assignment together, they'd worked as if they'd been with each other for years. They had a connection she couldn't explain. She only knew that when in the midst of action, they read each other as if they were of one mind. Noah had told them he wasn't about to mess with a winning team.

Riley reminded herself of her own competence. Even though she didn't feel particularly capable at this moment, she knew she could get herself out of any situation. She'd been through too much, escaped hell to become a lethal operative for the most well-known and admired rescue organization in the world. Not only would she not let LCR or her partner down, she refused to let herself down.

"Okay." Aidan pointed toward an abandoned, ramshackle structure. "There's the place where Malak told us to meet him."

"I'll let you guys out about a half block away, drive a few blocks," Sabrina said. "We'll be back to get you in five. Radio us if we need to get back sooner."

Justin gave Riley a quick once-over. "Stay beside me. If things go sour again, I want you to get out ASAP. I'll handle the jerks this time."

She wanted to argue, but now was not the time. Lives depended upon them getting this information and in a timely manner. They couldn't miss this opportunity. There would be a chance later to discuss this new autocratic position he'd taken.

Riley adjusted her clothing, then opened her door and stepped out. Justin got out behind her and then stood in front of her as he assessed the danger.

She huffed out an exasperated breath. "Dammit, Kelly, get out of my way."

"Zip it, Ingram. We can talk about my overbearing ways later. Right now your ribs are hurting and you're not at full capacity. I take the lead, or you get back in the car. Your choice."

"Fine," Riley snapped.

"Looks clear. Let's move."

They went down the broken sidewalk together, both appearing to stare straight ahead while still scanning for threats. Stopping at the meeting site, Justin took one more sweeping glance and then eased the door open. Riley stood at his back, her eyes roaming everywhere. She would not mess this up again.

As Justin stepped inside, he grabbed hold of Riley's belt and pulled her with him. She could complain later. For right now, he wanted her glued to him.

"Malak?" Justin called out.

"I am here, my friend. Sorry you had troubles."

Malak Salazar stepped out from behind a half-empty bookcase. Short in stature, with a heavy beard and wire-rimmed glasses, he appeared to be the least-likely candidate for intel sharing that Justin had ever seen. Which was exactly how he'd become one of the best in the business.

"No worries. We handled it. You have what we need?"

"Yes. Please follow me."

Justin's trust would go only so far. "Why can't you give us the info here?"

"Because I have something for you."

Justin shared a questioning glance with Riley. Malak had been a friend and ally to LCR long before either he or Riley had become operatives. Had something changed? Had he been bought out?

As if unaware of their doubts, Malak started ahead, apparently expecting them to follow.

"What do you think?" Riley asked softly.

What did he think? He thought he wanted to throw his partner over his shoulder and get the hell out of here.

"He's never done anything to make us doubt him before."

"You're right," Riley said. "Let's go."

Hoping they weren't making the worst decision of their lives, Justin walked beside Riley, following behind Malak.

Gun in her hand, ready to fight for both herself and her partner, Riley peeked inside the doorway where Malak had gone. Her breath caught on a gasp at the unexpected and new complication.

"What the hell?" Justin muttered softly.

Malak stood beside two young women, standing in a corner. "They are from a village close-by. Their father has sold them, and they are to be taken tomorrow. I'm asking you to rescue them."

Their low-risk, no-worries op had just become a major complication.

CHAPTER TWO

Swirls of steam filled the tiny bathroom. Riley stood beneath a scalding-hot shower and let the tension drain from her body. Even though the op hadn't been perfect and more complicated than expected, it had been successful. Thanks to McCall's connections, two young women who would have been enslaved for years had been relocated and were now out of harm's way. And she and Justin had gotten the information they needed. This time tomorrow, several more young women would be rescued from sexual enslavement and years of servitude.

This op was somewhat different than most. A few weeks ago, Taylor Vaughn, a freelance journalist embedded in the small community on the outskirts of Sinjar, had contacted Noah. An up-and-coming wannabe terrorist group had been causing trouble in the area. These men, about twenty in number, were apparently hoping to join the ranks of a much larger and more vicious terrorist group. It was rumored that they were rejects and cast-offs from a defunct Al-Qaeda cell. They were gaining strength and notoriety throughout the region by kidnapping young girls and women and selling them.

This type of horror wasn't new to the region. The journalist had originally come to the community to write a story about everyday life within the war-torn country. When Vaughn had learned of this new group, she'd known it was only a matter of time before they reached her location. With her help, as well as Malak's intel of when the kidnappings were taking place, the LCR Elite operatives would hijack the transport to rescue the women, as well as the reporter, who planned to allow herself to become a kidnapped victim also.

Despite the heat of the shower, a shiver ran up Riley's spine. Though she understood why the journalist felt the story was worth the risk, she wondered if the woman had really known what she was getting herself into. Volunteering to become a hostage to conscienceless and soulless men was a far cry from talking to sources about it. The ugly reality of enslavement, even with the promise of rescue, wasn't an experience anyone could understand unless they'd lived it.

Pushing those dark thoughts aside, she gathered her long, thick hair and scrubbed hard, relishing the clean feeling. Three days without a shower reminded her far too much of the days and weeks she'd been forced to go without. The refreshing scent of lemons and limes made her skin zing. She heard a tuneless, humming noise and almost dropped her soap in shock. The sound was slightly off-key but musical nonetheless. The most astonishing part of all was that it came from her. Simply amazing.

From the time she was five years old until she was eighteen, music had filled her heart and her world. When her parents had realized her talent, voice and piano lessons had followed. She had taken to both as if she were born to them. Music had been an essential part of her soul, feeding her creativity and giving her the freedom to fly.

On her eighteenth birthday, the music had stopped inside her head and her heart. Having no choice, she had continued playing, but music no longer filled her with joy and peace. It had become a duty, forced upon her. The possibility of music moving through her again had seemed as out of reach as the stars.

Shaking her head at this phenomenal occurrence, Riley rinsed the soap from her hair, applied a liberal dose of conditioner, and worked it through the long strands. She once again rinsed, and then, feeling squeaky clean and almost lighthearted, she turned off the water and exited the shower.

The tiny room was filled with steam, and she opened the door to allow some of it to escape. Breath left her lungs when she realized she wasn't alone.

Stumbling back into the room, Riley slammed the door shut and grabbed a towel to wrap around her body. "Dammit, Kelly. What the hell are you doing in my room?"

"Sorry, Ingram. I did knock."

He didn't sound the least bit apologetic. In fact, he sounded quite pleased with himself. Ever since her injury last year, she'd been struggling to get back on level ground with him. Things were different between them. While part of her felt a shimmering glow at that difference, another part wanted to squelch the change. Status quo was how she'd existed for so long. Her survival was tied to maintaining distance. If she let her guard down, would chaos erupt?

"Did the steam coming beneath the door and the sound of running water not give you a clue what was going on in here?"

The case they'd handled in New York a few months back had cracked open a door neither of them had walked through yet. It was like they both hovered on the doorstep, just waiting. Riley had told herself a million times that she needed to slam that door shut. If she did, she knew Justin would never try to reopen it. And that was something she didn't know if she could bear.

But here he was, invading her space, getting in her way, when a few months back he never would have considered such a thing. With one word, one look, she could stop this new familiarity—end it for good.

Realizing he hadn't answered her question, she bit her lip, wondering if he had left without saying anything else. "Justin?"

"Yeah?"

She jumped several feet back, startled at how very close he sounded. She swallowed her nervousness. For heaven's sake, this man was her partner. She had worked with him for years. She trusted him on every level. So why was she now so very aware of him in such a different way? Why did his voice cause ripples of delight to shimmy up her spine? How and when had she let her guard down?

"Why are you here? What do you want?"

The instant she asked, she regretted the words. They not only sounded unfriendly, but her voice actually quivered.

"I wanted to check and see how you're feeling."

Vulnerable, scared…needy. With only a towel wrapped around her wet, naked body and the man she dreamed of nightly on the other side of the door, that would be the truthful answer. But one she could absolutely not speak.

"I'm fine. Just need to get some rest."

"You think you damaged your ribs more when you were running? Should we bind them up before we head out tomorrow?"

"No…I—" She probably should repeat that she was fine and let him return to his room. It was the sensible thing to do. But having a conversation with Justin that didn't involve the details of a mission almost never happened. Call her weak, but she couldn't resist the temptation.

Without giving herself more time to think about it, she said, "Give me a sec. Let me throw some clothes on."

She dried off quickly, then wiggled into her underwear. Just as she was about to fasten her bra's front closure, she jerked to a stop. The stark light of the single bulb in the ceiling was as unforgiving as it was bright. It hid nothing. The scars would never go away. No matter how much time passed, she would always have them. Who did she think she was fooling? Justin Kelly had never seen her like this. He'd probably already figured out she was damaged on the inside. A girl with her kind of closed-off personality and snarky attitude usually had something painful to hide. But he couldn't know that that was only half her damage. The other half was on her body, the marks left by a fiend…a sadist, a monster. Marks that had scarred her both inside and out. Marked her for life.

She turned away from the mirror, pulled on a loose shirt and a pair of jeans. Justin would never be interested in someone like her…with so much baggage. She wasn't normal and never would be. She had stopped living in fantasyland on her eighteenth birthday. She could never return.

When Riley opened the bathroom door, dressed from head to toe and with that closed-off expression on her face, Justin wanted to curse at the change. When she'd opened the door earlier, he'd been stunned. For once, the expression on her face had been open and vulnerable. There had been a small smile on her mouth, and her eyes had held a dreamy quality.

Unfortunately, giving her time to get dressed had also allowed her the opportunity to put her armor on. LCR Elite operative Riley Ingram now stood before him.

"We're still leaving at oh-three-hundred?" she asked in that straightforward, businesslike tone.

"Yeah." His eyes raked up and down her body, assessing for himself before he asked, "You're sure you feel okay? You want me to bandage your ribs tonight?"

Alarm flared in her eyes, and though she didn't back away from him, he wouldn't have been surprised. Her wariness had never been so overt.

"My ribs are fine. I hadn't expected to have to run like that. Should've done some stretches to prepare. I'll be ready tomorrow."

Suggesting that she sit this op out wasn't an option. They would need every person on the team to rescue the women. He trusted her to tell him if she wasn't up to the task.

An awkward silence filled the room. He should be used to it. This had been their relationship for years. If they didn't talk LCR business, they didn't talk. He used to be okay with that. But things were changing between them. He knew it, and she did, too. Their awareness of each other on the job made for a great partnership. This awareness on a personal level was new and evolving. And one he wanted to explore.

Determined to get beyond the seemingly impenetrable wall she'd erected, Justin settled into the wooden chair beside the small desk. The chair squeaked in protest at his weight. "Where'd you grow up, Ingram?"

If he'd pulled his gun out and shot her, he didn't think she could've looked more shocked.

"Wh-what?"

"You've got a slight accent, just can't place it."

Midnight-blue eyes flared with immediate indignation. Justin had the fleeting thought that he was glad she wasn't wearing her colored contacts. She favored brown lenses, but he liked her real eye color. It reminded him of the night sky. And when she was angry, as she was now, her eyes could sparkle like stars.

"I do not have an accent," she snapped.

Yes, she did, but only when she felt tremendous stress, as she was apparently feeling now. Which made her all the more intriguing. Why did she need to hide an accent? Was that the reason she wore colored contacts so often, too? Why?

He decided to cut to the chase. "We've been working together for over three years now, and we still know almost nothing about each other. Don't you find that odd?"

Riley wasn't a tall woman—about five-four. She stretched every inch of that petite frame now as she went into haughty mode.

Justin held out his hand. "Before you get into your snooty 'my personal life is none of your business' mode, let me tell you a few things."

Her glare could've melted a glacier, but he continued, "I grew up in Parkersville, Ohio, right outside Cincinnati. My mom and dad still live there. My dad is a pharmacist. My mom is a schoolteacher. I've got three younger sisters. I joined the Army when I was nineteen, got tapped for some special assignments. Didn't make it home very often.

"A few years back, Lara, my youngest sister, was kidnapped by a gang of human traffickers. LCR rescued her."

That was more than he'd told just about anyone about his life. McCall and several LCR operatives knew because they'd been the ones to rescue Lara. His first meeting with Noah McCall and his team had not been a pleasant experience, but he owed them a debt of gratitude for rescuing his little sister. For that, and several other reasons, when he'd left the military, it had been an easy decision to join up with LCR.

"Why are you telling me this?"

"Because I want to know more about you."

"Why?"

"Because we're partners."

"We've worked together just fine without knowing anything about each other. Why do we need to change?"

She had him there. They did work well together. A few LCR people had joked that they seemed to share the same brain while on an op. It wasn't that close of a connection, but it was a good one. Did he really want to screw around with that? The answer came back, quick and decisive: Yes, he did. He wanted...needed to know Riley Ingram, the woman. Yes, he was attracted to her. She was beautiful, intelligent, and one of the gutsiest people he'd ever known. So yeah, he wanted to know her, but it wasn't just that.

He could lay some line on her about wanting them to work even better together. That wouldn't be the truth, though, and she would know it. "I want to know you, Riley. Not as a partner, but as a person."

Fear flickered in her face, and Justin told himself to drop it. He was about to do just that when she said softly, "I like music."

Her voice was soft, a little breathy...nervous. But she'd shared something personal, and he felt as though he'd been given a million bucks.

"What kind?"

"Ballads, mostly. The older ones. And the singers, like Lena Horne, Etta James, Billie Holiday, Nina Simone. Their music speaks to me more than any I've ever heard."

"Do you play an instrument?"

A small, wistful smile came and went so fast he almost missed it. "Piano. I could lose myself for hours."

Riley had opened up myriad avenues Justin wanted to pursue. He couldn't push her, though. This was the first time she'd offered even the slightest information about her past. If he asked something she didn't want to answer, he figured she'd shut down completely, and he'd never get her to open up again. This was a good start.

Deciding the best way to lower her fear was to talk about himself a little more, he said, "My parents love country music. They tried to get my sisters and me to love it, too. It didn't take."

"You don't like music?"

"Yeah, I do. Rock. Blues. And—" He could feel a light warmth creep up his face, and the thought of it embarrassed him even more. Hell, when was the last time he'd blushed?

She tilted her head. "And?"

He rarely shared this information. Most of the guys he knew would've given him hell for it, and even the women he'd dated had seemed to be put off by his preferences. But he wanted to share this information with Riley. "Opera."

His confession did something to her. If he'd thought Riley was beautiful before, he quickly amended that to breathtaking. Her face glowed, her eyes sparkled, and the most delighted smile he'd ever seen on her tilted her full lips.

"Seriously? My parents took me to see *Madame Butterfly* when I was eight. It was the most wonderful night. My father had season tickets. My favorite is *La Bohème*, but I loved *La Traviata*, too."

"Do your parents still go?"

Her expression went blank, and he knew he'd gone too far and asked a question she didn't want to answer.

She responded, but her voice was dull, lifeless. "My parents died when I was a teenager."

"I'm sorry. I—"

"It was a long time ago." Her gaze shifted to the bedside clock. "It's getting late. I need to get some shut-eye."

Though Justin regretted the change in her demeanor, he couldn't help but be encouraged by what he'd learned. He hadn't been sure he'd ever get to know anything more about her other than she was intelligent, courageous, and good at her job.

He stood and headed to the door. Before opening it, he turned back to her and said, "I had another purpose in coming here. To tell you again that you did the right thing today. Fighting back against those thugs was your only choice."

She nodded in that solemn manner he was accustomed to seeing. For now, that was okay, but if she thought they would go back to having monosyllabic conversations after this was over, she was wrong. Riley Ingram had opened several windows tonight. Justin intended to make sure they stayed open.

CHAPTER THREE

Justin crouched behind a boulder. A few feet away, hidden behind another large rock, was Elite operative Jake Mallory. A dozen yards below them, positioned strategically in the middle of the narrow dirt road, stood a dilapidated-looking truck. All traffic was blocked. Anyone wanting to get around the truck would have to first find a way to get the vehicle off the road.

Riley sat in the front seat of the truck. Beside her was Angela Delvecchio, Jake's partner and wife. As soon as the alert came, the women would emerge from the truck and play their parts. Then the fun would begin.

The plan was in place. Now all they needed was the target to arrive. Their lookouts, Fox and Thorne, were a few miles back. The instant the truck holding the abducted women was spotted, the two operatives would alert Riley and Angela, then follow at a distance. Even with the roadway blocked, the kidnappers wouldn't expect trouble until it was too late. Capture the kidnappers and rescue the women. Should be a simple rescue mission.

Justin had been involved in these ops too often to believe it would be as easy as it sounded. Careful planning could prevent disasters, but no one could predict every scenario.

Raising his high-powered binoculars, Justin narrowed his eyes in on his partner. Riley looked better today, as if she'd gotten a good night's sleep. When she'd come out of her room this morning, her expression had been exactly what he had expected. The implacable mask was back in place. He hadn't expected anything else, but the minute he saw her, he'd wanted to kiss her and see that expression melt into something else.

Frustrated, Justin shoved his fingers through his hair. Yeah, that would've gone over real well.

Jake Mallory's gruff voice broke into Justin's troubled thoughts. "Heard you had a little trouble yesterday."

"Got a little hairy. But we got what we needed. Got a couple of extra passengers, too."

"Yeah. Thorne told me about them. Good thing McCall's got the right connections."

"He's working to relocate all the families to a safe place. If there is such a place these days."

"Ain't that the truth." Jake jerked his head toward the truck. "Riley's ribs still bothering her?"

"Seemed to yesterday. Once we finish up this op, I'm going to recommend a few days off. She needs some downtime to recover."

A smile tugged at Jake's mouth. "Good luck with that."

Yeah, he'd need it. Didn't matter. He wouldn't back down.

The silence from Jake caught his attention. Justin glanced over to see the man's head cocked, speculation in his eyes.

"What?" Justin asked.

"She know how you feel about her?"

The question floored him. Not because he wasn't aware of his growing feelings for Riley, but because he'd worked so hard at masking them.

"That obvious?"

"Probably not to her. Or to most people." Jake's gaze went to the woman in the truck sitting beside Riley. "Maybe because I happen to be in love with an operative, too. I know what the symptoms look like." His smile grew. "Not the easiest thing in the world to handle, but damn worth it."

"You and Angela make a good team."

"Took some work, though. Still does. But like I said, damn worth it."

"Riley's got a lot of baggage."

Jake gave a derisive snort. "And you don't? Give me the name of an operative who says he doesn't, and I'll show you a liar."

Yeah, he had baggage. Hell, who didn't? And Jake was right. The majority of people working for LCR had been through their own hell. Still, the hurt he'd seen in Riley's eyes was something he couldn't yet reach. Didn't take a genius to know that someone had damaged her badly. Penetrating that thick veneer was like chipping away at granite with a plastic fork.

Static crackled in his ear, and then Aidan Thorne's voice came through their earbuds. "Two trucks headed your way, about a mile back. Two guys in each cab. Can't tell how many are in the back with the women."

"Roger that," Justin said.

From their vantage point, he and Jake would be able to spot them from at least a quarter mile away. Still, Riley and Angela would take no chances. Justin watched as they exited the vehicle and then lifted the hood. Angela climbed up on the fender, and within seconds a convincing head of steam rose, billowing through the air. By the time the trucks arrived, there'd be no doubt that the vehicle was disabled and unmovable by the women.

Would be interesting to see if the men would actually try to help or, being the dirt-wad, perverted creeps that they were, see two vulnerable women and try to kidnap them, too. Didn't matter really, because either way, these bastards were going down.

Both Riley and Angela were dressed in traditional Middle Eastern clothing, enabling them to hide their weapons. By the time the assholes realized the two women were anything but vulnerable, it would be too late.

Adrenaline surged through Justin. This was the reason he'd joined LCR, the reason he risked his life again and again. He couldn't think of anything he'd rather be doing. Years ago when Lara had been kidnapped, he'd been clueless about human trafficking. He'd heard about it, but he'd been immersed in following his own dreams, his own path. When she had been taken, his entire world had shifted focus.

When it came time to re-up, he'd chosen to leave the military and work for LCR. He hadn't regretted that decision for a moment.

A movement far in the distance caught his attention. "Targets spotted. Everyone, in position."

Justin watched as Riley, followed by Angela, went to the side of the road to wait. They looked exactly as they needed to—two helpless women in need of assistance. He'd never known anyone less a victim than either of these two women.

Riley rolled her shoulders to loosen them. She had been tense all morning while waiting for this op to go down. She'd been involved in dozens of these in her time with LCR. This one should be no different. She knew what to do. Her training was exemplary, and she was working with some of the most skilled operatives in the business. But she knew better than most that one should never take success for granted. Last year she'd almost been killed in what should have been a much less dangerous mission.

Since then she'd been hyperalert, anticipating trouble without the slightest indication that anything was wrong. She didn't expect problems but refused to let her guard down. On an op, it wasn't just her life on the line, but also her fellow operatives, as well as the victims they were rescuing. One second of inattention could mean disaster for everyone.

She glanced over at Angela who, as Riley had, had assumed a sad, defeated-looking demeanor. The more helpless they looked, the less likely the kidnappers would suspect they were anything but.

It was Riley's opinion that Angela Delvecchio was the epitome of the fearless female. Almost six feet tall, Angela had an exotic beauty that defied description and an energy that could plow over you if you got in her way. She and Sabrina Fox were the Amazons of LCR Elite, confident, strong—valiant in the face of danger. The two women could battle an army and win. Riley fought daily to remind herself how strong she was and how far she had come.

"Here we go," Angela said softly.

The trucks lumbered toward them, leaving a thick cloud of dust in their wake. Hidden in that dust would be Aidan and Sabrina. In the hills above them were Justin and Jake. By the time these men realized this was a trap, they would already be caught.

And, if anyone dared to check out the back of their truck, they would find a special surprise.

The lead truck stopped several feet from them. The driver stuck his head out the window and shouted, "Move your truck!"

Riley felt a lessening of tension in Angela and shared her relief. Though both of them knew the local dialect to some degree, neither of them was fluent enough to carry on a convincing conversation. The man who'd shouted had a British accent, which made communicating much easier.

"We can't," Riley stated with a British accent. "Our vehicle is disabled."

Letting loose a very American-sounding curse, a man jumped from the passenger side and stalked toward them. "Move it off the road, bitch."

Definitely American, Riley thought. Not only a sleazy human trafficker, but a foul-mouthed jerk, too. She looked forward to seeing him with a mouthful of sand when she kicked his ass.

"We cannot move it," Angela said. "We know nothing about repairs."

"Where is your man?" The one who'd first spoken to them was noticing the strangeness of the situation. Two women unaccompanied by a man was an unusual enough occurrence to cause suspicion. Fortunately, they had that covered, too.

"He is in the back of the truck. He is ill. We were on the way to the hospital when our vehicle stopped."

The two men glanced at each other, and the Brit headed toward the back of the truck to check out their claim. He jumped up into the bed of the truck.

Her hand on the weapon beneath her clothing, Riley waited for the noise that would erupt as soon as the man learned that beneath the blankets in the truck was Elite operative Brennan Sinclair, who was in no way ill or disabled.

A small groan and a thud was the only noise. Frowning, the American called out, "Tony? What's going on?"

The sound of a muffled voice made the man walk closer. As he drew nearer, the men in the other truck jumped out and headed toward them. The first man stuck his head into the truck.

Chaos exploded

The man flew back out of the truck, a look of surprised horror on his face. Riley and Angela revealed their weapons. Justin and Jake dropped from their hiding place behind the boulders, shouting for everyone to put their weapons down. Aidan and Sabrina ran forward, their weapons drawn. Brennan jumped from the back of the truck. Four men held their hands up as they realized they were surrounded.

Crying and muffled words were coming from the back of one of the trucks. Riley and Justin pulled the covering aside, unsurprised to see three women with their hands tied in front of them and their mouths taped shut. Riley climbed into the truck. In an instant, one of the women broke free, pulled a gun from beneath her clothing, and aimed at Justin.

"Kelly, watch out!" Riley shouted and dove toward the woman. The gun went off just before she tackled the woman to the bed of the truck.

Clocking the woman on her chin, Riley turned to check on her partner. Blood was blooming on his left shoulder. "You're hit."

"It's nothing," he growled. "Check and make sure the others aren't armed, too."

Riley did this by rote while her mind went over what she should have done and warred with what she wanted to do, which was go check on her partner and make sure he was telling the truth.

The two other women were not armed and looked to be as they had assumed, victims of the human smugglers. Neither of them spoke English, so Riley had to explain with her limited vocabulary that they were safe.

She tied up the woman who'd shot Justin. Leaving the other two women to comfort each other, she jumped from the truck to check on her partner. He was with the other women, four of them, explaining to them what was going on. Since Justin was fluent in Arabic, the women seemed to grasp the situation much easier. They knew they were safe.

"You sure you're okay?" Riley asked.

"Yeah. I'll get it checked out in a minute."

"No, you'll get it checked out now." Riley turned and shouted, "Thorne, we need you. Kelly's injured."

In seconds, Aidan appeared. "Let me take a look."

"He says it's nothing, but he's still bleeding."

"He's also able to talk for himself, Ingram," came Justin's wry reply.

Riley smiled to herself. If he was well enough to be sarcastic and grumpy, he wasn't hurt too badly.

She watched as Aidan pulled Justin's arm from the sleeve of his jacket. Blood now covered his entire arm, and Riley tensed up again. Maybe it was worse than she'd thought.

"He's right," Aidan said. "Got lucky. Just a bullet crease across the top of his shoulder. Probably needs a few stitches, though."

"Just slap a bandage on it. I'll get it checked out once we get this job done."

Riley blew out a gusty sigh. The op wasn't the cleanest on record, but for the most part, it had gone the way they'd hoped.

Sabrina appeared at the back of the truck. "We've got a problem."

"What?" Aidan asked.

"Taylor Vaughn isn't with them."

"Crap," Riley whispered. "Where is she, then?"

"The women don't know. Said when they were taken, a couple of the men grabbed Taylor, threw her in another vehicle, and took off."

Sabrina jerked her head in the direction of the handcuffed men lying on the ground. "They won't say where."

"Guess we'll just have to have a longer chat with them," Aidan said.

"And then what?"

"And then we go find her," Justin answered.

Turning over a band of human traffickers to the authorities wasn't as clear-cut as one would think. With the country being so fractured and sympathies split in various directions, LCR had numerous choices but was limited by one major obstacle—who did they trust? If anyone asked him, Justin's answer would have been an unequivocal *no one.*

Thankfully, McCall had worked out the logistics of who would get the prisoners, but once other people took custody, LCR could forget about questioning them. Getting information out of them would take time and skill. Fortunately, they had a master interrogator on the team.

"Any suggestions on where we can go?" Riley asked.

"Yeah." Refusing to grimace at the ache in his shoulder, Justin pulled a map from the inside of his jacket, spread it out on the truck's tailgate. "It's not fancy, but two miles up the road is another road that leads to an old shack. Used to be a lookout for the rebels. Been abandoned for years. It should give us enough privacy to get what we need."

Riley looked around at the barren but strangely beautiful landscape. "We'd better get moving. Being in the open like this is making me antsy."

"Agreed." He shot a look at Thorne. "You guys round them up. Ingram and I will head up to the shack. We'll make sure it's still empty and report back."

"Roger that," Thorne said.

Slamming the hood of the truck shut, Justin jumped into the driver's side. Riley got in on the other side.

"You ever seen Aidan interrogate before?" Riley asked.

"No. As far as I know, McCall and Fox are the only ones who have." He shrugged and then winced. "Whatever he does usually gets results, though."

"How's your shoulder?"

He moved it again, ignored the deep throb. "It's fine."

"You ever think about doing something besides LCR?"

He hid his surprise at the question. Riley Ingram asking a personal question was rare as the Houston Astros winning the World Series. It had never happened. Until last night. Had he finally broken through that impenetrable barrier?

He shrugged, regretted the movement. "At some point I'll probably want to get out of field ops, but I can't ever see leaving LCR. How about you?"

Instead of answering, she turned toward the window. He wasn't having it. She wasn't going to get away with shutting him out again.

"I asked a question, Ingram."

When she turned to face him, he expected to see anger. Instead, he saw vulnerability and an odd kind of fear. "LCR is my family. Families are forever. Right?"

"Yeah, they are."

They pulled to a stop in front of the shack. "This place looks worse than I remember. Shouldn't be anyone around, but let's check it out before we make the call."

Almost dizzy with relief, Riley pushed her emotions aside, her *do the job* mantra back in place. When this op was over and she was alone, she'd have time to sort through her feelings. And question why she was suddenly being so open when for years she'd been as closemouthed as a corpse.

Guns at the ready, they exited the truck. Justin headed to the front, Riley went around the back. Justin was right. This place was about as ramshackle as they come. The walls were a crumbling mass of clay and rotted wood. It could barely be called a structure, but it would suffice for what they needed.

She peeked inside a window, spotting a three-legged table leaning against a wall and two rattan chairs without bottoms. In the corner were a couple of soda cans and what looked like a used condom.

Scrunching her nose up at the revolting reason someone would have sex in such a disgusting place, she turned around and searched the landscape. Nothing but rocky hills and trees.

"Looks clear," Riley said into her mic.

"Yeah, looks good from here, too," Justin said, then added, "Thorne, bring our guests on up."

Riley stepped around front and watched as the truck holding the prisoners headed their way. She didn't envy them the next few minutes. She might not have ever seen Aidan conduct an interrogation, but one thing she knew for sure, the man usually got the information he was looking for. She had no clue how he did it, but the few times they'd had to interrogate hostiles, Aidan Thorne went in alone and came out with credible intel. And interestingly enough, not once had she seen a mark on anyone he'd questioned. That took some crazy skills.

Riley didn't know Aidan's background, had no clue what he did before he came to LCR, but one thing was for sure—the man knew how to get results. Fast.

The handcuffed group, four men and one woman, shuffled toward the small structure. Despite her training, Riley shivered.

Sometimes evil was concealed behind a façade. Other times, the wickedness was unhidden and apparent. She had seen and experienced it both ways. These people, with their dark expressions and eyes glittering with hatred, weren't bothering to hide who and what they were.

Getting information would not be easy, even for Aidan Thorne.

The last man in the line, the largest of the group, shifted his eyes to her briefly. She saw something in them, just a flicker. Her training kicked in before her mind comprehended. Just as the man's arm swept up, a slender knife in his hand, Riley lunged toward him. Swinging her arm upward, she knocked the knife from his hand, slammed her other fist into his face, and then whirled, finishing him off with a solid kick straight to his groin. Howling, he dropped to his knees, holding his crotch.

Justin grabbed his wrists and zip-tied them again. Looking up at her, he grinned. "You are one bad-assed, lethal woman, Ingram."

Her adrenaline still surging, she glanced around at the other operatives. All were giving her approving looks. She felt the glow all the way to her toes. Justin was right. She was badass and tough. She had not only come through hell and survived, she had become a force to be reckoned with.

She gave a small nod of acknowledgment and then turned away before anyone could read her expression. She had been focused on moving forward for so long, she had never realized that she had actually arrived. She had achieved what she'd always dreamed. Yes, she still had nightmares, still looked over her shoulder. But the stark differences in what she had been and who she was now were so phenomenal, it was as if she were two different people.

On the heels of that realization, came another one, even more startling and scarier. But she knew it was time. Time to stop running. Time to confront the most wicked of the wicked.

Riley Ingram was ready to face her past.

CHAPTER FOUR

LCR Headquarters
Alexandria, Virginia

Noah McCall read the information he'd received this morning from his source at the FBI. Their intel on Taylor Vaughn's abduction jived with what Aidan Thorne had uncovered from the kidnappers in Iraq. The journalist had not been taken by human traffickers or terrorists. Kidnapping the Iraqi women had provided the perfect opportunity for an abduction of a different kind. This one was all about payback and revenge.

Taylor Vaughn was an award-winning journalist. She had a reputation for infiltrating the most impenetrable organizations and gathering intel for her articles, making her one of the most admired, and reviled, journalists in the world. She had an incredible talent for deep cover, which had yielded her tons of information for her stories. Most times, the organizations she wrote about hadn't known they had a mole in their midst until the first headline appeared. Most never knew how they'd been compromised.

According to Noah's FBI source, several months ago, the journalist had infiltrated the organization of notorious crime boss Mateo Russo, one of the most-wanted criminals in the world. She had gained the trust of one of his generals and had apparently gotten access to a ton of information. For her safety and their investigation, the FBI had tried to stop her from writing her stories until Russo was apprehended. She'd resisted, but then it didn't matter, because she was discovered, and Mateo Russo was out for blood. But first, he would want to know what she knew, how she knew it, and who she had told.

Noah's gut told him that Russo wouldn't kill her until he believed he had all the information. And from what he knew about Taylor Vaughn, she would hold out as long as she could. She would know that the instant she was no longer useful, she would be killed. Noah hoped to hell she was as strong as she appeared. Mateo Russo was known for his ruthlessness.

The man had the money and connections to have dozens of hideaways throughout the world, which was one of the reasons he hadn't been captured. Mafia wealth could purchase both secret real estate and confidentiality. The man had been hidden for years, and unless something changed, he would stay that way.

LCR wasn't out to capture Russo. Their mission was to rescue Taylor Vaughn.

Noah had followed Vaughn's career and had read most of her articles. The journalist's ingenuity was impressive. At the same time, he was amazed that she had survived this long without anyone targeting her. With Mateo Russo, Taylor Vaughn's luck had run out.

Their biggest obstacle was finding where Russo had stashed her. The man had created an intricate web of hideouts that crisscrossed the globe. Many of the locations were fake, and a dozen or more were real. Finding the one where Vaughn was being held would take time. But just how much time did Taylor Vaughn have?

The buzzer on his desk sounded. Without taking his eyes from the monitor in front of him, he pressed answer. "Yes?"

"Noah, there's a William Larson on line one. I've taken the pertinent information, but he insists on speaking with you. I know that you usually like to read the background facts before you talk to a prospective client. It's just…this man…" She cleared her throat. "He's quite insistent."

Vicki Jackson was one of his most experienced screeners. As the wife of a law enforcement officer and the mother of two Navy SEALs, she wasn't easy to spook or rile. From the tone of her voice, Noah knew William Larson had managed to do both.

"Send me what you have on him."

Within seconds, Noah was looking at the bare facts on the case of a young woman who had been missing for eight years. Larson, a freelance computer consultant, was her father. The woman, Jessica Larson, was twenty-nine years old and had a long history of mental illness.

"Did he say anything out of line to you, Vicki?"

"No. Not really. There's just something about him that put me on edge."

Noah admired Vicki's instincts. If there was something off about the guy, Noah believed her.

"I'll take the call."

Seconds later, Noah pressed a button and said, "This is Noah McCall."

"Thank you for taking my call, Mr. McCall. That woman didn't want to put me through. She—"

"*That woman* is doing her job. How can I help you?"

There was a second of awkward silence, and then Larson said, "Of course. Of course. It's just that I'm at my wit's end. You're my last hope, Mr. McCall."

"I see that your daughter, Jessica, has been missing for eight years now?"

"Yes. We've tried everything trying to find her."

"And she has a history of mental illness? What is her diagnosis?"

"She's delusional, Mr. McCall. It started around her eighteenth birthday. Up until then, she was a normal, happy-go-lucky, young woman."

"Any history of self-inflicted harm or violence to others?"

"No, not really. Just mostly paranoia."

"She was twenty-one when she disappeared?"

"Um. Yes."

The hesitancy in Larson's speech could have been a normal response to Noah's somewhat intrusive questions. If Larson thought those few queries were intrusive, he hadn't heard anything yet.

"Where are you located, Mr. Larson?"

"Located? You mean, where do I live now?"

"Yes."

"Uh, um. Chicago."

"I have business in Chicago on Monday. I can meet you at one. Bring all the information you have on Jessica."

"Oh, couldn't we meet sooner? I can come to your office. Where are you located?"

"The Drake Hotel in Chicago. One o'clock Monday. That's my offer."

"Well, of course, of course. I just thought…" Larson gave a long, overly dramatic sigh. "I'm just so eager to find her, Mr. McCall, but I'll comply with your timeframe."

"I'll see you then."

Noah slumped back in his chair, frowning at the phone. Vicki's instincts were indeed sound. There was something off about William Larson. A fakeness to his tone had put Noah on alert and made him highly curious. Just what was William Larson hiding?

Pressing another button on his phone, he waited until one of his best researchers answered, then said, "Deidre, get me everything you can on a William Larson. Says he's in Chicago, but I have my doubts. Trace the number. See if it'll tell us his location. I'll send you what little I've got."

After he sent Deidre the sketchy information Larson had supplied, Noah leaned back in his chair again. A shadow of an idea niggled at the back of his mind. He wasn't going to jump to conclusions. But one thing he knew for sure. He was definitely looking forward to his one-on-one with the man calling himself William Larson.

CHAPTER FIVE

New York City

Riley slipped into the small, elegant room in the back of the church. The cathedral was well guarded, and she had wondered if she'd have difficulty getting inside. Thanks to the forethought of the bride and groom, she'd had no problem. Saying *LCR* had been the golden passkey.

The paparazzi surrounded the building but would not be allowed inside. Still, the number of reporters and photographers who had been allowed into the church was enough to make anyone nervous, much less a woman in hiding. Being photographed, even accidentally, wasn't something she could risk. Even dressed in a disguise, she was on edge. She had no idea if anyone was still looking for her. As helpless as she had been, they probably assumed she was dead. Still she would take no chances. The blond wig and thick glasses were an easy, uncomplicated cover-up.

"Kacie?"

The bride whirled around, and Riley caught her breath. She had never seen anyone lovelier. Dressed in a gorgeous, fitted white gown of lace and silk, Kacie Dane was the very definition of a beautiful, glowing bride. So glowing that Riley looked around to see if there was some sort of light shining above her head. There wasn't. It was all Kacie. Had any bride ever looked happier? Had any bride ever deserved happiness more?

"Hey!" Kacie's smile was both brilliant and welcoming. "It's so good to see you. I'm so glad you could come to the wedding."

"I hope you don't mind me coming in here."

"Absolutely not. Skylar was here but stepped out for a moment to help Gabe with his bow tie." She winked at Riley. "I like your disguise. Very retro."

That was another reason she liked Kacie Dane. Not one question of why she felt the need to wear a disguise. Kacie accepted people as they were.

"Your dress is lovely."

"Thank you. I was thrilled that Julian Montague agreed to design one for me." She glanced down at her dress and then grinned. "Brennan's going to love it."

"Yes, but not as much as the person wearing it."

"Oh yeah." Kacie expression softened.

"So, I just wanted to wish you well and...um..." Riley trailed off, belatedly realizing what a colossal mistake it had been to come here. Bringing up the worst experience of Kacie's life on what should be the happiest day of her life was not only incredibly insensitive, it was downright cruel. Even someone with her limited people skills should know that.

"What's wrong?"

"Nothing. I just wanted to say congratulations." She began to back away, toward the door.

"Thank you." Kacie held out her hand to stop her. "But there's something else isn't there? What is it?"

"No. Not really. We can talk another time. Maybe when you get back from your honeymoon." Seeking to change the subject, she asked, "Where are you two going?"

"I don't know. Brennan planned everything. He won't tell me until our plane lands. He even packed for me." Kacie laughed and added, "Considering the small suitcase, I have a feeling it's not a place that requires a lot of clothes."

Riley gave a strained smile and put her hand on the doorknob. "I'm sure it'll be great. Have a wonderful time."

Kacie grabbed Riley's hand and led her to a low settee. "Listen. LCR is my family, which means you're family. Tell me what's wrong."

"Nothing's wrong. I just—" Seeing the compassion and concern in Kacie's eyes, Riley swallowed and said, "I just wanted to tell you how courageous you are for what you did."

Confusion glimmered for a second, and then she said, "Oh, you mean spilling my guts at the press conference?"

"Yes."

"It was something I felt I had to do."

Thankful that Kacie didn't seem the least bit upset to be talking about her dark past, she said, "Why?"

"For several reasons. One, there was always a chance that someone would have found out the truth on their own and try to use it against me. Living under that kind of shadow wasn't something I wanted. Now, that risk is gone. And two, I was living a lie and I felt like a hypocrite. I'm a role model for a lot of young women. How could I tell other women who have been raped to come forward when I kept my past abuse hidden?"

"How did you find the courage to do it?"

Awareness flickered in Kacie's eyes, and Riley knew she saw the truth behind her questions.

"Part of it was Brennan. Having his love and support gave me the strength and courage to face my past."

"What was the other part?"

"The knowledge that I did nothing wrong. Nothing I did could ever make me deserve what happened to me. Even though I had recovered, I still felt shame for what I'd gone through. Even though I knew up here"—she touched her head—"that I'd done nothing wrong, I realized I still felt shame. I was raped and tortured by a monster. The shame was on him, not me."

Riley nodded. She knew all this. Had gone through tons of counseling herself.

"Do you regret making it public?"

"No. Oh, there were some nasty comments. Some calling it a publicity stunt. Online trolls looking for attention. Things like that. People whose opinion means nothing."

Save a handful of people, Riley didn't care about others' opinions of her. No, it wasn't her reputation at stake. It was her life, her sanity, at risk. But what would be at risk if she didn't take this next step?

Soft music sounded from the auditorium.

"Thank you. I'd better let you get back to getting ready." Impulsively, Riley hugged her and then jumping up, walked swiftly to the door.

As she opened it, Kacie said, "Riley?"

She looked back at the woman still sitting on the settee. The compassion on Kacie's face brought a lump to Riley's throat.

"If there's anything you need," Kacie said, "anything I can do to help, will you let me know?"

"I will. Thank you." Before closing the door, Riley added, "Be happy, Kacie. I wish you and Brennan the happiest of lives together."

***

Justin stood in the large foyer of the church, out of the way of the guests exiting the building. The wedding had gone off without a hitch. Brennan and Kacie had looked good together. As Brennan's best man, he'd been standing up front with him when Kacie had walked down the aisle toward her waiting groom. The entire church had exhaled with a collective gasp. Yes, she'd looked beautiful, but it had been more than that. Justin didn't think he'd ever seen anyone more joyful or more in love. Brennan's expression had been a mirror image of Kacie's.

Justin hoped all their dark days were behind them.

He'd been about to turn and face the front when he spotted a woman sitting in the back row. Even with the long blond hair, heavy makeup, and thick-rimmed glasses, he recognized his partner.

He hadn't seen her since their op in Iraq a week ago. He'd asked her if she would be attending the wedding, and she'd been noncommittal, saying only that she was unsure if she'd be able to make it.

The audience had been filled with LCR employees and operatives. Many of them in disguise. This wasn't an op, but because of their pasts, most needed to stay out of the limelight. It was something Justin understood and accepted. Seeing his partner dressed in disguise was something else entirely. It had been a punch to the gut. An abrupt, unpleasant discovery that revealed just how much he didn't know about her. Who was Riley hiding from and why?

The fact that they'd been partners for over three years and he hadn't known before about her need to stay hidden infuriated him. The anger was directed at himself, not her. Why hadn't he known this? Why had he allowed all these secrets between them? They were more than partners. They were friends. And hell, whether she was ready to admit it or not, they were more than friends.

It was way past time to find out the truth about Riley Ingram.

Before he could come up with a plan on how to make that happen, she came through the doors from the auditorium into the foyer. He watched in silence as she practically hugged the walls, staying in the shadows. He knew the moment she caught him looking at her. An awareness clicked in her eyes.

Weaving in between the hordes of guests headed toward the exit, he caught up with her. "Nice wedding, wasn't it?"

"Yes, it was."

"Are you going to the reception?"

"For a little while. I'm not much for parties."

"Yeah, me either." He gave her a look she couldn't misunderstand. "We need to talk. Want to meet me somewhere for a late dinner?"

"No."

If there was one thing he liked about Riley Ingram, she didn't prevaricate. If you asked her a question, she would either tell you the truth, tell you it was none of your business, or just not answer.

Deciding to go for broke, he said, "All right. Then you want to tell me who you're hiding from?"

Riley looked up at the man who'd come to mean so much to her. The black tuxedo fit his tall, muscular frame perfectly. He'd had a haircut since she'd seen him. His thick brownish-blond hair had just enough curl in it to make a girl think about twining her fingers through it. She had seen numerous women give him long, admiring looks. The two women in front of her during the wedding had whispered about how handsome the best man was, giggling about how much they'd like to meet him.

Justin Kelly was a handsome, ultra-masculine man whom most any woman would sigh over. Riley should know. She had done her share of sighing, especially in the last few months.

And now he wanted to know who she was hiding from. Just for a moment, Riley allowed a fantasy to take flight. In her imagination, she heard herself give him honest answers and explain what had happened to her. She watched his face darken with concern for her. There was no judgment, no condemnation. No disgust. Instead, she saw understanding, maybe compassion, but not pity. Never pity.

Then she returned to the real world and faced the truth. Speak the words she hadn't allowed herself to say in years? Tell him the truth in the middle of a crowd of mostly strangers? No. Way. In. Hell.

If she proceeded with her plan, he would know soon enough. Once he knew everything, would the admiration she'd often seen in his eyes be replaced with revulsion?

She could withstand a lot, but that was something she would not survive.

She gave him a smile that probably looked as fake as it felt, but it would have to do. "That's a discussion for another day."

"I see."

Now even more nervous as those slate-gray eyes seemed to penetrate straight through her bravado, she tugged her purse strap over her shoulder. "So. Guess I'll see you at the reception. Or, if not, on our next call."

Giving him no time to respond, she backed into the shadows, followed a group of people to an exit, and ran out the door. She told herself she wasn't being a coward. That it was ludicrous to have a discussion of such import with so many people milling around.

A hand grabbed her arm. She was so intent on escape that she snarled a curse as she turned around, her fist raised and ready to strike.

Justin let go of her arm and held up his hands in surrender. "Sorry. Didn't mean to startle you."

Mortified, she glanced around to see if anyone else had caught the unusual break in her cool façade. Fortunately, all the other guests were intent on enjoying themselves. No one had noticed other than the brooding man frowning down at her.

"We will talk soon, Ingram. This can't go on."

There were a lot of ways she could respond to that autocratic statement. Another time, she might have told him exactly what he could do with his arrogance. She opened her mouth to do just that and then saw the concern in his eyes. Justin played things cool most times but not on this. Not tonight. This man cared for her, and though nothing could ever happen between them, he deserved the truth.

"You're right. We will." She backed away again, saying softly, "I just hope we can handle it."

Turning, she ran out the door and into the night.

***

Aidan Thorne tugged at his bow tie. Damn thing was choking him to death. He'd much rather be fighting a three-hundred-fifty-pound bruiser with a knife than stand here in a monkey suit with a fake smile plastered on his face.

"Hi, Aidan, how are you?"

Recognizing the soft, female voice, Aidan flinched as his entire body tensed up. The one woman he'd been determined to avoid. *Hell.*

Polite mask frozen in place, he turned and gave a cool nod. "Anna, you're looking well."

Aidan groaned beneath his breath at his lame-assed words. *You're looking well* was what you told someone's elderly aunt. Not a beautiful, vibrant woman that made your mouth water and your skin feel like it was on fire. He told himself he should just be grateful for his ability to maintain a nonchalant air when his heart was thundering like a stampede of elephants. Anna Bradford looked nothing like the abused young woman LCR had rescued years ago. She had matured from an idealistic young college student who wanted to save the world to a lovely young woman. She was still too idealistic, though. And she was still trying to save the world.

Skin the color of light honey-gold, shoulder-length hair a mélange of soft brown and dark gold, dark brown eyes that gleamed with purity and hope, a light sprinkling of freckles across her small nose, and the sweetest, lushest mouth he'd ever seen. Anna personified every single quality that he'd sworn to stay away from.

"It was a beautiful wedding, wasn't it?"

He was in a dilemma. If he nodded curtly and walked away, he'd hurt her feelings. If he stayed, he greatly feared he'd give in to temptation, lean down, and see if the frosted-pink lipstick on her mouth was as tasty as it looked.

"Hey, babe, let's dance."

Even though he was saved from having to make a decision, Aidan glared down at the guy now standing beside Anna. He didn't recognize the creep, with his chiseled jaw, perfect hair, and I'm-too-cool-for-school demeanor, but he sure as hell didn't like the familiar way he'd grabbed for Anna's elbow.

Before Aidan could make his displeasure known, Anna gracefully twisted away from the guy, and with a diplomacy that would make the State Department proud, she laughed softly and said, "Stuart, there's no way I'm depriving all the girls lined up to dance with you." She tilted her head to the left. Sure enough, there were about five young women standing a few feet away who apparently had eyes only for this guy.

"They'll wait. I want to dance with you."

Though her smile lost a little of its shine, she didn't do what Aidan hoped she'd do and tell the jerk to go jump off a cliff. He was about to intervene and give a vulgar suggestion of his own when Riley appeared beside them.

"Anna, can I talk to you a minute?"

"Sure thing." She gave the Stuart guy a nod. "Go make those women happy."

"Yeah, whatever." Stuart headed toward his small adoring crowd.

"Who the hell was that guy?" Aidan asked.

"One of the top male models in New York."

Wasn't any of his business, but he had to know. "Why didn't you dance with him?"

Her burst of laughter was like a breath of fresh air, free and uninhibited. "Dance with someone prettier than me? Not a chance."

He liked her, dammit. Liked her self-deprecation. Her sunny disposition. Liked that even though she had once gone through hell, she still believed in goodness. She was everything he wasn't. Represented everything he couldn't have.

Aidan backed away. "Good to see you, Anna." He nodded. "See you later, Ingram."

Turning, he made a beeline for the door. If he didn't get out of here now, he would break every promise he'd made to himself to stay away from her. People like Anna Bradford did not belong in his darkness.

Riley watched Aidan stalk out of the room like he had a demon chasing him. Being familiar with running from her own demons, she recognized the act for what it was. She turned back to Anna and eyed her speculatively.

"He doesn't like me."

Anna's rueful statement caught Riley by surprise. Her friend was usually more perceptive than that. Knowing it would do no good to explain that Aidan's swift exit had more to do with liking her too much, Riley said instead, "I think having all these people around makes all LCR operatives a little antsy."

"But not you?"

Antsy? Yes, she was definitely that, but not because of too many people. Her disguise was a good one. No one from her past would suspect that the damaged and ravaged young woman they'd known would be at the star-studded wedding of a famous model and a former NFL quarterback. Those people most likely believed she was dead.

"I don't figure anyone would ever look for me here."

"Especially looking like that."

"What's the saying? Blondes have more fun?"

"Is it true?" Anna asked.

"Not yet."

Anna's gaze went to the door where Aidan had made his exit. "Not for me either." She scrunched her nose. "Maybe I should've gone all the way blond instead of just highlights."

It wasn't the first time her friend had indicated she had a thing for Aidan Thorne. There was a large group of LCR women who had a small crush on the Golden Adonis of LCR, as someone had called him. It was, however, the first time Riley realized her friend's feelings might be more than a simple crush.

"You think we could go somewhere and talk for a while?"

Pulling her gaze from the door, Anna brightened. "Let's go to my room, get these shoes off, and order room service. I'm in the mood for a triple burger, fries, and a chocolate shake."

As they headed out the door, the thought of food roiling her stomach, she was reminded of another difference between her and Anna. Riley enjoyed food, but decades of a strict, regimented diet wasn't something she had been able to overcome.

Anna believed in living life to the fullest and enjoying every moment. Riley's moments of joy were few and far between, but at least they now existed.

Would anything change once she confronted her past, or was she condemned to stay the same, running from her own shadow?

The uncharacteristic moment of self-pity almost stopped her in her tracks. Where had that come from? Hell, she had conquered more phobias than most psychology books even covered. She had defeated every obstacle that had been thrust upon her. She'd damn well not start feeling sorry for herself now.

Okay, yes. She had a big hurdle to get over. A damn big one. But just like all the other hurdles, she could and would put it behind her.

Chin set determinedly, she followed Anna out of the ball-room. Tonight she would allow herself a rare moment of happiness with one of the dearest people she knew. Tomorrow she would call Noah and tell him her plans. She had a feeling he wouldn't be the least bit surprised.

Justin sat at the table, the untouched beer in front of him now warm. The crowd had thinned out, but there were at least a couple of hundred people still here, apparently determined to dance until dawn or drink the bar dry. He had no desire for either. What he wanted and what he was going to do were in direct conflict. His heart told him to find Riley and get the truth from her instead of the vague excuses she'd given him earlier.

What he was going to do was sit here until he got bored enough to leave and go up to his hotel room. A crowd wasn't his thing, but it was a damn sight better than going to his room and staring at four walls.

"I can't decide who's the most miserable of us. You won't go after what you want, and I can't have what I want."

Aidan Thorne was slouched in a seat across from him. The usual good humor spark gone from his eyes. Thorne was one of the few people who knew what Justin felt for Riley. And as far as he knew, Justin was the only one who knew what Aidan wanted but wouldn't allow himself to have.

"I vote you," Justin said. "At least I have an excuse."

"You work with the woman every day. Spend hours alone with her, and she has no idea how you feel about her. How is that an excuse?"

"She's not interested in me. At least not in that way. You think I'm going to jeopardize our partnership by telling her?"

"You're sure about that?"

"What do you mean?"

"I just think Ingram might not be as immune to you as you think."

Whether it was because of his training or an innate gift, Aidan Thorne saw things others missed. He was a perceptive man with a strong tendency to see beyond bullshit, one of the reasons he was such a good interrogator.

So, was what he'd said the truth? Had Justin been so caught up in his own doubt that he hadn't seen that she felt something, too? He rubbed his chin and debated with himself, all the while aware of Thorne's amusement across from him. He ignored that, accustomed to the man's twisted sense of humor. So maybe things weren't as hopeless as he'd thought. Could he get her to admit feeling something for him? And if he could, would that strengthen their partnership or damage it for good?

His peripheral vision caught sight of McCall headed their way. The man's too-serious expression in the midst of happy wedding guests was a warning that something major was up. Positioning himself between their two chairs, he took in both men's gazes. "We got a location on Taylor Vaughn."

"Where is she?" Justin asked.

"Italy."

"Where in Italy?" Aidan asked.

McCall's mouth twisted in a grimace. "Good question. I'll brief you on the plane. Grab your gear. We take off in thirty."

CHAPTER SIX

Mother Nature was putting on quite a show for them as they rose higher in the sky. If time hadn't been of the essence, they probably would have waited till the storm quieted before taking off. Unfortunately, Taylor Vaughn was living on borrowed time. The longer it took to get to her, the less chance of her surviving.

"Let's get started," Noah called out loudly to be heard over the loud rumble of thunder and the drone of the plane.

Unbuckling her seat belt, Riley followed the other operatives to the large conference table in the middle of the plane. As she settled into her seat, she thought this had to be the most overdressed LCR meeting she'd ever attended. No one had taken the time to change. Though they might be dressed in fancy duds, all of them shared the same determined expressions.

"Here's what we've got. We know Russo has houses and hideouts all over the world. A dozen or more. Our intel has narrowed down the three most likely places he's got her stashed. All in Italy.

"We're fairly certain she's still alive. He's going to want to find out how much she knows, who she's told what." His voice went darker "He's going to want to talk to her."

They all knew exactly what this meant. Russo was known for his cruelty to his enemies. On occasion, he'd have someone killed, but more often, especially if he felt he'd been betrayed, he liked to mete out punishment personally. His methods were a clear indication that the man was a sadist. Riley shivered at the image in her mind, only it wasn't Mateo Russo she pictured but another man.

"Who'd we get the intel from?" Aidan asked.

"FBI and Italian government have been working together for years to capture Russo. They have someone inside his organization. I don't know if it's a snitch or one of their own people. However, they do believe this is credible intel."

"Do they think Russo will be there?" Justin asked.

"Doubtful. Word is he was in the middle of some kind of medical procedure when Vaughn was taken. The FBI believes he'll go to her in a few days, maybe a week."

"Making our window of opportunity very small," Justin said.

"Exactly." Standing, Noah went to a screen displaying a map of Italy. "We're going to make this as low-key and low tech as we can get. Our only priority is rescuing Taylor Vaughn. We'll let the feds worry about going after Russo."

He turned toward the screen. "Here are the three locations, all in separate parts of the country. We'll land in Rome. Each team will go from there."

He returned to the conference table and withdrew six folders. Sliding a folder toward each person, he said, "You'll find as much as we could dig up about the locations on short notice. Once we touch down, we'll have transportation, plus the supplies and weapons you'll need."

He leaned forward, taking in everyone's gazes. "Questions?"

"Yeah. When's this asshole going to get what's coming to him?" Aidan asked. "Sounds like he's been running everyone in circles for a long time."

Noah glanced over at Sabrina, who gave a small nod and said, "Declan's got him in his sights. Won't be long now."

Last year they'd learned that Sabrina's husband, Declan Steele, worked for Eagle Defense Justice Enforcers, a secret government agency.

"I thought EDJE only went after terrorists," Riley said.

"And those who help them. Russo is providing weapons and funds to at least a half-dozen small terror cells. They want him as badly as the FBI does."

"Be interesting to see who gets him first."

A small smile lifted Sabrina's lips. "I may be slightly biased, but my money's on my husband."

Noah gave a quick nod. "Hope it's soon. Bastard needs to be dealt with." He looked around the table. "Get some shut-eye if you can. We've got another five hours of flight time."

Riley waited for the other operatives to gather their folders and head back to their seats. As soon as she and Noah were relatively alone, she said in a low voice, "Noah, can I talk to you?"

"What's up?"

"I just..." She took a breath and let the words gush out. "I think it's time to try again."

Concern turned his eyes darker, his mouth straight-lined to grim. "You've remembered something?"

If only it were that easy. Her mind had never given her what she needed the most. Many details of her horror were etched into her brain, never to be erased. But the things she'd needed to know—such as names, places—were missing. One of her greatest fears was that they weren't even there.

"No, not really. I just think I'm ready to try again."

"Very well. We can set up more hypnosis sessions."

Years ago, she had tried hypnosis therapy, hoping to uncover what she had suppressed. It had done little good and only brought to the forefront the most awful things. The next step had been one she hadn't been ready to attempt. Until now.

"I think I'd like to go further this time. Maybe try the drugs."

The harsh frown on his face might have given others pause, but never Riley. She trusted Noah McCall implicitly. He had saved her life and her sanity.

"You're sure about that?"

Sure? Of course she wasn't. Being certain about something meant you were ready to deal with the consequences of a decision. What if the memory drugs brought out even more of the horror and nothing helpful?

She gave a little shrug. "I'm sure I need to try."

"Then you know I'll support your decision. After this op, come in and let's talk. I'll ask Samara to do some research on the most current treatments." He squeezed her hand, a rare gesture of affection. "You know we'll help you any way we can."

Riley whispered her thanks and went to her seat. Justin was sitting across from her, and even though he was sprawled in his chair and looked like he was sleeping, she knew he wasn't. Without opening his eyes, he murmured quietly, "We are going to talk, Ingram."

She knew he didn't mean here and now. This discussion would have to be when they were alone, when things could be said, secrets shared. She hoped they could survive the conversation.

***

Northern Italy

Riley adjusted her backpack to a more comfortable position. As trails went, this was one of the easier she had hiked. Someone had cleared a path long ago and used it often. Problem was, they had no assurance that it would lead to their target. They had the general location of the hideout but no pinpoint. And when they arrived, who knew what they'd find? They'd been walking for several hours without seeing any sign of a hideaway.

She cut her eyes over to her partner, who seemed just as preoccupied as she had been. Other than making a remark about the low humidity and pointing out a soaring hawk, he had been mysteriously silent.

Myriad issues occupied her own mind. She thought about Russo and what it took to make men such as him. About Taylor Vaughn and what horrors she had already no doubt endured. Was the journalist as tough as she seemed? And she thought about herself. About what would come after the rescue. Now that she had made a decision, a part of her was anxious to get started. Of course, there was another part of her that was just as eager to forget the idea and go on as she had been. Didn't she have a good life? Hadn't she accomplished more than she'd ever believed possible? Why stir things up now?

The too-silent man beside her was one of the biggest reasons to not do anything. She cared what he thought about her. She cared about him. Once he found out, things would never be the same. What if he lost all confidence in her? They had a winning combination right now. Did she really want to mess with that?

He had said they needed to talk. She was surprised he hadn't asked any questions yet. They were alone, with no one around to hear their discussion. Was he waiting for her to start talking? Could she just spill her figurative guts on a shady hillside in Italy?

Her foot slipped on wet grass, and she stumbled forward.

"Careful." A hand caught her arm before she could land on her face. "You need to take a break?"

She shook her head. "I'm fine."

When he said nothing more, she glanced up at him. The contrast in the tuxedo-wearing best man and the one beside her now was startling. How could someone who looked so sophisticated and handsome in formal wear also look just as good in an army green T-shirt and camo pants? The shirt stretched across his broad chest, not tightly, but snug enough to reveal the hard muscles underneath.

She had seen Justin without a shirt many times. You didn't spend days on an op with a partner without seeing each other in some stages of undress. Without a shirt, he was even more impressive looking.

Riley had always made sure she revealed as little skin as possible. Drawing attention to the marks on her body was always at the forefront of her mind. Justin had no such worries. She had seen several scars on his torso and back, but they didn't seem to bother him. Maybe it was because he'd gotten the scars heroically, whereas hers came from something altogether different.

Justin pulled a map from inside his jacket. "It'll be dark in about forty-five minutes. We're maybe a couple of miles from the first cabin." He jerked his head up toward a copse of giant pine trees a few miles ahead. "If it's not Russo's, we'll set up camp. Get started back at dawn."

"Sounds good." With a quick nod, she moved forward.

Justin held back a sigh. The furtive looks she'd been throwing him made him want to swear a blue streak. But not at her. He shouldn't have said what he said last night. Telling her that he was expecting her to spill all her secrets had done more harm than good. Yes, he wanted to know who she was hiding from and why. But he wanted to know because he cared about her. His stupid-assed comment last night—*We are going to talk, Ingram*—had sounded too much like a demand. Diplomacy had never been his strong suit. Neither was patience. But damned if he would push her into sharing things that might hurt her.

He couldn't say when he'd started looking at Riley as more than his partner. Their first meeting had been singularly unimpressive. If he'd been asked to describe her, he would have said brown and brown—brown hair, brown eyes. That was before he knew she wore a variety of colored contact lenses. She had delicate features and a small frame. Her facial expressions often alternated between blank and joyless.

She'd had little to contribute to the meeting, but when she did speak, it was in a halting manner, as if she had to force each word from her mouth. But then something had changed. She had shifted her gaze to his, and something had clicked between them. It hadn't been a physical thing—more mental. Whatever it was, it had stuck. From that day on, they'd developed an odd sort of communication. Words weren't necessary. He didn't believe in psychic connections, but hell if he could explain what their bond was. It defied description.

The more he worked with her, the more he admired her. No, she wasn't a great conversationalist, but she had the soul of a warrior and the heart of a lioness. He had watched her risk her life unflinchingly and with more courage than most people displayed in a lifetime. He thought maybe it was her courage that made him finally look at her. Beyond the solemn expression and dogged determination were a steeliness and firm resolve that came from within.

When had that admiration turned into something more? He wasn't sure. Maybe the attraction had always been there. She was beautiful, but in a quiet way. There was nothing flamboyant about Riley Ingram. But her dark brown hair was thick, lustrous, falling over her shoulders like expensive silk. She had creamy skin, and when she blushed, her cheeks took on a delicate pink. It always lifted his heart when she did that.

Riley didn't smile a lot, and he figured her life experiences hadn't given her much reason. Her eyes might be his favorite feature, because even though her smiles were rare, her eyes would often sparkle with humor. It didn't happen a lot, but whenever he saw the gleam, something tightened in his chest.

No, he couldn't say when his feelings had changed to something tender. He knew only that he wanted to chase away her shadows, see her smile with delight or laugh with joy. He wanted to hold her in his arms, kiss that unsmiling mouth, and make her moan for him.

She gave a soft sigh, and Justin glanced over at her. Riley had stopped walking. Raising her arms over her head, she stretched what he knew were aching muscles. The punch of attraction caused an immediate and unstoppable reaction in his body. Grinding his teeth together, Justin kept moving. Yeah, hard as hell, but what choice did he have?

The afternoon sun glinted off an object, and he jerked to a halt. "See that?"

Riley followed the direction of Justin's gaze. "What? No, I—" She broke off and then said, "Yeah." Grabbing her field binoculars, she peered at the area of the glint. "It's a cabin. Kind of small, though."

He pulled out his map, checked it again. "Yeah." Using his own binoculars, Justin took in the surrounding area. "Looks deserted."

"If this is his place and she's in there, there'd be guards."

"Probably. But it's out of the way and off the trail. Maybe they think they're safe." Justin made another sweeping glance with his binoculars. "Let's go, see what we see. If it's not his place, at least we'll have a roof over our heads for the night."

They exchanged a look that went far beyond agreeing on the plan. Both knew that if this was Russo's hideaway and something went wrong, either one or both of them could die. But this was a way of life for them. They'd chosen this career, and they accepted the risks.

Silent now, they had no need to communicate verbally. They knew each other's steps and what the other was thinking. Justin knew Riley would go to her left, to the back of the cabin. He would go to the right, to the front. If they couldn't see each other but needed to communicate, they would do so with a series of clicks on their radios. They'd devised this on their own, and it had worked so well, other LCR teams had employed the same method.

With cat-like quietness, Justin stayed low as he approached the front, on alert for any kind of trap. Even though they saw no one, that didn't mean squat. If this was Russo's hideout, then there could be any number of snares set to capture an intruder. Mateo Russo hadn't escaped the authorities for so long by being careless.

The ground was covered in new grass, with no indication that human feet had traversed the area in months. That could be a ruse, too.

Easing up onto the porch, Justin moved quickly to stand beside the door. Oddly enough, there were no front windows, but the door had a small glass pane. His gun at the ready in case bullets started flying, he leaned over and peered inside. The room was sparsely furnished, minimalistic but still comfortable looking. A sofa and an oversized chair faced a fireplace. On the other side of the large room was a small table with two chairs, and behind that a minute kitchen with a two-burner stove and a small fridge. In front of the oversized back window was a large but scarred desk and a surprisingly expensive-looking chair. Whoever the place belonged to hadn't skimped on this particular piece of furniture.

The place looked as though it hadn't been inhabited for months. A fine film of dust covered the kitchen table, and an intricate spider web stretched from the ceiling light fixture to a bookcase in the corner.

Unless Russo had gone out of his way to use spiders and dust motes to make the hideout look uninhabited, the cabin wasn't his.

A double click on his radio was Riley's all-clear signal. Justin answered back with one click.

Still cautious, he went back down the steps and met Riley on the side of the cabin. "Looks like we've got a place to stay for the night."

She gave him a solemn look, and he saw the questions in her eyes, along with the trepidation. They'd been alone with each other many times before, but this new awareness of each other put things on a different level.

Justin wanted to assure her that he wouldn't push, but at the same time, he wanted her to feel like she could tell him anything. Did she think he would judge her? Think less of her?

Was there a way he could make her realize that there wasn't anything she could tell him that would make a damn bit of difference in his feelings for her? Didn't she know he was already lost?

***

Her nerves on edge, Riley sat in front of the fire Justin had built and struggled with herself. For the next few hours, they had nothing but time on their hands. Using the excuse of sleeping would work for only a few hours. Pretending he wasn't there wasn't an option. Though the cabin was well equipped, it wasn't overly large. There was no way to avoid him.

Getting inside had been no problem for Justin. The lock had been flimsy enough for a child to pick, much less a man with her partner's skills. After exploring the place, Justin had checked in with headquarters and reported their location and their plans for the night. Noah had advised that Angela and Jake had checked in and had come up empty also, but he was still waiting to hear from Sabrina and Aidan.

After talking with Noah, they'd begun their setup for the night. Justin found a stack of wood beneath a tarp and soon had a roaring fire going. Riley rummaged around trying to create something edible with the MREs they'd brought with them. Such a domestic scene made her nervous. Domesticity was not her strong suit. For whatever reason, her training had not included cooking. She tried to not think too hard on the reason for that. Whenever she did, nightmares ultimately followed. Having Justin close-by when gripped by one of them was something she needed to avoid at all costs.

After consuming a nutritious but bland meal of beef stew and slightly stale bread, they cleaned up any mess they'd made and then settled before the fire. They were silent, each lost in their own thoughts. Maybe it was her own over-imaginative mind, but Riley thought the room held an air of expectation. How did you start out sharing a nightmare? Especially one that made no real sense?

She was saved from having to make that decision when their radio crackled with static, and Noah's tense voice exploded in the room. "Target has been located. Thorne and Fox found the site. We'll keep communications open."

Meaning everyone would be able to listen in on the rescue.

"By the way, Ingram and Kelly," Noah said, "the cabin you found belongs to a writer. Deidre contacted him, gave him a few details. He said you're welcome to use it for as long as you need."

"Good to know," Riley said.

Aidan Thorne's voice came through, low and tense. "We're about to go, McCall."

"Stay safe, you two," Noah answered.

Riley pushed her personal worries aside as they waited to hear the rescue. Listening to one was so different than being in the midst of it. She held her breath, waiting to hear a *go* signal. After that, all she and Justin could do was wait and listen—and pray—as the rescue of Taylor Vaughn went down.

CHAPTER SEVEN

Western Italy

"I don't like it. They're too relaxed." Aidan's voice was a low rumble, as he spoke into his mic to his partner.

"They're in a remote area. Think they're hidden well. I'd say they're not worried about being found."

"Maybe so, but could be an act."

Sabrina made a tsking sound and sighed. "So distrustful of bad guys, Thorne. Where'd that come from?"

"Guess I've known too many of 'em."

"Yeah, me, too."

"Want to do more recon?"

"No. Nothing's changed in the last hour. That guy on the back porch is snoring loud enough to wake the bears. We'd better do this before somebody comes out and gives him the heave-ho."

Glad they were on the same page as usual, Aidan went left, Sabrina to the right. The structure was too large to be called a cabin. Nestled within a forest of evergreens, it rose an impressive two stories. Aidan figured Russo probably stayed here on occasion. What he'd give to find the jerkwad here tonight. He gave a mental headshake. *Not your mission, Thorne.* Rescuing Taylor Vaughn was the only thing they needed to concentrate on. He told himself the same thing that had been sustaining him for years. *The bad guys always get what's coming to them, and some got it sooner than others.* He refused to allow himself to believe anything different. If he gave up looking for justice, then he'd lose. Damned if he would lose this fight.

"Thorne, you copy?" Sabrina's soft voice came through his earbud, jerking him out of his dark thoughts.

"Copy, Fox. What do you see?"

"Two males in the kitchen, playing cards. I can take them by surprise. They've got their guns holstered, so shouldn't have any issues."

"Roger that. The guy on the porch is still sleeping. I'll help him sleep a little longer."

"Let's get this done."

"We'll go on three. Meet in the middle. Watch your back, partner."

"Back at you," Sabrina said.

"One, two, three."

Aidan stepped out from behind the bushes and eased up to the porch. The first three steps were silent, the fourth gave an annoying squeak. The sleeping man opened his eyes.

Flying at the man on the porch, Aidan tackled him before the guy could go for his gun. They grappled all over the porch, grunts and curses filling the air. Aidan finally pinned the bastard, face down. Bending his arm behind his back, he put just the right amount of pressure to give him a taste of what a broken arm might feel like. The guy grunted. He'd most likely be yelling if it weren't for the fact that his mouth was pressed down against wood.

"I'm going to let you raise your head just a bit so you can talk. You try to yell for your friends, I'll rip your arm from your shoulder. You got that, asshole?"

When the guy continued to struggle, Aidan repeated his threat in Italian. The man gave a frantic nod of understanding.

Easing the pressure a bit on his head, he heard the guy release a loud puff of air and groan again.

Continuing in Italian, Aidan said in a low tone, "So far, so good. Now tell me how many men are inside."

"It's just me. I swear."

"Wrong answer, asshole." Lifting the guy's head up by his hair, Aidan slammed his face into the porch. He pulled a zip tie from his pocket, secured the unconscious man's hands and feet. For extra insurance, he slapped a wide swath of duct tape over his mouth and then rolled him off the porch into the bushes. "That'll teach you to tell lies."

Getting to his feet, he peered into the window and saw nothing other than some comfortable furniture and a number of grisly animal heads adorning the walls. Guy was not only a criminal, but he had shitty decorating taste, too.

He eased the door open and stepped inside. Noises in the back of the house told him his partner had struck. Aidan glanced around, again saw no one. He headed toward the kitchen to lend a hand. The cold steel of a gun pressed against his temple.

"Who are you?"

"No one," Aidan said.

"Well Mr. No One, you've landed in the wrong place." He pushed Aidan toward the kitchen. Since it was exactly where he wanted to go, he didn't fight him. Yet.

The ruckus Sabrina was causing registered in their hearing at the same time. The man ground the pistol against Aidan's head again and said, "Who else is with you?"

"My girlfriend. We're just looking for a place to get it on. You know…have sex. I got horny…and well, you know how it is, amico." Aidan wiggled his eyebrows for effect.

Guy wasn't buying it. "Let's go."

They moved forward again. One of the men in the kitchen bellowed, startling Aidan's captor. Aidan took his opportunity. Bending and turning, he slammed his left forearm into the hand holding the gun, as his right fist smashed into the man's face. As if he didn't know, or didn't care, that his nose was a bloody mess, the guy let out a low roar and jabbed his fist into Aidan's gut. Aidan saw it coming and deflected the hit to his face. The bracing pain only pissed him off.

Shoving the man up against the wall, Aidan grabbed him by the neck and squeezed with just the right amount of pressure. The guy went limp, and Aidan helped him to the floor.

Turning, he saw that his partner had subdued the other two men into unconsciousness. Their eyes met. They grinned their triumph at each other and then headed upstairs.

***

Riley and Justin sat in tense silence, listening as the rescue went down. She couldn't tell how many men Sabrina and Aidan had confronted so far. What amazed her was the stealth and quietness. Other than a few grunts and one bellow that had been cut off almost before it sounded, they'd managed to secure the ground floor.

Now the only sounds were the operatives' quiet breaths as they moved to the second floor. Having worked with them on numerous ops, Riley knew much of their communication was nonverbal.

Seconds later, Sabrina's voice, calm and quiet, said, "Found her."

"How is she?" Noah asked.

"Alive," Aidan said, the bleakness in his voice telling them even more.

"Do what you can for her, Thorne," Noah said. "I'll have a medical helicopter at your location in approximately twenty minutes."

"Roger that." The radio clicked off.

Riley sat back in her chair and let loose an explosive sigh of relief. Now that it was over and everyone was safe, they could all relax. She refused to consider what Taylor Vaughn had endured while in captivity. There was no telling what those fiends had done to her, and dwelling on it was pointless. What one human being could do to another didn't surprise her. She'd lost her faith in humanity years ago. Last Chance Rescue had restored some of that faith. Not enough for her to let her guard down, though. Never again.

Pushing those dark thoughts away, she glanced over at Justin and then swallowed hard. The fire had chased away the icy chill in the room, and the air had gotten downright balmy. Justin Kelly, who'd never had a modesty problem in his life, had stripped down to a pair of loose shorts and nothing else.

Being attracted to a man wasn't something Riley had ever believed would be possible. She hoped many of the memories in the dark recesses of her brain never emerged, but the ones that had were horrible, vile. Sexual desire had seemed as far out of reach for her as a kitten flying a plane. Utterly impossible.

But then she'd met Justin Kelly, and all her preconceived notions evaporated.

"She's safe now, Ingram."

"What?"

"You have a worried look on your face."

Yes, she was worried, but it had little to do with the journalist's rescue. Justin was right. Taylor Vaughn was safe and would get the medical care she needed. This had been the best kind of outcome. No operatives injured and a successful rescue. It didn't get better than that.

So no, she wasn't concerned about that. What troubled her was the man sitting across from her. Those intelligent, piercing eyes saw too much. And now endless hours were ahead of them with nothing to do but talk. Oddly, talking was the lesser of her worries. The biggest were the nightmares.

They had been with her from the beginning. Some were so obscure that when she woke, the memories of them were like wisps of thin fog, disintegrating instantly. Others stuck with her longer. Still others had her waking up screaming. What if she had a screaming nightmare? How the hell was she going to explain that?

This wasn't the first time they'd spent the night together out in the field. They'd been on missions where the accommodations were a hard ground and a small fire. On those occasions, she'd slept lightly, waking frequently. This time would be different. She'd had almost no sleep in over twenty-four hours. That and a long day of hiking had worn her out. Sometimes, exhaustion meant she slept like the dead. Other times, if her body was too tired, she couldn't fight the demons that invaded her sleep.

And now, having decided to do something about confronting her past, would her subconscious do everything within its power to stop her by reminding her what hell was like? Hiding those violent episodes from Justin was going to be difficult, if not impossible. Just how long could she stay awake tonight?

Justin clenched his fist to keep himself from reaching out to his partner. The wary glances she was giving him were breaking his heart. Addressing them might not be the best idea, but dammit, he had to know.

"Ingram, do you have doubts about me?"

"What do you mean?"

"I mean, do you think there's some kind of flaw in my character that gives you cause for concern?"

She jerked back as if shocked that he could say such a thing. "Of course not. I have total faith and trust in you."

"Then you have to know you can tell me anything."

She looked away from him, and he figured he'd gone too far. He waited, though. They'd come this far, could they go further?

"Justin, it's not a lack of trust. It's just… I don't know. Saying it's complicated sounds like a cliché, but in this case…" She sighed. "Sometimes I can hardly believe it myself, and I'm the one who lived through it."

"Did what happened to you occur after your parents' deaths?"

An odd expression flickered on her face. The answer she gave was even more enigmatic. "Yes, I guess you could say that."

"Are the people…or man who hurt you still alive?"

"I don't know. Probably. I don't usually worry about being out in public, but Brennan and Kacie's wedding was international news. I felt I had no choice but to disguise myself."

"Can you tell me how you started with LCR?"

"No," she whispered. "I can't."

Before the disappointment could even register, her next words cracked his heart open wide. "Have patience with me. Please, Justin? This is really hard for me."

"You take all the time you need, sweetheart. Just know I'm here when you're ready."

The endearment was deliberate. He wanted her to accept the transition, if she hadn't already. This was no longer Ingram and Kelly having a discussion. An intimacy had developed between them. One that he wanted to grow and expand.

The response to his comment was more than he could have hoped for. Her eyes took on a soft, dreaminess, and her mouth lifted in a rare smile.

Justin's heart was beating like the bass line of a hard rock song. If he said anything more, asked anything else of her tonight, he was certain she'd close down.

He said the first thing that came to mind. "Fox and Thorne have a good partnership."

The relief on her face told him he'd said the right thing.

"Noah's good about pairing up people who work well together." She tilted her head. "Did you worry he'd made a mistake with us?"

Surprised but pleased that she'd asked something even remotely personal, he nodded, knowing she wouldn't take offense. "Yeah, I did. We didn't seem to have a lot in common."

"Until that first op."

Their first op together had been an eye-opening experience in many ways. Riley had seemed so closed-off and distant, he had anticipated major problems, even a failed op. He'd voiced his concern to McCall, who'd told him to give her a chance. He was damn glad he had.

"Why do you think we work so well together?" she asked.

He had some theories but doubted she'd be interested in hearing them right now. Baby steps were his only choice. The caution, however, didn't stop him from countering. "Why do *you* think we work so well together?"

She sent him a teasing grin, a rarity for her. "Really bad deflect, Kelly. And I don't know why either. We train together a lot, so that might be one reason. But other than I can somehow read what you're going to do before you do it, I think we complement each other. Our strengths somehow mesh."

"Yeah. Did you have skills before you came to LCR, or did you learn them all from McCall's training?"

Skills? Riley almost laughed out loud at that. She'd had no knowledge of how to defend herself, physically or emotionally. When Noah had found her, she'd barely been able to function as a human being, much less as a confident, skilled operative.

Since telling him that would create a multitude of questions she wasn't close to being ready to answer, she responded truthfully if vaguely. "All LCR training. What about you?"

"Already had military training, but my hand-to-hand needed some work."

"Logistical planning of a mission was a breeze for me. I did pretty well on shooting, too, but my hand-to-hand sucked."

He flashed her one of his teasing grins. "Bet that creep you took down in Iraq a couple of weeks ago thinks differently."

Riley felt an unusual burst of pride. She had taken the cretin down, and with minimal effort. If she'd had this skill earlier in life, everything could have been so different.

"A smaller size can be an advantage, because most people underestimate you."

"That's what Noah said."

There was no need to go into detail about how her size had nothing to do with her difficulty in learning how to physically defend herself. It had taken her months to allow anyone to touch her. Putting herself into a training exercise in which physical contact was a must had been unbearable. But with her therapist's help and Noah McCall's incredible patience, she had overcome that fear, along with a multitude of others.

A giant yawn took her off guard. The lack of sleep plus the hours-long hike today, along with the additional stress of Justin's questions, had taken their toll.

"Why don't you take the bathroom first? I'm going to do a quick perimeter check."

She stifled another yawn. "Call me if you need help."

Justin watched her walk away, almost stumbling in her exhaustion. He'd learned a lot tonight. Not so much actual information, but a whole lot more about what was in Riley's mind and heart. First, she did trust him. He had known that, but he'd wanted to hear her say the words. And second, she was having the same thoughts he was about their relationship. He'd seen the spark of attraction from her before, but tonight there had been more. Even though he told himself to take it slow, that anything this good would be even better if it wasn't rushed, it was still damn hard to hold back.

He took a little longer than normal to check their surroundings and then lock up. He wanted to give her a chance to settle down. Hopefully, she'd be asleep when he went back inside. There was only one bed in the cabin, and no way in hell was he going to sleep on the too-short couch or the floor. If she was already asleep when he got in bed, it would make things less awkward. He wouldn't do anything without her permission, but neither did he want her to worry about it. As he had told her, she could take all the time she needed.

Didn't mean things were going to be easy, but anything worthwhile was worth waiting for. And he was learning, Riley Ingram was definitely worth the wait.

***

Why did the dreams always begin the same? Even as she told herself she was falling into one, she couldn't prevent the descent into darkness.

First, there was only pitch-black nothingness, then the fear came, almost overwhelming in its intensity. What would he do this time? What could she do but allow it to happen and pray it wasn't as bad as last time? But she knew those prayers were pointless. She had defied him. The other times had been about his pleasure. This time…this time it would be about her punishment.

Could it be worse than it had already been? A secret, evil voice cackled inside her. Yes, yes, yes, it could and would.

She heard the sounds first. Soft little scratches, then the pitter-patter of tiny little feet. What was that? What was he doing now? She struggled against the ties at her wrists and ankles. She had expected pain and fear, but this was almost worse. Not knowing fed her imagination until her fear was at a fever pitch. The noise grew louder and louder, and then the squeals came. It sounded like an army of rats! He was going to let rats devour her, feed on her? This was her punishment? So it was to be death this time.

Screams built inside her, but he had filled her mouth with a ball gag, which only allowed muffled sounds. Why couldn't he have allowed her the release of screaming? She struggled, the bindings on her wrists and ankles becoming unbearable as she fought to break the bonds. Blood dripped down her arms, and her panic grew. The rats! They would smell the blood! They would be on her in seconds, feeding, devouring! *Help! Help! Please!* Her mind pleaded for a faceless, nameless person to save her, but there was no one to care. Even if she had been able to utter a word, no one gave a damn about her. She had learned that final truth today.

A sob built in her chest, and she made an anguished sound. Lights flooded the room. She looked around. It was empty. There were no rats. Nothing to fear. She was safe.

A voice boomed above her. "You think your misery is over, my sweet? It's just getting started."

The room went pitch black again. At first, there was nothing. Complete silence, emptiness. Then sounds, like something sliding. Then she heard them. Rattling? Rattlesnakes? It was only sound effects, just as the rats had been. She could deal with noises. Sound couldn't hurt her. He was just trying to scare her.

The rattling grew louder, and she ground her teeth together, determined not to give in to the fear. She could handle psychological torture. It was the hideous pain that destroyed her. Sounds wouldn't kill her. Couldn't hurt her. She would endure.

Light burst forth again. The room was empty, as she had surmised. Taut muscles went lax with relief. Her breath settled. She could handle this. She could.

"You think you're home free, don't you? You think your punishment is only this? You don't know what suffering is. Once I'm through with you, the very thought of trying to escape will sicken your stomach. You'll do anything to stay with me."

The light went off again.

I can do this. I can do this.

Just because he'd threatened something worse, she told herself, as long as physical torture wasn't used, she would be fine.

The horror continued. She stopped struggling. Though her heart still pounded, and each new sound was worse than the last, she forced her mind into another place. She no longer heard anything. Music filled her head, and she was swept away in its beauty. Her mouth moved up in a smile. She would destroy the darkness with music. It had always brought her light…it would again.

The noises stopped, and silence again filled the room. The music in her head became stilted. *No, no, no. Bring it back. Bring it back.* His torture wasn't over. As long as she had an escape in her head, she could survive.

New sounds penetrated the silence. A door opened and closed. Footsteps came closer. Was he here, or was this just another new way to terrify her? Lights exploded once more, and she squinted her eyes against the blinding brightness. Blinking away the tears, she saw an image. It was him. He was here. Would he finally free her? It had been hours. Surely her punishment had passed.

He pulled the gag from her mouth. "Have you learned your lesson?" he asked.

She nodded as vigorously as her bindings would allow. She tried to speak, but her throat and mouth were dry from fear and lack of water. She managed a croaking, "Yes, sir."

"I don't believe you have."

For the first time, she realized he held something behind his back. Before she could comprehend, prepare herself, an agony unlike anything she'd ever felt swept through her.

She screamed. Cried. Kicked. *Stop it. Stop it. Stop it. Please. Please. No more!*

"Riley? Wake up. Riley, it's me. It's Justin. Stop struggling, baby. You're fine. You're fine."

She woke, screaming, crying. "It hurts, it hurts."

"I've got you, sweetheart. Nothing's going to hurt you. I promise."

She became aware of several things. She was gripping Justin's shoulders with a finger-numbing clench. He was holding her shivering body against his. And somehow she felt safe, protected.

Breath shuddered from her, and she buried her face against his chest. "Sorry. Nightmare."

She felt a kiss pressed to her head, and he squeezed her harder. "You're safe now."

She nodded. "Yes. Thanks."

"Want to talk about it?"

Talk about a horror she did her dead level best to never remember? *No. Just no.*

She shook her head. "It's just residual junk. Guess it's been one of those days that brings out the night monsters."

"Night monsters?"

Releasing her grip on his shoulders, she lay back against the pillows. Though it was dark in the room and she could see only the silhouette of his head in the shadows, she felt no fear. This was Justin. And though her secrets weren't ones she could share with him yet, there was no one she trusted more.

"You didn't have night monsters when you were a kid?"

"You mean like the boogeyman?"

"Yes."

He laughed a little. "Not really. I was mostly afraid of my dad and his belt."

"He hurt you?"

"On occasion. I deserved most of it. I was a bratty kid."

"You?" She gave an exaggerated gasp. "Surely not."

"Yeah." She heard the grin in his voice. "Defies all logic, I know."

"Your parents. They were good to you?"

"Yes. They're good people. Good parents. Didn't have a lot of money, but we had love."

"That's nice."

"Riley?"

"Yes."

"We've already established that you can trust me. Right?"

"Yes," she whispered.

"Can I kiss you?"

The question didn't surprise her. She had known they were heading to this place. Her heart consented before she gave her answer with a soft sighing, "Yes."

She watched his head lower slowly, the anticipation almost more than she could bear. His mouth touched hers, tender, soft, light. A feather of a kiss. A mere taste on her lips. It was sweet and perfect. She wanted more.

Lifting her hands, she brought him closer to her for a deeper connection. As if understanding what she needed, he licked the seam of her mouth. She opened, and he took control.

Justin groaned beneath his breath. He had meant their first kiss to be a soft, light initiation into exploring each other, their lips becoming acquainted. Riley had a different idea. And though he was on board with giving and taking more, he noted one specific thing. She kissed as if she'd never been kissed before. Unskilled, unpracticed. Riley was always so reserved, but not with this. And while she kissed with innocent passion, Justin's body throbbed with an unrelenting want. His heart and mind told him to go slow, but his body had a completely different goal. Didn't matter. He was a man, not a boy. He controlled his urges. Besides, frightening her was the last thing he wanted.

Riley apparently had other ideas. Though unskilled she might be, she made up for it with enthusiasm, with generosity. She held nothing back. And like everything Riley tried her hand at, she learned fast.

Groaning again, Justin lifted his head, surprised to find himself breathing hard. He had long since accepted his attraction for Riley and that he wanted her. What he was just now realizing was he wanted more than just a physical relationship with this maddening, indomitable woman.

Unsettled and at a loss for how to adjust to this astonishing revelation, he gave a somewhat standard, albeit sincere, compliment, "You're so damn beautiful."

Little did he know it was the one thing he never should have said.

He felt the change in her immediately. She'd been pliant, soft in his arms. Now she was stiff, unyielding. "Beauty matters to you?"

"It's not the most important thing, but it's part of being attracted to another person."

"If beauty is what you're looking for, we have nothing in common after all."

"You don't think you're beautiful?"

"It's not important to me. Beauty is a shallow, ridiculous premise. It's not important to me. It apparently is to you."

Admittedly, it had been a trite thing to say, but never had he considered she might be offended. Reaching over, he flipped on the bedside light. He needed to see her face. Maybe then he could figure out where he'd gone wrong.

She jerked her face away from him. "Let me up."

"No. Not before we talk this out."

She wiggled beneath him. "Let me up. Now."

"Look, I obviously upset you, and I'm sorry. Most women—" He cut off his words, wincing the moment they came out of his mouth. If he'd thought she'd been offended before, the look on her face told him this was even worse.

"If you haven't already figured it out by now, I'm not most women. Now let me up, dammit."

Rolling over onto his back, he blew out a sigh of frustration as he watched her disappear into the bathroom. Never in his life had he met a more puzzling, infuriating, and maddening woman. Wasn't it just too damn bad he was falling in love with her?

The kiss had been a dumbass move on his part. She'd had a violent nightmare. He should've held her, consoled her. But no, what did he do? He kissed her. Yeah, she had responded like a wildfire, but that didn't make him any less of a sleazeball.

A few minutes later, she returned to the bedroom. Her mask was firmly in place. He also noted regret and embarrassment in her eyes.

Figuring she would grab a pillow and go sleep on the sofa, he was stunned when she switched off the lamplight on the night-stand and then crawled back into bed. He waited until she had settled beside him, then said, "I'm sorry, Riley."

"There's nothing to forgive. I just have a few million hang-ups, which I'm sure you've already noticed."

"If I promise to never tell you you're beautiful again, will you let me hold your hand?"

She gave a small huff of laughter, and he felt her hand on his. He gave her hand a gentle squeeze and then heard her breath even out. He wondered if she were sleeping or merely faking it to keep him from asking questions. She didn't need to worry. He had pressed her too much already. He told her she could take her time and he meant it.

He closed his eyes but it took him a long time to fall back to sleep. He could still hear her screams. The childlike cries of "It hurts!" made him feel physically sick. Who had hurt her? And just where was the son of a bitch now?

CHAPTER EIGHT

Drake Hotel
Chicago, Illinois

"Thank you for agreeing to see me, Mr. McCall. I know your time is valuable."

Noah shut the door of the small conference room, then angled his head slightly, acknowledging the comment. He had been highly anticipating this meeting with William Larson.

After hundreds of interviews over the years, he'd learned to read people. He'd dealt with a sea of humanity across every spectrum. None was perfect. Most of them had good and bad qualities, and he'd learned over time that, for the most part, the good outweighed the bad. Because he saw many of them at their absolute lowest point, he tried not to judge too harshly.

And then there were those who he knew immediately were pure evil without a hint of real humanity. The moment he met William Larson, he knew his instincts had not failed him. William Larson was one of those people.

"I'm a little surprised we're meeting at a hotel. I thought we might meet at an office. I am assuming you do have one?"

Yes, he had an office, in another city, but not one this asshole would ever see.

"I meet all prospective clients at a hotel." Noah didn't bother to explain why.

"I see… Well, nevertheless, thank you for seeing me. As you might imagine, we've used every resource available to find our little girl. Her mother and I refuse to believe she's lost to us."

"Little girl? When we talked on the phone, I understood she was a grown woman."

"Oh, she is. It's just…" A self-conscious, ingratiating smile slid like an oil spill across Larson's mouth. "Do you have children, Mr. McCall?"

"I don't share that kind of personal information."

"Oh…of course. I understand. I was just trying to explain that when you have children, no matter how old they get or how far they roam, they'll always be your babies."

He pulled a slender wallet from the inside of his jacket. Like any proud, doting father, he withdrew a photograph and slid it across the coffee table toward Noah. "She was our pride and joy. So sweet, so smart and talented. We miss her so."

Noah took the photograph, thinking most people's photos of their kids were on their phone these days. He dropped his gaze and took in the image of Jessica Larson. Grateful for his ability to hide all emotion, he said, "What age is she here?"

"Almost eighteen."

"You said she disappeared when she was twenty-one. You don't have anything more recent?"

"No. We—" Another slick smile, this time tinged with grief. "I'm ashamed to say we were angry with her for years, believing she just ran away. That anger made us do the unthinkable. We destroyed almost all of her photographs."

Bullshit.

"And you no longer think she ran away?"

"We're still not sure, Mr. McCall, but time has softened our anger. What we want more than anything is to be reunited with our precious girl."

"I'm surprised your wife didn't come with you."

"Loretta's not well. I'm afraid the trip might have been too much of a strain. Besides, she needed to stay behind with Keira."

"And Keira is?"

"She's our other daughter. We adopted her a few years ago."

Oh, holy hell.

"How old is Keira?"

"She turned sixteen just a couple of months ago."

Two years younger than when Jessica's life went to hell. Was the bastard raising Keira for the same damn thing?

Not noticing Noah's utter stillness, Larson continued, "Besides, talking about Jessica upsets Loretta so much. We've exhausted ourselves trying to find her, and I'm just not sure she can take much more. It's been years since we've seen her. A mother's heart is fragile. Loretta's is almost broken."

"You don't believe Jessica's dead?"

"No, I can't accept that. We've searched for her for years, though, without any hope. As your organization's name implies, Mr. McCall, you are our last chance…our last hope. We must find her."

The last line was said with such conviction and emotion that Noah would've probably believed the man loved his daughter if he didn't already know better. So why the emotion, almost desperation? His gut was telling him the reason, and he didn't like the answer.

"Do you think she could she have been abducted? Was she dating anyone? I'm assuming you checked with all her friends. Is she staying away because she doesn't want to come home? Could she be afraid to come home?"

Larson was too skilled to show his surprise at the rapid-fire questions, but the dilation of his pupils gave him away. The idiot apparently thought he could give the barest facts and Noah would take him at face value.

"She has nothing to fear. Her mother and I love her dearly."

"I see." Noah allowed just a tinge of doubt to color his tone.

The slight twitching of his mouth was Larson's only sign of irritation. That was okay. Noah would put him at ease later if necessary. For right now, putting him on edge would reveal more of what he wanted to know. Despite only just meeting him today, Noah already knew more than this man could ever fathom, but there was still more to learn. Like, why?

"Why don't you tell me about Jessica?"

"We always called her Jessie." Larson expelled a sad sigh. "She's a bright, intelligent young woman, but she's disturbed, Mr. McCall. So very disturbed."

"In what way?"

"She's quite delusional. Made all sorts of heinous accusations about her mother and me. We tried so hard with her." He paused to allow a little sobbing breath. "So very hard."

"And her doctors? What did they say?"

The sound he made, between a snort and a *pfft*, made it clear what he thought about doctors. His words bore that out. "They know nothing. A few act as if she's just a disobedient child."

Noah cocked his head. "Not one of them gave you a medical diagnosis?"

He shifted his eyes away. "Of course they did."

"And?"

"I don't see why her mental diagnosis has anything to do with you being able to find her."

"If we have no idea what's she suffering from, it makes it almost impossible to narrow down where she might have gone. We need everything we can get on Jessica. In fact, I'd like to see her full medical history. If you can't share, then I'm afraid this meeting is at an end."

"That's ridiculous! I'm not going to—" A cold, dark look entered Larson's eyes as he leaned forward. "Do you know how much money I have, McCall? I could bury you without blinking."

"Please try, Mr. Larson," Noah said softly. "I would love to take you on."

Larson's face puffed up like an angry blowfish and turned red. Noah couldn't deny he was enjoying the show. Apparently, Larson had only a limited ability to play the concerned, loving father before his real nature surfaced.

A giant, rasping sigh released, bringing a more normal color to Larson's complexion. "My apologies, Mr. McCall. My love for my daughter is so overwhelming sometimes that I tend to lose my temper. Your request, of course, is reasonable, but I'm afraid I don't have that information with me. Would it be appropriate to send those documents to you at a later date?"

"That would be acceptable. Why don't you, in the meantime, tell me more about Jessica? Where did you last see her? Where would she feel the safest place to hide? Does she have any relatives or friends she might have turned to?"

Larson leaned back in his chair. Having regained his composure, the man was now in his element. Both eloquent and emotional, the act was impressive. No doubt, all the practice he'd had over the past few years enabled him to recite the details from memory.

The pitch of his voice, the husky tone when he talked about his little girl, the sheen of tears in his eyes—all a masterful performance. There were many reasons Larson wanted to find his daughter, but love, especially a father's love, had nothing to do with it.

If this bastard and his wife ever found their beloved Jessica, Noah could only wonder who would try to kill her first—her loving father or sainted mother?

No. That didn't make any sense. No way would the man spend money on trying to find his daughter just to murder her. Killing Jessica would not be his ultimate goal. He would do to her again what he'd done when she was eighteen years old. He would turn her over to a monster.

It was Noah's responsibility to make sure none of them ever found her.

But now there was a new concern, even more alarming. Someone else was in just as much danger as Jessica had once been in, perhaps even more so, if that was possible. If what he feared was true, then they had only a short amount of time to act.

The question was, when this was over, would he have destroyed a young woman he had once saved? But he had no choice in the matter. Besides, if there was one thing he knew for certain about her, Riley Ingram would face this challenge head on.

CHAPTER NINE

Alexandria, Virginia

Her knees were knocking as she readied herself for her meeting with Noah and Samara. All morning long, she'd been telling herself that this was her choice. No one was making her take this step. She could still call Noah and tell him she'd changed her mind. Things could stay as they were. She didn't have to do this.

But didn't she?

The trip down the mountain yesterday had been excruciating. The trek up had been no gabfest, but going down she hadn't uttered one word. Justin had made a few remarks, but when she'd barely responded, he gave up. Her lack of words had been from extreme embarrassment and shame. She supposed Justin's had been from bewilderment and confusion.

A normal woman would not have been offended by being called beautiful. A normal person would have taken it as a compliment and moved on. Or maybe blushed, giggled, simpered. Whatever a normal woman did when she was told she's beautiful.

How stupid for her to try to pretend to be someone other than the damaged woman who wouldn't recognize normal if it came up and kicked her ass. She had learned to live with her limitations.

She told herself that her strengths far outweighed her handicaps. She could shoot like a pro. With some well-targeted fist strikes and kicks, she could bring down a three-hundred-pound man. Her logistical skills were excellent, and she could strategize an op to perfection. And when called upon, she could assume any role LCR set out for her to play. She had saved numerous lives and would continue to do so until she died. Those were the things she needed to concentrate on, be proud of. The other things were superfluous.

She bit her lip as she acknowledged the truth. No, those other things weren't unimportant. Her feelings for Justin were real, as authentic as any she'd ever had. But he deserved someone who could be normal, not someone so messed up that the very words *you're beautiful* put a cramp in her stomach and had her heart pounding in horror.

Dropping down into her kitchen chair, she propped her elbows on the table and buried her face in her hands. It had been so perfect until she'd messed it up. Never had she imagined a kiss being so wonderful. Why, oh, why couldn't she have just let his words slide off her? He had meant them as a compliment. What girl didn't enjoy hearing nice things said to her?

Disgusted with her indecision, she grabbed her keys and headed out the door. It didn't matter. Either way, it was long past time to deal with her past. Hypnosis had been moderately successful. She would try that again first. Maybe there were new techniques that would work better for her. If that failed, drugs were her only other option. She would do what she had to do. The nightmare at the cabin had been one of the worst she'd had in years. Maybe if she finally remembered everything and was able to bring the sick, twisted fiend to justice, she could find some peace. Maybe she and Justin could—

She stopped that thought before it could be completed. No, she and Justin couldn't. They were partners and nothing more. Romance and intimacy were for other people. Normal people. Wasn't it just too damn bad that normal had never been part of her life?

***

LCR Headquarters

"Do you think you should give her some notice before she arrives?"

Noah gazed at Samara, who'd been pacing his office floor for over an hour. She showed nervousness now, but he knew when Riley arrived, she'd be the calm, supportive friend and counselor Riley needed. It was one of the many reasons he loved her.

"I'd prefer telling her in person. She didn't return until last night. We'd already set up this meeting."

"She's going to be blindsided. Devastated."

Noah held out his hand for Samara to join him at his desk. They'd been married a little over six years now, and not a day had gone by since then that his heart didn't melt when he looked at her. His life had been far from easy before he met her, having gone through more hells than he could count. But he knew to his soul that if going through those same experiences again would lead him to this woman, he'd do it in a heartbeat. She had been and would always be his greatest blessing.

Settling onto his lap, Samara locked her arms around his neck and held him close. They were both unsettled. They had watched a traumatized young woman grow into a strong, independent adult. Her incredible strength had surprised them. Neither of them wanted to see her hurt.

"We knew she'd want to delve deeper at some point. And even though this isn't the way I would have chosen, at least she won't have to endure more hypnosis or resort to drugs. If this way works, we can find the bastards without putting her through additional trauma."

Every LCR operative at some point made a choice to deal, or not deal, with their past. Some chose to go on as if nothing terrible had happened to them. Most, however, chose to confront their demons.

For just about anyone besides Riley, Noah would encourage the latter. He'd faced his own demons, and though it had almost gotten both him and Samara killed, in retrospect, he was grateful that the most painful part of his past had been settled.

But Riley? Riley was different. Would this destroy her or make her even stronger? After yesterday's meeting, there was no other option. Whether she was ready or not, it was going to happen.

Apparently seeing the worry in his eyes, Samara hugged him tighter, now trying to reassure him instead. "She's stronger now than she's ever been."

Noah acknowledged that truth with a nod. Yes, she was. When he'd met her years ago, Noah had never seen anyone more beaten down or broken. At that first meeting, he'd feared that she would barely be able to function as a human being, much less have a reasonably normal life. She had surprised the hell out of him and Mara at every turn. Not only had Riley recovered her spirit and her courage, she had become a force to be reckoned with—a formidable opponent of evil. She might not be his most-skilled operative or his strongest, but what Riley possessed couldn't be taught. And since her parents were, in his opinion, the spawns of Satan, she'd definitely not inherited her strength of character from them.

"She is strong," Noah agreed. His mind went back to several months ago. They'd been on an op to rescue Kacie Dane. He remembered the look of distress on Riley's face when she'd seen the chains and handcuffs on the bed, her small moan of pain. In her time as an operative, she had encountered similarly horrific scenes, but that one in particular had brought a memory to the forefront.

What would happen to her when she was forced to confront the man who had inflicted those wounds on her soul, those scars on her mind and body? Would she endure, or would they lose her to the darkness?

He wished they had a choice or more time. They had neither. If what he suspected was true, all hell was about to break loose. He just prayed to God that it didn't destroy Riley in the process.

***

Riley stood outside Noah's office, feeling the need to remind herself once more that this decision was hers. It always had been. She could turn and walk away. No one would think less of her, especially Noah and Samara. They knew what she had endured, knew how far she had come. She knew they admired her. Though, in her estimation, much of that admiration was undeserved. She had overcome a lot, but every day she had to fight a battle not to succumb to the terror.

Having no roommates or lovers gave her the ability to hide certain facts. Such as, she woke almost every night in extreme panic. Not always from nightmares, at least not ones she could remember. But she'd often wake in a cold sweat, thinking that he had found her, that he would force her to go back with him. On occasion, she would wake in extreme pain, as if she actually felt the sting of the whip tearing into her skin. Other times, she would wake gasping for breath, the claustrophobic feel of imprisonment literally pressing the air out of her lungs.

But even more frightening were those rare nightmares in which she hadn't really gotten away from him after all. That her life with LCR was merely a dream. That she would open her eyes and she would still be with the monster.

Most times, after walking around her apartment for a ten or fifteen-minute pep talk, she was able to go back to sleep, reassured that he had no idea where she was or what she had become. Occasionally, the pep talk didn't work. On those nights, she forced herself to do something, anything to take her mind off her past.

No one knew that she often felt as though she were on the very precipice of a cliff, and with one slight nudge, she would fall into the deepest hell pit where he would be waiting to devour her. She fought her demons every single day. Probably always would.

So if she turned around and went home now, no one would blame her. Except she would know. She, who had come so far, overcome so much, would know that she hadn't taken that final step. And if she didn't take the step, she would have to acknowledge that she had failed. That even if she never saw him again, he had won. He had already taken so much from her. Damned if he would be in control of her any longer.

She knocked on the door and Noah called out for her to come inside. Shoulders erect, chin set with determination, Riley opened the door.

There was no turning back now.

Chapter Ten

The minute Riley walked into his office, Noah felt instant reassurance. The expression on her face was that same determination he'd watched develop over the years. Her eyes held not just the will to survive, but also the glint of purpose. They said she was ready to go to battle. She would persevere, no matter what came her way.

"Come on in. Mara's already here."

She gave Samara a quick hug and, after refusing coffee or soda, sat on the sofa. Noah watched as she visibly tried to relax. He knew she wasn't nervous about meeting with him or Mara. Her real nerves came from what she had come to tell them.

She surprised him, however, and said, "I've asked Anna to be here, too. Hope that's okay."

"Of course it is," Mara said. "I didn't get to talk to her at the wedding. I looked for her at the reception but didn't see her."

Riley gave one of her rare smiles. "That's because we went to my room and ordered room service."

Samara laughed. "Excellent idea."

"I didn't get to spend a lot of time with her, though, since we got the call about Taylor Vaughn. I texted her yesterday to see if she could come to Virginia. Turns out she's in DC for some meetings so she's heading over on the Metro. Since she was instrumental in my recovery, too, I thought it best that she join us."

Those few sentences told Noah something else. Despite her calm demeanor, Riley was nervous. Her explanation about Anna might sound normal coming from another person, but not Riley. She had a uniquely economical way of speaking. Five sentences in a row from her was unusual.

Knowing there was no other way around this other than to reveal what had happened and let her begin to process it, Noah sat in a chair across from her. "You need to know something before Anna arrives."

"What's that?"

"I had a meeting with a man yesterday. His name is William Larson. Does that ring a bell?"

"No." Her brow wrinkled as she tried to recognize the name. "No," she said again. "Why?"

"He's looking for his daughter. Showed me a picture of her. Said her name is Jessica Larson. It was a picture of you, Riley."

Her face went bloodless, and her pale lips whispered a shocked, "What?"

"He said his daughter went missing eight years ago. That she just one day disappeared. Said she had a history of mental illness. Even claims to have doctors' reports."

She was quiet for several seconds, and Noah gave her that time to digest the news.

She drew in a small, shuddering breath, gave a brief nod. "So, apparently Lloyd King became William Larson. That's why we were never able to find him. And my mo—" She gave a rapid shake of her head. "His wife. Was she with him?"

"No. She stayed at home. Goes by the name of Loretta Larson. They live in Los Angeles. I met with him in Chicago. Mia and Jared Livingston helped me out and followed him. Jared flew back on the same flight with him, followed him to his house."

"You know where he is," Riley said softly, her voice trembling slightly. "After all these years, you know."

"Yes."

She straightened her shoulders, sat up in her chair. "So why, after all these years, is he trying to find me?" Her eyes went wide. "You don't think he knows I work for LCR, do you?"

"Absolutely not. I have a few suspicions about his reasons for wanting to find you. But believe it or not, that's not my biggest concern now."

"What is?"

"He claims he has another daughter. Her name is Keira. She's sixteen."

"I didn't have a sister."

"Exactly."

He went silent again, allowing her to take in the information and grasp its implication.

As it hit her, Riley closed her eyes. *Oh no, oh no, oh no.* The shock of learning that her father was searching for her shrank to minuscule portions as she absorbed the meaning of Noah's words.

"They have another young girl. They're going to do to her what they did to me."

His answer was a grim, "Yes."

"We can't let him do that."

"No," he said very gently, "we can't."

"We need to get her out of there. You know where he lives. We can—"

Noah held up his hand. "Hold on. Jared and Mia have already scoped out the house, and there's no sign that any children live there. We're assuming he has her stashed somewhere else.

They'll stay there and keep eyes on him until we decide how to proceed."

Before she could respond, the buzzer on Noah's desk sounded, and his receptionist's voice called out, "Anna Bradford is here to see you."

Standing, Noah went to his desk and answered, "Send her on up."

He turned back to look at Riley. "Are you okay?"

Saying yes would be a lie of major proportions. Of course she wasn't okay. Everything was spiraling out of control. She had been set on a specific course, determined to see her plan through. And now that plan had taken off on a completely different trajectory. She was crumbling like decayed bones as her stomach churned like a wild sea.

Making the monumental decision to find her abuser and bring him to justice had been difficult enough. Now she would have to face the people responsible for handing her over to him. The people she should have been able to trust above anyone else, who had betrayed her in the worst possible way.

She had been focused on finding Dimitri and making him pay. And now this. She felt adrift, unfocused and confused.

"Ingram?"

Noah saying her last name, in that way, brought her focus back to where she was, who she was now. Not who she had been.

She straightened her spine and answered him. "I will be okay. I have to be."

Samara sat on the arm of her chair, put an arm around Riley's shoulders. "We'll get through this together. You're not alone. You'll never be alone again."

Riley allowed herself a rare moment of self-indulgence and leaned into Samara. She could only imagine what would have happened to her if she had not met Noah. Without him and then later Samara, Riley was almost certain she would be dead.

The day she'd left that monster's house, she had assumed she would go someplace and die. There had been no hope of ever having a life. She had just wanted to escape. The news he had imparted to her on her twenty-first birthday had been the final act…the final impetus to get her to leave. She had been determined to escape or die trying. Surviving hadn't really been on her radar.

Stowing away on the ship bound for France had seemed like her only chance. No one had noticed the small shadow that had flitted about during the night, looking for a place to lie down and die. She'd recovered from most of her injuries by then, but she'd been a broken woman. Dying in privacy, away from the demon, had seemed like her only chance at peace.

She had landed in France, surprised that she was still alive. The voyage had taken over two weeks, and if anyone had noticed her, they'd been kind enough not to out her. At night, she would steal into the kitchen and rummage for food and water. She hadn't taken much, just enough to keep from starving. Despite feeling as nonhuman as one could, she had a core of ethics that hated the idea of actual theft.

The day they'd docked in Marseille, she was stronger but still so weak that if Dimitri's men had been waiting for her, she wouldn't have been able to fight them. But when she'd slipped onto the pier, not a soul had looked at her. She'd walked away, free for the first time in years.

A knock on the door pulled Riley from her memories. The door opened, and Anna Bradford stepped inside. Lovely, lighthearted Anna, who always looked for the best in everyone, was Riley's opposite in almost every way possible. And from the moment they'd met, they'd been fast friends.

After hugging everyone, as was Anna's way, she sat across from Riley and said, "So what's up?"

Riley had to smile. That was Anna's way also. Where Riley was cautious, weighed every word before she spoke, and trusted almost no one, Anna dove in and got to the point. Considering she was one of LCR's rescued victims, it was astounding. But Anna had used her experience as a victim to fight for others.

Noah and Samara sat side by side on the sofa. It didn't surprise Riley to see them holding hands. It wasn't until she'd met them that she saw what true love and devotion really were. Their commitment to each other was one of the cornerstones of her life.

"What's going on?" Anna asked again. "You were very mysterious on the phone."

She tried to smile, decided it took too much effort. "I asked you here because I wanted to tell you that I decided to try more hypnosis and, if that didn't work again, drug therapy."

"What? Why?" Her face a mask of concern, Anna jumped to her feet, pulled her chair next to Riley's and took her hand. "Are you sure? I mean, after all this time." Her gaze went to Noah and then Samara. "Can't you guys talk her out of it?"

Riley squeezed Anna's hand. "That's not important anymore. Things have changed."

"Changed how?" Anna's gaze went from Riley's pale, determined face to Noah's grim one and Samara's worried one. "Okay, seriously, will someone please fill me in on what's going on?"

"My father..." Riley almost strangled on the word, "came to see Noah. He's searching for me."

"Oh shit."

Anna cursing was rare. As an advocate and counselor for traumatized children, she was hyperaware of her image with her young clients. To avoid cursing, she often invented words to use as substitute curse words. This time, Anna didn't mince her words. "Why the hell didn't you take the jerkwad down, Noah? You had him in front of you. You could've had him bound, gagged, and on the way to jail within minutes. Why in the world would you let him leave?"

Riley held up her hand to stop her tirade. "There are complications. Noah will explain."

In short, succinct sentences, Noah gave Anna the details of his visit with Larson, including the news about the young girl, Keira.

"They'll do to her what they did to you," Anna said.

"That's what we believe," Noah said. "We can't risk him knowing that we're on to him until we can rescue her. Larson said they adopted a child a few years ago. We can't find any records of adoptions, closed or otherwise. Nor can we find a birth certificate for her.

"We've known for years that there are online auctions for children. With the dark web, they've become more prevalent."

"So you're thinking Keira was either abducted by this guy, or she was sold to him on the dark web," Anna said. "If it's the latter and we take him down, we could take down a whole bunch of other guys like him."

"Job one is to rescue Keira," Noah said. "Regardless of how he got her, we need to move on him as soon as we can."

"Noah." Riley almost hated to ask, because if it was true, a whole new avenue of hope, along with the specter of hurt, opened up. "Do you think it's possible that's what happened to me? That I was stolen, and these people pretended to be my parents?"

"I think it's a strong possibility. I did some research when you first came to LCR, but it led nowhere. Once we rescue Keira and bring Larson in, we'll make him tell us the truth."

Riley didn't doubt that for a moment. William Larson aka Lloyd King didn't know what he had unleashed by contacting LCR. She couldn't wait to see his face when he realized how badly he'd screwed up.

"My plans haven't changed for Dimitri. Think Larson will give up his location?"

A small, grim smile played around Noah's mouth. "I believe we can arrange that. Are you ready to take on the Larsons, too?"

If he'd asked that question when she first arrived, her survival instinct would have urged her to say no. What Dimitri had done to her was brutal and inhumane, but in a weird way, understandable. He was a sadist, a monster, the epitome of evil. Since then, she had learned to battle monsters. She knew how to win, how to overcome evil. But the people she had called her parents were a different kettle of fish. For eighteen years, she had thought they were her biggest supporters, her champions. The people she'd trusted the most in the world. Their betrayal had been worse than any pain Dimitri had ever inflicted.

She saw no judgment on anyone's face. Knew there would be no urging for her to even be involved if she said no. But then, what would that make her? A coward? Less than what she had become? A victim once again, too afraid to face her demons? She was a rescuer. She did whatever it took to save lives. In LCR, the victim always came first. Personal grudges had to be put aside for the greater good. Larson had to be stopped before he destroyed another life. There was no other choice to make.

She took a breath, this one soul-deep, and said, "Let's bring these bastards down."

CHAPTER ELEVEN

Mediterranean Sea

With silky elegance, the yacht sailed through velvety smooth water. Majestic and sleek, the Jewel of the Sea was the largest of its kind. Two hundred and fifty tons of graceful steel, the vessel was the envy of every man in the world. Dimitri Soukis took pride in that fact.

Though he had inherited some wealth, Dimitri still considered himself a self-made man. Through his vision, perseverance, and sheer doggedness, he had been able to maintain that wealth as well as amass more. Times were tough for many. Most of his acquaintances had lost everything. The jealous ones accused him of dishonesty, of taking advantage of the less fortunate. He laughed in their faces. Less fortunate? Through grit and strength, he had gained his wealth. While others whimpered and whined as they saw their riches dwindling away, he swooped down and took what he wanted. The spoils of victory were always the sweetest.

Was it any wonder that he'd been nicknamed The Vulture? He enjoyed the comparison. He had no sympathy for those he had taken from, those he had destroyed. They had been too stupid to retain their wealth—bad luck for them. Luck had nothing to do with Dimitri's success. He saw, he wanted, he took. To hell with the rest of the world.

There were two rules he'd set for himself when he'd taken control of his family's empire. He swore he would never break them, and to his knowledge, he hadn't.

The first rule: Be ruthless in all things. If his father were still alive, he'd cut his feet out from under him if necessary. To win, one had to be ruthless. Dimitri had no real friends…didn't want any. He had business associates who liked to call themselves his friends. Did they know he could have them destroyed with barely a wave of his hand? He hoped so.

He'd learned long ago that there were two kinds of people in the world. The ones who wanted what you had and the ones who wanted you to give them a handout. The first kind he enjoyed destroying. The second kind he used to his advantage. Amazing what people would do for you for money.

His second rule was just as important as the first: Be willing to dump the garbage. No. Matter. What. He had eliminated more than a few relatives, several business acquaintances, and if a servant displeased him, Dimitri didn't give him a second chance.

And then there was Jessica.

In his most private moments—ones he would never reveal to anyone—he considered her his only failure.

She had been pure and perfect. His beautiful girl. His to remold and remake into what he needed.

Making her into what he expected had been a time-consuming, sometimes grueling endeavor. Not to say there hadn't been times he hadn't enjoyed the training. Especially during the first year. Later on, when she realized how much he enjoyed her tears, she learned to withhold them. He'd had to work even harder on her then.

When she had left him, the embarrassment had been much worse than his heartache. He had offered her everything, and she had practically spit in his face. People, most especially women, did not leave Dimitri Soukis and live.

He had searched for her, discreetly, of course. His business rivals didn't need to know what went on in his personal life. They especially didn't need to see that he hadn't been able to control one slight female. In private, he raged and roared his fury. In public, he was amused, blasé. A woman who didn't appreciate the gift of living with Dimitri Soukis was deserving of pity. How stupid she must be to leave everything behind.

He had been misled. She had not been what he had expected—what he had been promised. Oh, she'd put on an act, he had to give her that. She had pretended to be malleable, obedient to his commands. Then what had she done? She had betrayed him, had tried to call out for help. He had punished her for that infraction.

That one punishment had been exactly what both of them had needed. After her recovery, she had been docile and meek. He had realized his leniency with her had brought on her need to flee. Any softness he'd shown her before was gone. In its place was strict discipline. At last, she had been becoming exactly what he'd hoped she'd be. He had been on the verge of giving her the greatest gift any woman could receive. And then, without any warning whatsoever, she had disappeared.

He had gone on with his life. People might speculate in private what had happened, but they would never have the audacity to ask him or speak of it in public. He would never stop wanting her, though.

None of her replacements had held up near as well. They were all gone now and he was alone. His wants and needs unfulfilled. It was so damn unfair!

Jessica would return to him one day—this he vowed. And when she did. Oh, when she did, she would pay for every day that she had been away from him. And then, if he was feeling merciful, he might let her die.

But then again, what fun would that be?

"Mr. Dimitri, sir. You have a phone call from a Mr. Larson."

About damn time. Dimitri held out his hand for the phone. Snatching it from the servant, he put the phone to his ear. "Well? Do you have news or not?"

Los Angeles, California

William Larson stood on the balcony of his multimillion-dollar mansion, blind to the spectacular scenery below. Bitterness and fury kept him from appreciating the view. Hearing Dimitri Soukis's slimy, pompous voice on the phone, William could almost feel his blood pressure shoot up the charts.

His teeth grinding against each other, he forced calmness into his tone. "I'm making arrangements to find her, to have her returned to you."

"It's about time. Any reason you're doing it now?"

William held back his snarl of anger. The asshole knew exactly why he was working so hard to find the girl.

"You're ruining my reputation," William said. "People are wary of buying from me. They say my products are inferior."

"With good cause. You've never delivered what I was promised."

It took every bit of control William had left not to let loose on the man. As it was, he could barely get the words out. "I have provided you with several others since Jessica."

"None of them held up."

Telling the brutal beast that it was his own damn fault would do no good. The man wanted what he wanted. And he had paid an astronomical amount for Jessica. Not for the first time, William cursed her for escaping. Dammit, why couldn't she have just died like the others?

Finding women, especially young healthy ones, who could survive Dimitri's particular needs was difficult. Since Jessica's defection, William had sent others—three of them. And hadn't charged Dimitri one single cent. Two of the girls had died within a year of delivery. The other had lasted almost two years before she had sliced her wrists and bled out.

"Jessica was the best one and she left me."

The whine in Dimitri's voice was both childish sounding and creepy.

"We trained Jessica to entertain and please. She was to be an obedient companion, a lovely, useless ornament. Her sales profile described her talents and abilities. If you had indicated you wanted a full-time slave with strong masochistic tendencies, you should've said so. We could have accommodated you with someone else at that time. But finding that particular type of woman takes time and a goodly amount of training. We—"

"You dare blame me for Jessica's inexcusable behavior?"

William held his temper. Alienating the man would be even more detrimental. He had to find and return Jessica to redeem himself in the eyes of his clients. With three pieces of merchandise to move within the next six months, he had to play this just right. This would be his biggest payoff ever. He couldn't screw this up.

"I have six different agencies working to find her."

"I won't pay a penny more to you."

"I'm not asking for money. I just want to make this right."

"How do you plan for this to work?"

"Once I hear that she's been found, I'll arrange a meeting. I've had medical records created to show she has severe mental problems. They'll turn her over to me without difficulty. I'll contact you and make arrangements for transfer."

"What makes you think she's even alive? She was a half-wit who could barely take care of herself. Plus, she's been gone eight years. She could be at the bottom of the ocean, for all we know."

William wanted to growl that it was the asshole's fault that she had been in such poor condition. Jessica had been his best, his brightest star. Intelligent, talented, but with a pleasant, amenable personality. He'd spent more time and money on her than any of his other pieces. Therefore, she had brought the biggest price.

When Dimitri had bid for her, William had pushed aside his thoughts that maybe it wasn't a good fit. The man had a reputation for being too abusive to his women. But the money had been too big of a temptation.

It was just too damn bad that Dimitri hadn't killed the girl instead of allowing her to escape. Then it would be all on his head and not William's. It wasn't fair that he had to do all this extra work, plus bear the expense of finding the bitch when it should've been Dimitri's responsibility.

"She may have been in poor condition, but since she somehow managed to escape, her survival instincts were apparently still working."

"If you do find her, she won't be treated as well as before."

"Having been out on her own, she may be even harder to control."

"Then I'll enjoy breaking her again even more. I've finessed some particularly enjoyable new methods to ensure obedience."

Probably the same methods that had caused the deaths of the three girls William had provided after Jessica's escape. He couldn't care less. All he wanted to do was get the bitch back to Dimitri and move on.

"Return her to me and I'll make sure you regain your reputation. I'll be satisfied and you'll never hear from me again."

Those words, more than any others, was music to his ears. "I'll contact you when I have something." William ended the call.

He hadn't even known that Dimitri had put out the word that William's products were defective. He'd been so immersed in doing his job, readying and perfecting his merchandise, that he hadn't realized how severely damaged his reputation was until he had begun the preliminary advertising for his upcoming sales. After years of supplying some of the most beautiful and talented pieces of merchandise on today's market, people were questioning his professionalism. Even his most frequent clients were acting hesitant.

He had to fix this and fast!

"Well, what did he say?"

William looked at the attractive blond woman standing in the doorway. She was one of his most trusted business associates, had done some phenomenal work, but she was becoming beyond tiresome. Lately, she had taken on a more assertive attitude. As if she was his equal, his partner. It wasn't an attitude he appreciated. He didn't care that she had provided one of his best pieces of merchandise. He paid her well for her work. Her duties did not extend to more than he allowed.

If he could score just a few more good sales, he wouldn't need her or the other women he used for trainers. He'd take the money he made and disappear for good. With millions in the bank, a new name, and maybe a new face, he could live the good life somewhere and never have to worry about working again.

This one would give him trouble, though. He already knew it. She'd worked for him longer than anyone else. Because of that, she took liberties. Some he ignored. Occasionally, he had to show her who was boss. If she gave him too much trouble, he'd just eliminate her for good.

William waited to see if that thought caused even a twinge of guilt. She'd given him years of dedicated service, along with the use of her body from time to time. After a few seconds, he decided he was perfectly fine with killing her if need be.

Wouldn't do to alienate her now, though. She had another six months to train their "daughter." When Keira went on the market, he'd make sure she stayed where she was supposed to be. No more screw-ups like Jessica.

"Dimitri said if we bring her back to him, he'll alert everyone that we made good on his investment."

She gave a derisive snort. "It's all his fault in the first place. When she called me that day, it should've been a wakeup call to him that she wasn't in line."

"True, but telling him that would do more harm than good."

Pulling out her phone, she clicked on a text. "I've got three potentials waiting in the wings after Keira's gone. A six-month-old boy in Australia, a three-year-old girl in Canada, and a five-year-old girl in Russia. Infants are a pain in the ass. Even if we hire a nanny for a couple of years, it'll be easier if we get an older kid. Five years is almost too old. How about we split the difference and take the three-year-old? My contact says she'll be an easy one to snatch."

Once again, William held on to his temper. This was yet another reason this woman had to go. She had started taking on more responsibility without his asking for it. This was his business. She was an employee, not a partner.

Yes, she would have to go. But that would have to wait until Jessica was found and Keira was ready to go to auction. Then he'd show the bitch who was boss.

CHAPTER TWELVE

Justin stood outside Riley's apartment door. His hand raised, poised to knock, he hesitated. He wasn't one to second-guess his decisions, except when it came to his partner. She made him as unsure as if he were a teenager in the throes of puberty. In most everything else in his life, he went full speed ahead. Not with Riley. This slip of a woman, with her acerbic tongue, giant chip on her shoulder, and courageous spirit, made him feel like a pimple-faced kid with his first crush.

He had screwed up the other night, and he still didn't get why. The kiss hadn't been a mistake. Nothing so damn fine could ever be called a mistake. Okay, yes. It had been piss-poor timing. He should've waited, talked to her, held her. But she had responded to the kiss like a house on fire. It hadn't been the kiss that had screwed things up.

The compliment was where he'd gone wrong. He'd told her she was beautiful, and that had destroyed everything. Okay, so she didn't want anyone to think she was beautiful, even though she was. He could live with that. What he couldn't live with was not knowing why she felt that way. Who had made her hate the very idea of physical beauty? No, being attractive wasn't the most important attribute, but neither was it something most women would run from either. She'd taken his remark as an insult instead of a compliment.

That wasn't all. Her nightmare had sounded as though she were in hellacious agony. Whatever she had gone through, whatever had been done to her, he wanted to help her, be there for her. She would push him away. He already knew that. But he cared too much to let her.

But still he debated whether to knock on her door. He wasn't even sure why he was here right now. He'd been finishing up a run, one of his longer ones that he did on his days off. Normally, he'd go home, take a shower, put on some music, and wind down. That had been his intention tonight, but during his last mile, he'd gotten the extreme urge to check on Riley. He'd had the oddest sensation that she was in trouble, that she needed him.

"What are you doing here?"

Justin turned to see Riley walking down the hallway toward him. Not exactly a welcoming greeting, but he hadn't expected that she would be all that happy to see him. They had left things unsettled between them. Riley knew him well enough to know he was here for answers. Answers she didn't want to give.

Tough shit.

With anyone else, he might not have made the effort. Might've said to hell with it and walked away. The shadows beneath her eyes told him she hadn't slept well last night, but it was the deep pain glimmering in their depths that told him to stand his ground.

"If you're not ready to tell me everything, that's fine. I can wait. But you need me, Riley, whether you want to admit it or not."

"You're right."

He couldn't hide his surprise at her easy agreement. A small smile played around her mouth, as if she had enjoyed shocking him. She unlocked her door, pushed it open, and went inside.

Justin walked in behind her. All the apartments in this area had been converted from warehouses. They were expensive, but with LCR's generous salaries, operatives could afford the best.

His first thought was that for a woman in hiding, she had an amazing amount of windows. Riley's apartment was large, airy, and filled with so much natural light he wondered if she ever had to wear sunglasses inside.

"You must really like natural sunlight."

Dropping her keys on the coffee table, Riley looked around her home. Few people had been invited into her sanctuary, her place of peace. Her home was her escape, her refuge, the place she felt the safest. She had no real talent for decorating. Her apartment was an eclectic collection of all the things she remembered enjoying. Books and music brought her comfort. On her days off, she spent hours in book and music stores. She also loved antiques—things that had a history. The refurbished grand piano in the corner was one of her first buys. That she had yet to play it didn't mean anything.

And yes, bright sunlight and openness were as important to her as air. They made her feel safe. An assurance that she was not and never would be a prisoner again.

If one paid close attention and read between the lines, they would see the real Riley Ingram here.

"It's nothing fancy, but it's home."

She turned to him then. Justin stood before her like an immovable boulder, the expression on his face granite hard, the look in his eyes not cold but very determined. Getting her partner involved in her hideous past was something she'd resisted for as long as she'd known him. And while a part of her still resisted strongly, she knew she couldn't do this without him. But it was more than that. She didn't want to do this without him. No, maybe they'd never have the storybook romance she'd dreamed of as a kid. They might never go beyond what they'd already had—a passionate, unbelievable, wonderful kiss. Because she'd messed things up.

But she trusted this man more than anyone in the world. She couldn't, wouldn't do this without him. And since LCR would soon be involved, she had no choice. She was grateful that she would be the one to explain things. Having him learn the truth in a room filled with other operatives would be wrong. He deserved to hear this in private, from her.

She opened her mouth to begin and then froze, her throat clogging with fear. Recognizing the signs of a full-fledged panic attack, she said quickly, "Have a seat. Be back in a moment," and dashed into the bedroom.

Shutting the door behind her, she leaned back against it, closed her eyes, and breathed through the panic. Now that the time had come to tell him the truth, her brain was stuttering, trying to find a way out of the promise she'd made.

If she told him everything, he would never look at her the same way. Justin saw her as a strong, capable woman—courageous. If she told him the truth, she would become a victim to him, an abused woman so beaten down by a sadistic fiend that at one time she had barely been able to mumble a word without permission. How could she explain that the woman he trusted to watch his back in the field had at one time fallen to her knees on command? Had barked like a dog, crawled on her hands and knees, following behind her master? Had worn a collar and a leash? Had performed like a trained animal to the amusement of his friends?

Bottom line, she couldn't. She just could not do it. But that didn't mean she wouldn't tell him the truth. He just didn't have to know all the gory details.

Turning the doorknob, Riley opened the bedroom door and returned to the living room. Justin was standing at the bookshelf against the wall. Her book collection was as broadly eclectic as everything else in her apartment. Poetry, world history, and biographies blended with suspense, romance, and children's books.

She had read each book with a deep appreciation for not only the beauty of the worlds the authors created but for the sheer loveliness of the words. Early in her captivity, Dimitri had banned both books and music. He had known they provided an escape from her misery, and if there had been one thing Dimitri didn't want, it was her escape, either physically or mentally. Everything she loved, he'd wanted to destroy. On occasion, he had demanded she perform, either by singing or playing the piano.

Being forced to do something you previously loved was a special kind of hell all on its own.

"You have quite the collection," Justin said.

"This is just a small amount. I have more in storage. I hope to have a house one day with a library big enough to hold them all."

"Are you looking?"

"Looking?"

"For a house? Are you in the market for one yet?"

She was about to say no and then stopped herself as a disturbing thought came to her. She had wanted to buy a house for years, even while she still lived in Paris, but she had put it off. It wasn't because she couldn't afford one. Had she put off purchasing a house because she was afraid it might be too permanent, too settled? If she grew complacent, happy, it might mean she'd let her guard down, and then he would come for her. Destroy everything again.

At that moment, she made her up mind to start looking for a home to buy. Dimitri had no control over her. She refused to allow him to influence her choices ever again.

"I'm going to start looking soon."

"What kind of house would you like? Traditional, contemporary? You want to build or buy an older home?"

Those were things she didn't even have to think about.

"An older home. At least twenty-five years or more. With a yard. Some acreage, so I can have a garden. Not so far from the city that I'd have a long commute, but far enough into the country for scenery and landscapes."

"And lots of windows?"

She gave a small, solemn nod. The windows were the most important. They represented more than just light. They let her see what was coming. "Yes, lots of windows."

"Sounds like you've put some thought into it already."

That had been part of her therapy. Dream of beauty, grace, elegance. Imagine all the things you want to have, to surround yourself with. Replace the ugliness of your former life, a nightmare, with the beauty, the dream, of what you wanted your life to be.

She wanted the house she bought to have been a home, a place where people had loved each other, had been happy. She didn't know very much about love, but she knew it was powerful enough that it could linger, that it could stamp itself on a heart, a life. Why not a home?

She knew all about evil. That it lingered and tainted, even grew. Why couldn't its opposite do the same? Why couldn't love destroy evil, replace it?

Aware that she'd gone down a rabbit hole that often led to darkness, she shook herself a little and nodded toward the kitchen. "You want some coffee, something to drink?"

"Water."

Grateful for the short reprieve, she went to the kitchen and poured two glasses of ice water from the pitcher in her fridge. She swallowed half of one, relishing the bracing burn of the icy cold liquid as it slid down her parched throat.

Returning to the living room, she handed him the full glass and then sat on the edge of the chair across from him. She took another sip of water.

For the first time, she noticed he was wearing gray running shorts and T-shirt that were slightly damp. "You've been running?"

"Yeah. Should've gone home and showered before I came over." His gaze bore into hers. "I didn't want to wait."

"I see."

Justin forced himself to sit, even though he'd do much better pacing. But he had a feeling that would make her nervous. She was finally ready to tell him what she was dealing with. No way did he want to make her uneasy.

She didn't say anything for the longest time, just stared above his head as if lost in the past. Justin forced patience.

"For almost eight years, I have been hiding from a man."

She stopped so abruptly, Justin cocked his head slightly, almost sure he'd missed something. But no, she'd clamped her mouth shut as if she had said what she intended to say and nothing more.

"And?"

"I've decided to stop running."

At this rate, it would be another eight years before she finished explaining. Her face had gotten paler in the last few minutes, and his gut clenched. Riley was no coward. Whatever this man had done to her was bad. And it was clear she was hesitant to tell Justin the truth. Every fiber within him wanted to go to her, hold and comfort her. The look on her face said she was closing herself off. He figured she might need to do so to get through this conversation.

He held himself back and said the one thing that might give her the spark she needed. "Spill it, Ingram."

The snapping of Justin's voice did exactly what he had hoped. Color bloomed in her cheeks, and she glared at him. "I grew up in what I thought was a normal household. My parents weren't affectionate people, but I hadn't known anything different. I thought everyone was like us. I was homeschooled. Had no friends. Wasn't allowed to watch television. My parents were my world. I never questioned that life should be any different."

Her throat worked as she swallowed hard. "Remember I told you that my parents were killed when I was a teenager? It's not true. They're still alive. They gave me to a man, a stranger, on my eighteenth birthday. I never saw them again."

Every bit of breath left his body. Oh holy hell. He wanted to say that was ridiculous, that no parent would do anything so cruel or unfeeling, but he couldn't because he knew she was telling the truth. Riley's parents had given her to a stranger, apparently a sadistic stranger, and then just left her with him?

"I escaped from him when I was twenty-one. He's been looking for me ever since."

Three years she was with the creep. What had he done to her? What had she endured? And how the hell had she survived?

"What about your parents? What happened to them?"

"After I escaped…and was able to articulate…things, LCR searched for them. They had disappeared. Apparently, they changed their names."

Of all the things he had thought had happened to her, this didn't come close to any of them. Yeah, he figured she'd been assaulted or abused in some way. But to have her family betray her in the worst possible way? The people who were supposed to support and care for her no matter what?

The details she had given him were ridiculously sketchy. Who was this bastard, and how the hell did he get away with this crime for all these years? But if he pressed for more, she would shut down. His only option was to allow her to tell her story at her own pace.

"What made you decide to stop running?"

She jerked her head up, frowning a little. "That's all you've got to say? No questions about how or why? You believe me?"

"Believe you? Riley, you're my partner, my friend, my—" He broke off, took a breath. "I trust you with my life. Why would I question you about this?"

"Maybe because it's so damned unfathomable?"

"I've seen the shit people can do to each other, even families. Not much shocks me anymore."

She slumped down onto the chair as though exhausted.

"The son of a bitch who did this to you. What happened to him?"

"I don't know."

"What? Why not?"

"When I was found, I remembered three things. The man's name is Dimitri. He lives in Greece. And he's wealthy."

"So you have, or had, amnesia?"

"Selective. The counselors told me I remembered only the things my mind could handle. I remembered my parents and what they did to me, leaving me with that bastard. I remember screaming, crying, and a sting in my neck. He must've drugged me. I remember waking up in a completely different place."

Her voice went softer. "I remember some of the things he did. Too many, really. Years ago, I tried hypnosis, hoping to remember something that would be of use. I wanted to find Dimitri, make him pay. The things I remembered weren't really helpful for that kind of information. Most of my memories were of pain and fear. Nothing beneficial, so I stopped."

She swallowed hard, continued, "Remember last year when we were searching for Kacie?"

"Yes."

"The chains in the bedroom. The blood. We'd come across scenes like that before, and though they disturbed me, I never related to them. But that one scene triggered something for me. Since then, I've been having more nightmares. I'm remembering more and thought I could try hypnosis again. If that didn't work, I was ready to try some of the new memory drugs. Hoping something would spur a memory that would lead us to Dimitri."

He didn't know if he'd ever admired anyone more. She had to be the strongest, most courageous person he'd ever known. Instead of allowing what that bastard did to her destroy her, she was still fighting, still determined to win.

"Turns out, that's not going to be necessary," she said.

"How's that?"

"A man named William Larson contacted Noah a few days ago. He claimed he was looking for his daughter. He showed Noah a photograph. It was me."

"William Larson is your father?"

"When I lived with him, his name was Lloyd King."

"He changed his name so Lloyd King would no longer exist."

"Yes. Noah figured he and my mo…" She shook her head. "He and his wife did that after I escaped Dimitri. They could take no chances. If I survived my escape, they knew the authorities would come looking for them."

He had so many more questions, but the exhaustion on her face told him she was near the end of her reserves. But he had to know one more thing.

"So how are we going to get these bastards?"

Her mouth twisted in a mockery of a smile. "Expect a call to come in on an op soon."

"This is going to be an LCR op? Why can't they just be arrested?"

"Because Larson told Noah they have another 'daughter' at home. She's sixteen."

Comprehension came quick. "You believe they're going to do to her what they did to you."

"That's our theory. We've got to rescue her before that happens. If they wait until she's eighteen, like they did with me, we've got time. But there's no guarantee. We have to move now."

"I'm sure it's occurred to you that those people most likely aren't your parents."

"Believe me, out of everything I've learned today, this might be the most joyous news of all. I just hope I can get the truth out of them."

"Knowing you don't have their blood in your veins has got to be a relief."

"What if my real parents are just as bad as Larson?"

"Could they be any worse?"

"No."

"Then don't borrow trouble. You could have been kidnapped. They might still be trying to find you."

That was a possibility that hadn't hit her yet. Could she actually have family somewhere who wanted her? Who might actually be decent people? Her memories of her childhood were sketchy at best, but she didn't remember any other parents, didn't remember the trauma of being kidnapped.

She pushed that worry aside. It was way down on her list of priorities. Right now their focus was on the young girl in the clutches of monsters who might sell her to the highest bidder without a hint of hesitation or remorse. She was the important one now.

"What's the plan?"

"We haven't talked logistics yet. But since Larson requested LCR's assistance in locating me, it should be simple enough. Noah can contact Larson and tell him I've been located. We come up with a convincing story of where I've been for the past eight years. Depending on how that plays out, we'll go from there. Either way, a team will be in place to get the young girl away from the Larsons."

"And Dimitri?"

"It's Noah's belief that Larson will contact Dimitri and tell him I've been found. We'll set up a sting. As soon as I'm in his presence, I'll take him down."

The dichotomy of the outrage in his eyes and the calm expression on his face was an interesting study in Justin's personality. She knew he was opinionated and could be as outspoken as anyone. However, Justin had learned to temper his responses with caution. He could and would explode if pushed, but more often than not, he hung back, waited, and watched. If he struck, it was with swift and brutal force. That didn't happen very often. She'd only ever seen him completely lose his cool once. They had rescued a kidnap victim from a human-trafficking ring. The child had been so badly beaten, they'd thought he was dead. Justin had broken away from the LCR group and gone after the man who'd hurt him. It had taken three people to pull Justin off the man's unconscious body.

She had always relied on her partner's restraint, recognizing it as one of his greatest strengths. But the grim look in his eyes told her he was fighting hard to hold on to it.

"Dimitri doesn't know what I'm capable of now, Justin. Eight years ago, I was a timid, weak young girl who couldn't defend herself against a puppy. He will have no idea that the young girl he abused can and will kick his ass to hell and back."

"He'll have men to protect him. You said he's wealthy. He might have an army. You can't protect yourself against an army." His voice, though calm, held a hard edge. "If he tries to hurt you again, I'll rip him apart."

She nodded. Dissuading him would do no good. Telling him that Dimitri was hers to take down would only inspire an argument that neither of them would win.

A chime sounded, and Justin pulled his phone from his pocket and clicked a key.

"What is it?"

"Text from McCall. Briefing tomorrow afternoon.

She shivered. It had begun. Soon, everyone would know. She began to back away from him both mentally and physically. She needed time to regroup, settle herself down, and prepare for tomorrow.

"It's late. You probably need to get home. Get some rest."

"No."

"What?"

"I want to stay here with you."

"Justin. I—" She swallowed hard. "I… Why?"

"Because we have something, Riley. We're not just partners, not just friends. Something even more real is going on between us. For just a little while, push all of this aside and think about the here and now. About us."

"I know. I feel it, too. It's just…" She was overwhelmed, almost breathless. Her heart pounded with both exhilaration and fear. "I don't know that I'm able to—I've never…"

His eyes were an exhilarating mixture of tenderness and heat. "It doesn't matter. We'll work that out together. You matter to me, Riley. It's been so damn long since I've felt anything real, so believe me, I know the difference. Don't shut me down. Let me stay. Let me hold you. Be with you."

Taking what might be the most difficult step of her life, Riley went to him and held out her hand. "Come with me."

"I need to shower. Take one with me?"

Her heart was beating so hard, she barely heard her own whispered words. "I have scars."

"I have them, too, both inside and out." He pulled her close, spoke against her mouth. "Let's heal each other."

CHAPTER THIRTEEN

If anyone had told her an hour ago that she would soon be leading Justin Kelly into her bathroom and taking a shower with him, she would've told them they were either delusional or they had been inside her daydreams.

She stood in the middle of the bathroom without any idea how to proceed. Intimacy was foreign to her. She knew all about rape and abuse. What body parts could cause fear, revulsion, extreme pain. But the pleasure and delight one person could give another was beyond her realm of knowledge. She was twenty-nine years old and hadn't a clue what to do next.

Fortunately, Justin knew. He gathered her into his arms, gently, tenderly. She felt no threat, no fear. The instant his mouth touched hers, any remaining anxiety ceased. Yes, this was what she wanted, what she needed. This was Justin, and despite all the impediments in their way, she was going to take this gift, this precious, ageless moment in time, and savor the magic.

Wrapping her arms around his broad shoulders, she stood on her toes and leaned into him, giving herself up to the beauty she hadn't believed existed outside of her own dreams. Heat suffused her body, inside and out. She whimpered, glorying in the incredible, delicious heat of him. He was a unique blend of solid steel, hot desire, and melting tenderness. And for just this moment, he was all hers.

Releasing her lips, reluctantly, slowly, he growled, "Let's take a shower before it's too late."

She knew he wasn't talking about the time. She'd felt the hardness, the evidence that he wanted her as much as she wanted him. Yes, she was scared, even embarrassed, but the need overwhelmed her fears.

With quick efficiency, Justin stripped out of his clothes, dropping them on the floor. Even though she told herself to do the same, she couldn't move a muscle as she watched him. He was built for strength and endurance. Powerful muscles, sleek, golden skin. Every inch spoke of discipline and determination. His erection stood hard and vital, jutting up toward his belly button. It should have scared her. Her body and mind had known violence. The appendage should have triggered horrific memories. It didn't. She didn't need to ask herself why. She knew. This was Justin. He would never do anything to hurt her.

Tentatively, she reached out and touched him there. A sharp, inhaled gasp of air told her she'd surprised him. She glanced up at his eyes. They gleamed with tenderness, humor, and heat. He liked her touch.

She cleared her throat. "I know how this works. The… uh, mechanical side of things. But I'm definitely not an expert on techniques."

"Look at me." When she did, he took her hand and kissed the palm. "You have nothing to fear from me. We stop any time you say so. You want to go slow, fast…whatever you need. Got that?"

She nodded, and then with barely a quiver of nerves, she let go of his hand and stripped out of her shirt, shoes, and jeans. In less than a minute she was standing before him, completely bare.

Justin took in her beauty. She was slender, small-framed, almost delicate looking. With small, perfect breasts and brownish-pink nipples. A flat stomach and toned legs. Yes, she had scars. They probably looked worse to her than they did to him. To her, they were marks of horror and fear, remnants of the shameful things that had been done to her. To Justin, they were a badge of courage, of fortitude and strength. The scars didn't define her. Her strength and resilience were revealed through them.

"I know that being told you're beautiful isn't something you want to hear. But hear me on this, Riley Ingram. In every way that counts, both inside and out, you are the personification of the word beauty."

He worried the words were the wrong ones, but she smiled widely. "Thank you. I didn't realize how much I needed to hear you say that."

He held out his hand, and they stepped into the shower together. It was a large one, and the image of them standing beneath the spray as they lost themselves in each other was a strong temptation. He told himself that could come later. For now, their first time, when she was feeling both vulnerable and awkward, they would give themselves to each other in the traditional way. That didn't mean, however, they couldn't get to know each other more intimately. To him, part of the enjoyment of sex was the journey of discovery.

With that in mind, Justin soaped up his hands and slid them down Riley's wet, silky body. She was a joy to touch, firm in most places, exquisitely soft and malleable in others. Within seconds, he heard her moan. He smiled at the delightful sound.

His hand slid down her legs and then up again. Pausing at the juncture of her thighs, he touched the soft curls between her legs, waited and watched. If she panicked or jerked away, he'd stop. Instead, to his amazement and pleasure, she moved her legs farther apart.

Wanting to praise her for her bravery but not wanting to break the intimacy they were creating, Justin gently pressed his hand against her sex. The heat he found there almost brought him to his knees. Gritting his teeth, he gently spread the lips of her sex and washed her tenderly. He was pleased to hear her breathing become erratic, and her fingers tightened on his shoulders. He glanced up at her face and smiled. She had the glazed look of need and showed not an ounce of fear.

Backing away, he handed her the soap and waited to see what she would do. Her hands glided up and down his torso, and Justin groaned.

Dreamily, Riley decided that he was hard everywhere. Even the places she thought he might be soft felt like steel beneath her fingers. How many nights had she fantasized about Justin, never believing her dreams might come true? From the tips of his very large and narrow feet to the top of his thick head of hair, he personified masculinity in its most basic form. She lingered on the indentations in the hard planes of his stomach, marveling at how wonderful they felt beneath her fingertips.

Her hands moved up and down, not realizing how much she was turning him on until his voice ground out the words, "Touch me, Riley. Please, baby."

"What?"

"I'm dying for you to touch me. Will you?"

She knew what he was asking. Taking both her hands, she wrapped them around his hard length and slid them up and down. He hissed out a breath. She glanced up at his face and was glad to see the sound he'd made was from pleasure. She felt an enormous amount of pride in that. She, Riley Ingram, a girl who should be too damaged to even consider an intimate relationship, was gladly giving pleasure to a man. Because he was her man.

As if realizing they'd both had more than enough stimulation, Justin moved to stand beneath the spray, pulling her with him. Seconds later, he turned the faucet off and opened the door. Before she could even contemplate his movements, he was sliding his arms beneath her and carrying her. Laying her gently on the bed, he whispered, "I couldn't wait."

"Then don't." Holding her arms out to him, she said softly, "Make love to me, Justin. Make me feel whole."

Following her down on the bed, he started at her mouth, tenderly kissing her, then moved down to her throat, and then her breasts, pausing to suckle each one. Kissing down her torso to her stomach, the juncture of her thighs. Without waiting to see if this was okay, taking it as approval that she didn't say no, he spread her legs and buried his face between her legs, lapping gently.

The heat intensified, burning hotter, faster, out of control. Riley arched her body, reaching for something and unsure of what she might find when she got there. Without warning, a wild, intense, outrageous pleasure washed over her. Suspended in ecstasy, she reached for and found the stars. Long moments later, she lay panting on the bed, overwhelmed by the enormity of what she had just experienced. How had she not known?

Raising his head, his eyes glittering with more emotion than she'd ever seen in him, he growled softly, "You're perfect in every way."

Whispering words she never thought she'd be able to utter to anyone, she said, "Come inside me, Justin."

He hovered over her, hesitating.

"What's wrong?"

"I didn't come prepared for this."

Thankful that she had an answer, she whispered, "I'm protected."

Groaning his approval, he covered her body with his, slid inside her and thrust deep. Riley wrapped her legs around his hips, relishing the closeness, finding joy in his need to reach fulfillment. He plunged in, then out again. Then, with a groan that came from deep in his chest, he let go, releasing inside her.

Not wanting to crush her, but not willing to let her go either, Justin collapsed onto his back and pulled Riley on top of him. She snuggled into him, resting her head on his chest. No woman had ever felt so right or so good in his arms.

"I never would have believed anything could feel that good."

He heard her shyness and wonder in the soft words.

"You've never dated, been intimate with anyone before this?"

"I've never trusted anyone enough to date. Besides, when we're on an op, we don't necessarily come in contact with the best of humanity."

"What about when you're not on an op? Your free time. Do you go out?"

She propped her forearms against his chest and raised her head to look at him. "If you haven't figured it out already, I'm not exactly normal, Justin."

"What the hell does normal even mean or look like?"

"Good question." She huffed out a small laugh and put her head back on his chest. "I don't really know."

"What do you do in your free time? I know you have friends. Anna Bradford's a friend of yours, isn't she?"

"Yes. Samara McCall introduced me to her not long after LCR rescued her. We clicked immediately. We see each other when we can. Since we both travel a lot in our jobs, it's not as often as we'd like. She stays in touch with me when she's on the road. She's better at being a friend than I am."

"How so?"

"Relationships are hard for me. They involve emotions. I kept myself shut down for so long. It's easier to stay frozen. Hurts less."

"It's a lonely place to be."

"Yeah, it is."

He pressed a kiss to the top of her head. "Get some sleep."

She yawned and stretched, then settled on him like a small, snuggly blanket. "Hold me?"

"I'm not going anywhere. I'll hold you all night long."

He felt her lips on his chest in a small kiss and thought that might be the sweetest touch he'd ever received. A small, uninhibited act of affection from Riley meant more than a grand gesture from anyone else. When Riley gave, she gave freely.

Justin lay awake awhile longer. He'd been so immersed in Riley and what she did to him both physically and emotionally, he'd had little time to absorb all he had learned about her past. There was still so much he didn't know. How had she escaped? How had LCR come across her? Why didn't she know more about this monster named Dimitri?

His thoughts whirled like tornadoes before they settled on one irrefutable fact. This woman meant more to him than anyone ever had before. Riley believed she should be the one to take Dimitri down. And it was definitely her right. But if she couldn't do it, then he would do it for her. It was as simple as that.

CHAPTER FOURTEEN

Darkness surrounded her, its nothingness a comfort. There was safety in the solitude, peace in the oblivion. Silence sheltered her. She held on to the dark abyss of emptiness as long as she could.

Stay quiet. Stay silent. Stay still. Be good. Shh. Shh. Shh.

She'd been down this road before. Panic would set in soon. But for right now, she could ignore the fear. She could pretend that her eyes were closed. That she was anywhere else in the world other than where she was. That she had choices. Options. Freedom.

Shh. Stay quiet. For just a little while longer, don't think. Just pretend.

A door opened and closed. Footsteps sounded. Every cell within her froze. She had only been here for a short while. Barely an hour. He wouldn't be ready to release her yet.

Shh. Stay quiet. Be good.

Torn between the dread of what faced her if she was suddenly released and the terror of remaining here for hours, if not days, she waited to hear his plans.

"Are you uncomfortable?"

"Yes, sir," she whispered.

"Do you know why you're being punished?"

"Yes, sir. I was disrespectful."

"And?"

"I didn't answer you immediately, sir."

"Do I take good care of you?"

She knew better than to answer with the truth. "Yes, sir."

"Do I demand too much from you?"

"No, sir."

"Then why were you disrespectful when I am so good to you and take such good care of you?"

She shut her eyes tight against the threat of tears. They would only make him happier. He was like a demon who fed off her tears and screams. The more she gave, the more he wanted.

"I asked you a question, Jessica."

She jerked alert. *Don't make him angry!* She gave him the answer she knew he wanted. "Because I am a willful, disobedient slut who doesn't appreciate what she's been given, sir."

"What should I do to you?"

"You should punish me, sir."

"Worse than the punishment you're receiving now?"

Since she was currently locked in a four-by-four wooden box with one small air hole, the answer would be obvious to most people. No one deserved this kind of treatment. However, if she answered no, she would still be punished and probably much worse. If she answered yes, that she should receive worse punishment, the chances were fifty-fifty that he would go easier on her. What choice did she have?

"Yes, sir, worse than the punishment I'm now receiving."

"Excellent answer." She heard his joints pop, telling her he was now standing. "We're expecting guests this evening. If I punish you the way you deserve, you won't be able to stand, much less do what I require of you. Therefore, I will table your punishment until the time of my choosing. Who knows? Maybe in a few days I might be more forgiving."

She knew better than that. He would wait until he thought she was comfortable again. Until she thought she was safe. Then he would mete out his punishment. But he didn't know her little secret. She knew she was never safe. Never comfortable.

"What do you have to say to me?"

"Thank you, sir. I appreciate your leniency and understanding."

"And?"

"And your love."

"Very well. I will be back in a few hours to let you out. In the meantime, dwell on your disobedience and think of ways you can make it up to me. I'll allow you your chance tonight after our guests leave."

No matter what he had planned, hell awaited her. Tears sprang to her eyes, and she could no longer hold them back.

Shh. Don't let him hear you cry. Don't. Don't. Don't.

Breaths shuddered from her body, and she shook her head.

Stop. Stop. Don't let him hear. Don't let him see.

A sob escaped. Evil laughter. He heard her! Lights exploded above her as the lid was lifted.

She swallowed a scream of anguish.

Riley jerked awake. Heart pounding, body drenched with sweat, breath gasping from her lungs. It had been so real. Too real.

Light was filtering into the room, telling her it was just past dawn. The dreams were becoming more realistic. Was that because she was allowing the memories to return after years of blocking them, or was it something more? Did her subconscious, knowing that she would be facing him soon, want to prepare her, perhaps warn her?

She didn't know which she feared more.

Moving her arm slightly, her hand brushed up against a warm, hard body. Terror seized her mind. He was here! Reacting on instinct, she reached for her Glock on the nightstand and sprang to her feet.

Waking up next to a naked woman had always been a delightful experience for Justin. Waking up and finding one standing above you holding a gun on you diminished the enjoyment considerably.

Figuring she was still half asleep and not wanting to startle her, he chose to play it light. "Is this the part where I say, 'Wasn't it good for you?'"

He couldn't see her face, but she went stiff, stopped breathing.

"Riley, sweetheart," he said softly, firmly, "it's me, Justin."

She blew out a gasping, "Justin?"

"Yeah. I—"

The gun dropped to the floor with a thud and she backed away. "I could have killed you," she whispered harshly.

He snorted. "When have you ever taken an unjustified shot?"

Instead of laughing it off, she ran to the bathroom.

His head fell back onto his pillow and Justin let out a huge sigh. He had known going in that a relationship with Riley wouldn't be easy. She had been too badly hurt not to have issues adjusting to a new relationship. Especially an intimate one. Waking up next to a man had to be disconcerting. The possibility of it triggering a memory might always be there. None of that mattered. They could work through each and every one of them.

He set his feet on the floor and stood. They needed to confront this now, before it got any bigger. Knowing her, she was blowing the event way out of proportion.

Pulling on his shorts and shirt, he padded barefoot to the bathroom and pushed the door open. Wrapped in a thick white robe, she was sitting on the edge of the tub, her face in her hands.

"Want some coffee?"

She raised her head and stared at him as if he were crazy. "I just tried to kill you, and you're offering me coffee?"

"Well, technically, it's your coffee. But I'll make it."

She shook her head. "You need to leave."

"No, I don't. I need coffee. So do you."

She stood and headed toward the door. "I'll make coffee, and then you need to leave."

He grabbed her arm as she tried to pass him.

"Don't, Kelly. Just don't."

"Not going to happen. Call me Justin. Call me Kelly. Call me asshole. I don't care. I'm not leaving until we get this settled."

"Get what settled? I can't even sleep beside a man without trying to kill him. What's to settle?"

"Hey." He pulled her against his chest, but she remained stiff and unrelenting. At least she wasn't pulling away or fighting him. He pressed a kiss to her forehead. "This was a first for us. It's not going to be without a few bumps along the way."

"Bumps are finding out my coffee tastes like mud or your feet smell like Limburger cheese. It's not waking up beside a lunatic holding a gun to your head."

He shook her shoulders gently. "Some bumps are bigger than others. We're complex people with dangerous jobs. We're bound to have big-assed bumps.

She gave him a strained smile. "You're right. I'll go make coffee."

He let her go, hoping some of what he'd said stuck with her. Last night had opened a door for both of them. He wasn't about to let it close again.

Riley worked on automatic as she made coffee. Justin hadn't followed her into the kitchen. She wouldn't blame him if he just left without saying anything else. But she knew he wouldn't do that.

Her mind refused to dwell on what had happened or Justin's reassuring words. There would be plenty of time to think on these things once he left. There were truths she had to face whether she wanted to or not. She had lived in fantasyland once before, and it had almost destroyed her. She refused to believe in fairy tales ever again.

"Smells good."

She pulled two coffee mugs from a cabinet and filled both with the steaming brew. Turning, she handed one to Justin and took a sip of her own.

Justin took a long swallow. "Doesn't taste like mud. So does that mean my feet don't smell like Limburger cheese?"

She wanted to smile, joke with him. He was trying to alleviate the tension, assure her what had happened wasn't that big of a deal. He had no idea how wrong he was.

Since it was what he wanted and it would be easier, she gave him a teasing look. "Maybe not Limburger. Cheddar. Very sharp cheddar."

He grinned. "I like cheddar."

"Me, too, but I don't think I'll be nibbling on your toes anytime soon."

He took her cup from her and set it on the counter along with his. Pulling her into his arms, he gave her a hug. "We're going to be all right, Ingram. I promise. We'll get these assholes in jail where they belong, and then we'll concentrate on us."

Unable to get into a long, complicated discussion of why there could be no *us*, she nodded and said, "Guess I'd better get ready. Noah wanted me to come in this morning to talk about a few things."

"You want me to come with you?"

"No, that's okay. You need to go home and get ready, too. I'll see you at the briefing this afternoon."

He pulled away to look down at her. She'd been pretending for most of her adult life. Playing a role was what she did best. So she put on her best *everything is fine* expression and smiled up at him.

Only, Justin now knew the real Riley Ingram. His eyes dark with concern, he whispered, "I promise you it will all work out, Riley."

Instead of giving him more words he probably wouldn't believe, she pulled his head down to hers and kissed him with all the feeling and fervor in her heart. If this was their last kiss, she wanted the memory to be one she could take out on long, lonely days. He tasted like coffee, toothpaste, and Justin. Perfect in every way.

Finally, he pulled away from her. "That should last me until tonight." He dropped another quick kiss on her lips and turned around. "See you soon."

She waited until the door closed behind him to say, "No, that's a kiss that will have to last a lifetime."

Even after Dimitri and the people who'd claimed to be her parents were in prison, who she was or what had happened to her wouldn't change. She was damaged beyond all hope. Justin deserved a whole person, not the small pieces of humanity she'd managed to mend together to create Riley Ingram. And he certainly didn't deserve the Riley Ingram who'd pointed a gun at his head after he'd shown her such love and tenderness. It was better for both of them if they went ahead and faced that fact.

CHAPTER FIFTEEN

Last Chance Rescue Headquarters

Noah stood at the front of the large conference room. When he'd moved LCR headquarters to the States a few years back, he hadn't anticipated needing a lot of space. Much of LCR's mission planning took place in their satellite offices. If more space was needed, the Paris office, run by LCR operatives Eden St. Claire and Jordan Montgomery, was used. This was different. Not only would they be running two ops, possibly simultaneously, they were involving more than LCR operatives. Both Samara and Anna were here, not only to help in planning but as moral support for Riley.

Since space was limited, all seats were taken. At some point, he might need to call in more operatives, but for right now, the people sitting around the table would be the primary agents.

His gaze moved around the room. Some of the brightest and best of LCR were here, every one of them focused on the mission. Though they had risked life and limb on numerous operations over the years, the knowledge that this mission involved one of their own made the stakes even higher. There wasn't a person here whom he didn't trust with his life.

The conference table was long and narrow. On the right side sat Samara and Anna, along with Sabrina, Aidan, Justin, and

Riley. The left side held Eden, Jordan, Angela, Jake, and McKenna Sloane. They were some of his most experienced people, but he had additional reasons for bringing Eden and McKenna in on the mission. Their considerable experience would be important for the op, but it was the trauma they had both endured that might be of more use to Riley.

"We all have varying degrees of knowledge about this case. I'm going to start at the beginning so we're all on the same page."

He glanced over at Riley. They'd discussed this a few hours earlier. Nothing would be held back that was pertinent to the case. The specifics of her imprisonment and what had been done to her were, in his opinion, not pertinent. If she wanted to share any of those details, that was her choice. Still, certain facts were going to be uncomfortable for her. He had every faith that she would tough it out and be fine.

"A couple of days ago, I met with a prospective client. He indicated his daughter was missing. Had been missing awhile. He said he and his wife were close to giving up hope. As with many of our cases, he said he believed Last Chance Rescue was his last hope.

"I talked to him on the phone and got a strange vibe. The minute I met him, I knew something was off. He said all the right things, but it was practiced, staged. I believed he was looking for someone, perhaps even his daughter, but the more I listened, the more I realized that her well-being wasn't his primary concern. When he showed me a photograph of his daughter, my suspicions were confirmed. The photograph was of Ingram.

"I got as much information as I could, assuring him we would do all we could to find his daughter."

Noah shifted his gaze to Riley again. Though she was paler than normal, her mouth was set in a firm line. She would see this through.

"I've asked Ingram to fill us in on as much as she feels comfortable sharing. If I feel additional information should be revealed, I'll do so."

He felt rather than saw Riley take a deep breath, and then she began to speak, her voice matter-of-fact, as if she were discussing a stranger.

"I was raised in Atlanta as Jessica King. I thought we were a normal family. My father was a strict man but not harsh, my mother seemingly kind. I was homeschooled. I never questioned why I didn't have friends. My parents kept me occupied. I believed my father was a consultant. Although I can't recall what he might have consulted anyone about, he wasn't at home but a few days a week.

"I wasn't deprived of anything other than social contacts. I had an aptitude for music, and my father paid for piano teachers and voice coaches. Looking back on it now, I realize their sole concentration was on me. I thought it was because they loved me. On my eighteenth birthday, I discovered they had been preparing me."

When she stopped, no one said a word. Was it shock that kept them silent? Riley didn't want to know. She glanced up at Noah. They had an agreement. If she gave him a certain look, he would continue her story. She was giving him that look now.

As if he'd intended to continue all along, he said, "Riley was taken to a hotel room and introduced to a man named Dimitri. She believes he was approximately forty-five to fifty-five. Her parents left her with him. She hasn't seen them since."

Odd, but it sounded less shocking when Noah told it that way. No need to tell them the other details. Like, she'd thought her parents were having some sort of surprise party for her. Which, looking back, would have been extremely weird, since she'd had no friends to attend a party. And no one but Dimitri knew that after they left, she had tugged and pulled on that damned locked door, screaming to be let out. Crying for her parents, immersed in an unimaginable hurt. Her bewilderment at her abandonment was so immense, the terror of her situation didn't hit her until it was too late.

With the prick of a needle, she'd fallen into the arms of a monster, a sadist whose only source of enjoyment was the agony he inflicted on her.

A large hand grabbed hold of hers. She looked down to see it was Justin's. Another hand, smaller and softer, took her other hand. Anna.

Emotion clogged her throat. She hadn't had friends then, but she had them now. Her determination renewed, she nodded at Noah and said, "I woke up in a mansion. Needless to say, my stay was not a pleasant one. He held me prisoner for three years. I escaped on my twenty-first birthday."

"How?"

The question came from McKenna. Though there were no tears in the other operative's eyes, Riley saw the compassion and the understanding. It hit her then, perhaps more than ever before. Every person in this room had been through their own version of hell. She was no different. What an odd thing to find comfort in, but she did. She wasn't alone anymore. She hadn't been alone since Noah rescued her.

"Dimitri held a dinner party. After it was over, he told me to leave the room. The servants left, too. They were distracted for a moment and didn't see me hide under a food cart that was covered by a cloth. They pushed the cart into the kitchen. It was late, and the staff decided to wait until the next day to clean up. The instant they left, I got out and followed them. I knew how to be small and silent. There were at least a half dozen of them. They never noticed me following them. They went through an outside door. I caught it before it could close, waited a few seconds, and then walked out."

She gave a wan smile. "Seems unbelievable now. It was so damn easy."

She didn't add the obvious. Couldn't verbalize it. Had it been that easy all along, and she just hadn't tried, timid, beaten-down mouse that she was? She hadn't tried to escape simply because she'd been too afraid. She had accepted that the abuse was her lot in life. Then Dimitri had made that one announcement—so profound and frightening it had woken her up, jerked her out of her frozen, mindless acceptance. She had realized she had no choice. Leaving had become her only option. If she had been caught, he might have killed her. Death had been preferable to what her future held if she had stayed.

"That was a very brave thing to do."

This came from Eden St. Claire. One of the strongest, bravest women she knew.

"Not really. It was done out of necessity and fear."

"That's what being brave is about, Riley."

She managed a strained smile and then glanced back up to Noah for him to continue.

"Here's what we know about William Larson. He lives in Los Angeles with his wife, Loretta. We believe Loretta is the same woman Ingram knew as Lorraine King.

"We haven't seen her, but discreet questioning of the neighbors has confirmed they have a teenage daughter named Keira. They stick to themselves. No friends or relatives visit them."

"How'd you get this info so fast?" Aidan asked.

"The minute Larson walked out of the hotel, he had a tail. I rarely meet a prospective client without having an LCR operative standing by. I don't usually need one, but in this case, I did." He shrugged. "Mia and Jared Livingston followed Larson to the airport. Jared purchased a plane ticket and flew to LA on the same flight that William took. Jared watched him hail a taxi at LAX and followed him to his home in Lakewood.

"Since then, we've discovered a few more things about Larson's operation."

"Operation?" Aidan said.

"Yes. Seems Larson has two other families besides Loretta and Keira. In each location, he has a wife and a teenager. One is a girl about fourteen. The other is a young boy, around twelve. One home is in Pasadena, the other in Cypress."

"He's got his own damn factory," Justin snarled.

"Close to it."

Even though Noah had given her this information earlier today, her head was still reeling. Did this information perhaps confirm their suspicions that these people were not her parents? She prayed fervently that that was the case. Having their blood both revolted her and scared the hell out of her.

How many times had Larson done this? Had he had multiple families when she was living with them? Had that been why he was away from home so much? Were there other people even now enduring a hell he had sold them into?

"We're doing more recon. He may have more houses, more families than the three we know about. In the meantime, I have

Shea and Ethan Bishop monitoring one of the houses. Gabe Maddox and Cole Mathison are watching the other one. And Jared and Mia have eyes on the house where Keira is living. If more houses are found, I'll send more people.

"Here's where the speculation comes in," Noah continued. "Since we know what Larson did with Ingram, there's no reason to believe he's not done this several times before. Multiple dwellings, multiple families, who knows how many children."

"He's selling them." The anger in Jordan Montgomery's voice was all the more evident by its seething quietness.

"Yes," Noah said simply. "My belief is that he's training them for specific purposes, possibly for specific people."

"The return on his investment would have to be huge to spend so many years on them," Sabrina said. She glanced over at Riley. Fiery anger made her green eyes glint like emeralds.

"True. He may have varying degrees of involvement before he makes a sale. We won't know everything until we're able to question him."

"Please say that will be soon," Jake said.

"Not as soon as we'd like. But we'll get there. This will be a two-pronged mission," Noah stated. "One team will concentrate on William Larson, along with the women posing as his wives. That team will rescue any children in his custody now.

"Another team will take on Dimitri, once we find him."

Noah glanced at Riley. He had thought to spare her by making her just another team member but with a specific job. Thanks to Samara and Anna, he had changed his mind. Putting Riley in charge gave her the distance she needed. If she could look at this mission as just another job of rescuing innocents and taking down bad people, her focus could be on her mission, not her emotions.

"Ingram, if you'll get everyone up to speed on some of the specifics."

Her game face on, Riley stood and faced her fellow operatives. If she felt the least bit embarrassed or uneasy about what this mission was about, she hid it well. When he had offered her the lead on the job, he had reminded her of two very important points. One was that every operative on this mission had faced their own hell in some way. That this was hers had no bearing on who she was to them. Secondly, she was a professional operative with years of experience under her belt. If he didn't trust her to do the job, he wouldn't put her in charge of the op. Period.

"Jessica remembers very little, other than her captor's name was Dimitri. After her escape, she remembers hearing what sounded like Greek being spoken and seeing signs in Greek. She spoke to no one. She managed to stow away on a cruise ship bound for France.

"In the two weeks it took to get to France, as well as a few more days there before she was rescued, Jessica's so-called parents had ample time to disappear. Until a few days ago, when William Larson met with Noah, we had no clue where they might be."

Riley took in a silent breath. Pretending this was just another op by referring to herself in the third person brought attention to her discomfort of the situation. Noah was right. She needed to get past this and focus on the op. Just because they knew she had been a victim at one time didn't mean they knew the brutal facts of what had been done to her. Besides, she was no longer a victim.

As if she wasn't revealing difficult details, Aidan said, "So if you've been missing for eight years, why's Larson just now coming to LCR?"

"Since we didn't know where he was until last week," Noah said, "it's hard to say. Something has obviously happened to compel Larson to search, or renew the search, but we don't know what this is."

"If he's getting ready to sell another child," Eden said, "perhaps he feels the need to clear this matter up."

Riley shrugged. "Dimitri may have asked for a refund."

As a joke, it fell flat. There was an awkward silence in the room until Justin growled, "Bottom line, we're going to get the son of a bitch."

"Oh yes, we most definitely are," Noah said softly.

"And we're sure that Larson has no clue that Riley is one of us?" Sabrina asked.

A small glow ignited at Sabrina's words. Yes, she was one of them. They still saw her as their team member. Nothing had to change. She was a valuable member of Last Chance Rescue, an operative with considerable skills. She needed to remember that.

"We're the only ones who know who and where Jessica is," Noah said. "We control the situation. We manipulate them into playing our game. We set the players in motion. Then we strike. Our mission is to not only rescue the teenagers Larson currently has, but also everyone he's sold through the years. We will also identify who and where this Dimitri is. I don't care if he's on the moon, we will find him."

"Are local authorities in LA aware of Larson?" Eden asked.

"Not yet," Noah said. "When it's time, I'll ask operative Honor Stone to make contact. She's still got close ties to the FBI and can smooth the way for us. However, until we get our plan in place, we're keeping everything within our LCR family."

Riley knew Noah's reference to family was no accident. He had told her, as had Samara, that LCR was her family, that she would always be one of them.

Even though she felt frozen inside, a small glow continued to burn within her. Revealing her past to her co-workers might have been the most difficult thing she'd had to do. Telling it to her LCR family hadn't been nearly as tough.

Justin didn't think he'd ever seen anyone braver in his life. Riley continued to amaze him. She'd sat, calm and matter-of-fact, and described the hell she'd lived as if it were just another case. Other than the slight stumble when she referred to herself as Jessica, she'd been in total control of the meeting without a hint of emotional baggage to impede her. He had already known he was in over his head. Last night had confirmed that for him. He'd never known anyone who could drive him crazy with both frustration and desire the way Riley did. And he'd never admired anyone more.

He could read her better than anyone. Much of her calm demeanor was an act, but hell, where did she get the courage? He was damn sure if he'd been in her shoes, he would've been belligerent, sarcastic, and furious.

Needing to get up and moving, do something to move forward, Justin said, "So where do we go from here?"

McCall stood and joined Riley at the front of the room. "I'm going to wait a few more days, then contact Larson with a possible lead. I won't give him a lot of information. I'll tell him things are fluid, but there could be a break soon.

"Depending on his reaction to this news, I may tell him I know about the other organizations he's got looking for Jessica and ask him to back away from them." His mouth gave a grim twist. "I'd rather these organizations use their limited resources to focus on victims who actually need saving. We've got this covered."

McCall walked over to a map of California. "As mentioned, we know about three of Larson's houses. There could be more. Jared and Mia are monitoring his activities.

"Once I alert Larson that there may be a break in the case, I anticipate he'll want all the details. I'll give him only enough to keep him hooked until we're ready to go to the next step.

"In the meantime, we'll be setting up a cover in East Tennessee. The offices we used for the Wakeford sting a couple of months back are still available. It's a good, easy cover for us. Once we're set, I'll feed him enough information for him to locate Jessica.

"We're figuring he'll play it one of two ways. Either Larson will have someone abduct Ingram and take her to Dimitri. Or he'll tell Dimitri where she's located, and Dimitri will have his people take her."

"I've agreed to have some trackers implanted," Riley said. "Once I'm abducted, LCR can track me to Dimitri's location."

"What's to keep Larson or Dimitri from having her killed?" Thorne asked.

Riley answered, her voice both calm and confident, "Dimitri's got a lot of fury stored up, saving it for the day he finds me, but if he wants me dead, he won't kill me right away. He'll want me to suffer. That will require time alone with me."

"He'll want to take you somewhere that's safe for him," McKenna said. "Cowards like that think of their own skin first."

Justin appreciated that McKenna kept the conversation moving forward so the operatives didn't get mired in the horrific images that Riley's statement conjured.

There wasn't an operative at LCR who didn't know what McKenna had gone through years ago. Both McKenna and her husband, Lucas Kane, had helped bring down the man who'd hurt her. Justin hoped for the same kind of scenario for Riley, with one exception. He wanted to see Dimitri hurting. Bad. And he wanted to be the one to give it to him.

"Now that everyone knows the basic plan, let's talk strategy and undercover assignments." Noah passed out individual assignment folders to each operative. "Our initial setup will include undercover assignments for Riley, McKenna, Justin, and Anna. Depending on what we learn and how things develop, I may involve several more of you.

"Over the next few days, we'll get everyone into place and settled. Everyone else is on call until this is over. We'll communicate frequently and stay—"

"Wait," Aidan said. "Why the hell is Anna working an op? She's not an operative."

Though there had been a few surprised expressions when Noah had mentioned Anna, Aidan's reaction and blunt words raised several eyebrows.

"You have a problem with the assignments, Thorne?" McCall asked.

Never one to back down, Thorne said, "Hell yeah, I do. Anna's not trained to handle something this dangerous. She's not—"

"Anna is right here and can speak for herself," Anna interrupted. "I'm not going to get in the way of the big, bad LCR operatives doing their jobs. Got that, Thorne?"

As if she hadn't spoken to him, Thorne kept his focus on McCall. "Why the hell would you put an untrained civilian on an op?"

"Anna has participated in several LCR training scenarios. She isn't a full-fledged operative"—McCall shot Anna a quick smile—"despite my many offers for her to join our team. She is, however, a highly skilled individual who can not only defend

herself and others, she'll be there for moral support for Riley."
McCall paused, cocked his head. "That ease your mind, Thorne,
or do we need to discuss this further?"

Admirably ignoring the ice-cold glare from Anna, Thorne
jerked his head in a stiff nod. "Whatever you say."

Taking him at his word, McCall went on to discuss the
others' roles. The tension eased out of the room. Justin opened
his assignment folder. He read quickly, nodding with approval.
He was familiar with the location. It was a good cover. Setup
time would take a few days, giving him time with Riley. She kept
throwing up barriers, insisting things wouldn't work between
them. He had every intention of breaking down those barriers
and making sure she understood one important thing: He was
here to stay.

CHAPTER SIXTEEN

"Kelly, can I see you a minute?"

Noah had waited until Riley disappeared into the elevator.

Kelly gave a frustrated look as the door closed on Riley's pale, determined face, and then he turned back to Noah. "Yeah. What's up?"

"Let's go to my office."

As soon as Kelly followed him into his office, Noah closed the door and, in an uncharacteristic move, locked it.

In silence, he went to the bar against the wall, pulled out a couple of cold waters from the fridge, and tossed one to Kelly.

The operative caught it one-handed but didn't open it, the expression on his face wary.

Going to his desk, Noah leaned back in his chair. He was about to break a half-dozen self-imposed rules, and even as his gut churned, he saw no option.

"I talked to Riley this morning, before the briefing."

"Yeah, she told me she was meeting with you."

Noah leaned forward. "Let me be blunt. I know that you and Riley are involved, that you slept together last night."

"Not that it's any of your business, but yeah, we did."

"You're right. Normally, I'd stay out of your personal lives. It's not my business who you choose to sleep with."

"Then why the hell am I here?"

"Because you need to be aware of a few things."

The look became warier. "Like what?"

"I can name on one hand the confidences I've broken in my life. I'm not bragging. It's just I get pissed off if anyone does that to me. I figure I owe them the same courtesy."

"And you're going to break that rule for me?"

"Hell no. I'm breaking that rule for Riley."

"Why?"

Instead of giving a direct answer, Noah said, "Do you know why I paired the two of you as partners?"

"We work well together. Have a connection."

"That's one of the reasons, but a lesser one. The biggest reason is you don't put up with bullshit."

Kelly frowned. "That's true, but I can't say as I've seen a lot of LCR operatives put up with bullshit. We tend to get pissed off with bullshitters."

Noah went to his feet and started pacing. He didn't usually have trouble communicating, but in this instance, maybe because he wasn't sure he was doing the right thing, he was having difficulty putting the right words together.

With a growl of frustration, Noah whirled around and started talking. "Eight years ago, I got a call from a minister in Marseille by the name of Francois DePaul. He and Milo Evans, the man who helped me create Last Chance Rescue, had been friends for years. Milo had just been killed, and I assumed he was calling with condolences."

Realizing he was putting off the inevitable, Noah plunged forward. "That wasn't the reason for his call. He had a ministry for the homeless and indigent. A young woman had been found, brought to him. She was so malnourished and unhealthy, he feared for her life.

"Usually, he would only have seen that she got medical care or tried to care for her himself. He hesitated doing the usual thing. He got the strong impression she was hiding from someone. She wouldn't speak, but he knew she was terrified. He was concerned that if he kept her at his shelter, whoever she was afraid of would find her. So he called and asked for my help."

Justin's teeth were clenched as he listened to McCall. Despite his surprise and concern that the LCR leader was breaking protocol and sharing this with him, he couldn't and wouldn't refuse to listen. McCall wasn't doing this for himself. Justin had never seen him look so uncomfortable or ill at ease.

"I agreed to see her and went to Marseille." McCall cleared his throat. "I had never seen anyone more broken or damaged in my life. Not so much physically, though she was certainly in poor health. But emotionally…" He shook his head. "She was in bad shape.

That was saying a lot. McCall had probably seen the worst of the worse.

"She wouldn't communicate. Would barely raise her head. Refused to look anyone in the eye. Touching her was out of the question. I made the mistake of touching her shoulder, and she made the most god-awful sound I'd ever heard, like a wild animal in severe pain.

"I couldn't leave her there. I agreed with Francois. She was deathly afraid of someone. I brought her back to Paris and arranged for her to live in a small health care facility. It was a temporary arrangement at best.

"I told no one about her. I tried to visit her each week, and though she never spoke, I could tell that I was getting through to her. She didn't smile, but her demeanor seemed to change. She grew a little more relaxed each time I saw her. She began to eat and grow stronger. She still wouldn't communicate with me."

McCall voice went thick. "After I married Samara, I told her about the young woman. And Mara, being Mara, wanted to meet her. We went together. I introduced the two and then walked out the door. Half an hour later, Mara came out of the room and said, 'She's coming home with us.'"

He smiled a little. "And that was that. She came to live with us. She still wouldn't communicate other than with an occasional nod or a few hand gestures. Mara thought she might be mute and tried to teach her sign language. That didn't last long. She got frustrated one day and told Mara that if it was all the same to her, she'd rather just speak."

Justin's heart lightened. That sounded like something Riley would do.

"After that, she made amazing progress. She managed to tell us what she remembered. She had a wealth of information on the people who raised her. I immediately started looking for them, but by then they were in the wind.

"The information on her captor was minuscule in comparison. She knew his name was Dimitri. She knew how she came to be with him. And she knew how she escaped. That was it. She agreed to hypnosis, but either the information is just not inside her or she's repressed it. The hypnosis was doing nothing other than upsetting her, so we stopped.

"One day, Mara was headed to a self-defense class and invited Riley to go with her. That day, probably more than any other day, was a revelation."

Justin wondered if McCall realized he'd finally started referring to the "young woman" as Riley. Since the man didn't do anything without cause, he thought it was probably a purposeful maneuver.

"Why a revelation? Had she already been trained or something?"

"No. It was clear she had no skills. In fact, I don't think I'd ever seen anyone with less self-preservation skills."

"Then why the revelation?"

"Because she was a natural. Once she understood what she needed to do, you only had to tell her once. It took a while to develop the killer instinct to go with her training."

McCall went silent. Justin wondered if he was reflecting back or considering what more to reveal.

"Thing is, I never expected that she would be capable of much more. She had come so far, but I knew she was still hurting. A year and a half after she moved in with us, she told us she wanted to get her own place. Get a job."

McCall cleared his throat. "We arranged for a new identity and background. She chose the name herself. Said Riley Ingram sounded both strong and normal.

"She moved out and got her own place. Got a job at a gym. She'd kept up her self-defense classes and started teaching them.

"One day, she came to see me and dropped a bombshell on me. Said she wanted to be an operative. Wanted to rescue others like herself. I tried to talk her out of it, but she wouldn't budge.

"Mara and I...we both worried she wouldn't be able to handle seeing other abuse victims. That it would trigger memories. I agreed to give her the full LCR training, thinking that once she accomplished that, it would be enough. It wasn't. She surpassed all my expectations once again."

"You talk about her almost as if she's your daughter."

McCall gave a half smile. "I've worked hard not to show any favoritism. I have a deep admiration, and even affection, for all LCR employees. But Riley got to me."

She'd gotten to Justin, too, and that was before he'd known what she'd endured and overcome.

"So what's the real reason you told me all this, McCall?"

"Each time Riley's faced with a challenge, she meets it head on and conquers it. She's never shown the least interest in developing a romantic relationship until you."

"You think I'm a challenge to her?"

"No. I think you could be her downfall."

"What the hell?"

"Riley isn't going to be one to have a lighthearted affair and move on."

"I'd say it's up to Riley and me to decide what kind of relationship we're going to have. She's an adult."

"Contrary to popular belief, involving myself in an operative's love life is not a common occurrence. I pair operatives together who I believe will bring out the best in each other. Falling in love is their own doing."

McCall went silent again. Justin could tell the man was struggling. Even though he resented the interference, he couldn't work up any anger. What Noah and Samara had done for Riley was incredible. They had saved her life, given her a new one. So hell yes, this was an uncomfortable conversation, almost a lecture, but he'd sit here and take it. And when it was over? Hell, right now all he wanted to do was find Riley and hold her, not only for the remarkable woman she had become but for the abused, neglected, and damaged young woman she'd once been.

"I asked you earlier why I partnered you and Riley. It's true you two have a connection that causes you to work well together. That's not the biggest reason, though. When I first hired you, I encouraged you to use the anger you have inside you. You were and probably always will be bitter about what happened to your sister."

An understatement. Every time he thought about what she'd gone through, what she hadn't been able to handle, his guts boiled.

"Using rage to save others is something most LCR operatives can identify with, but your rage went deeper, because in the end you weren't able to save your sister. And she couldn't save herself."

Justin clenched his fist. Even now, years later, the fury could engulf him. His baby sister had been kidnapped, and although she had been rescued by LCR, she had never recovered.

"Whether you want to admit it or not, some of your rage is directed at Lara for not being strong enough to overcome her trauma."

Justin was on his feet and in McCall's face before he realized it. "Listen, you can psychoanalyze people all day long, but you damn well leave my sister out of this."

McCall never flinched. "And there's your answer," he said softly. "You've got a rare blend of compassion and anger. I knew you wouldn't let Riley back down, because you saw her as a warrior from the start. But you also have a unique perspective. One that can see beyond a façade to the pain beneath."

He needed to get the hell out of here before he either knocked McCall's teeth down his throat or hugged him. This touchy-feely shit was more than he could handle right now.

Backing away from the man, Justin headed toward the door. "I don't know if you're insightful or bat-shit crazy. You know I'm grateful that you rescued Lara and what you tried to do for her later. And I'm damn grateful for what you've done for Riley. And for teaming me up with her. Beyond that…" He shook his head.

"I probably made a muck of what I was trying to say, Kelly, another reason I don't like to interfere in the personal lives of my operatives. All I'm asking is that you give Riley time to deal with everything. And if you're not serious about this new relationship, then you damn well be upfront and honest with her and then back away."

McCall's eyes seared him. "Because it might not be politically correct or legal to threaten an employee, but if you hurt her, Kelly, I'll beat the ever-living shit out of you. Then I'll turn Samara loose on you."

"Hurting Riley is the very last thing I plan to do."

"Our plans don't always turn out the way we think they will."

Justin walked out of McCall's office. Every particle of his body told him to find Riley, hold on to her, and never let her go. He wouldn't. Because if he did, she'd read him, see the pain he was feeling for her. She needed his strength right now, not his sympathy.

But he had to get rid of this rage. The bubbling fury that was consuming him would make him no damn good for her or this op.

Sliding his phone from his pocket, he pressed a speed-dial number. Without giving the man a chance to speak, Justin growled, "You up for a spar?"

"You looking to beat the shit out of something?"

Justin gave an abrupt, humorless laugh. "Yeah."

"Just so happens I'm in the mood to give it right back. See you at Bruce's in ten."

Ending the call, Justin headed out the door. Bruce's place was a dirty, gritty gym a few blocks away. He and Aidan had discovered it by accident one day and frequented it at least a couple of times a month. It was a great place to de-stress. Bruce had only one rule: Nobody dies.

Oddly enough, that was one of McCall's rules, too. Too bad about that, because once they found Dimitri, Justin had every intention of breaking that rule. And one thing he could guarantee. The bastard would not die an easy death.

Chapter Seventeen

Riley couldn't remember a time when she wanted to be alone more than she did today. Even though she'd deliberately withheld the gruesome details about what had happened to her, these people were LCR operatives. They could easily fill in the blanks.

Embarrassment was a small price to pay to finally have the opportunity to destroy the people who had tried to destroy her, but it was still draining. More than anything, she wanted to go back to her apartment, her sanctuary, and hide.

Too bad she had a friend who saw things differently.

"This wasn't exactly what I had planned today."

Anna threw her an easy grin over her shoulder. "It was either this, or make you watch me eat a triple-fudge sundae."

Riley's stomach roiled at the thought. Still, climbing a damn mountain hadn't been on her agenda either. "You know, I climbed a mountain a few days ago."

Anna wiped sweat from her face, not one bit daunted or discouraged. "Not with me you didn't."

No, it had been with Justin. Just the thought of him caused her heart to squeeze. The expression on his face when they'd left the meeting today hadn't been difficult to read. He wanted to singlehandedly find both William Larson and Dimitri and kill them. That was a sentiment she shared, but she couldn't let her anger get in the way of doing her job. Her job sustained her, made Riley Ingram who she was. If she allowed her need for vengeance to take over, then she'd lose herself all over again. They'd taken too much from her already. Damned if she'd let them destroy her a second time.

"Okay. You've gone from sad to dreamy-eyed to angry in the matter of a few seconds. Talk to me, Riley."

"I had sex with Justin."

Anna stumbled, and Riley grabbed her before she could fall down the hill. "Hell's bells, Riley. Don't be telling me stuff like that when I'm halfway up a freaking mountain."

Mountain wasn't exactly the correct term for the hiking trail, but it was steep enough to work up a nice sweat. She and Anna had hiked it a half-dozen times since she'd moved here.

Anna glanced around and, seeing nothing remotely comfortable to sit on, shrugged and plopped down in the middle of the dirt. "Okay, I'm sitting. And now I can calmly say, shut my mother's freaking front door. Are you kidding me?"

Despite her whirling thoughts, Riley couldn't help but grin. Anna had a creative way with words.

"No."

"So, how did it go?"

"Depends on what you mean by the word *it*."

She snorted and rolled her eyes. "Don't get vague on me now. I don't need details." Grabbing Riley's hand, she pulled her down to sit beside her. "Just tell me the highlights."

"It was..." Fabulous. Wonderful. Monumental. None of those insipid words could describe how absolutely phenomenal it had been.

Realizing Anna wouldn't let it go until she gave an answer, she shrugged. "It was nice."

"No flashbacks?"

"Surprisingly, no. At least not then."

"What do you mean?"

"I had a nightmare. One of my more vivid ones. When I woke up and felt a body next to me, I freaked."

"Freaked how?"

Riley closed her eyes in humiliation. "I held a gun on him."

"Ha. I'll bet he didn't even need coffee after that."

"Did you hear what I said, Anna? I could have killed him."

"No, you couldn't. You're better trained than that."

She said the words with such confidence that they hit Riley exactly where she needed them. She *was* better trained than to shoot without thought. And it reinforced Justin's comment that she would never take an unjustified shot.

"Still, no man wants to wake up to a naked woman holding a gun to his head."

Anna laughed. "Actually, I know a few who might. But that's beside the point. How did he react?"

A smile tickled at her mouth. "He joked about it. Asked if this was where he was supposed to ask if it wasn't good for me."

Anna nodded her approval. "Good for him." Tilting her head, she said, "So was it?"

"Was it what?"

"Good for you. You used the word *nice* before. Nice is a picnic without ants. Not the way one describes a hot night of sex with a gorgeous LCR operative."

"It was everything I've ever dreamed of. Everything I needed."

Squealing her glee, she grabbed Riley for a hard hug. "I'm so happy for you. No one deserves it more."

"Wait. I said the sex was nice. After I pulled the gun on him, it kind of went downhill."

"I thought you said he was cool with it."

"He was. I wasn't."

"You're too hard on yourself, as usual. What did you do? Tell him it was over?"

"Basically, yes."

"Do you trust him?"

"Of course I do."

"Do you love him?"

"I—"

"This is me, Riley. We've never lied to each other. Don't start now. Do you love him?"

"More than I ever thought possible. And that's why—"

Anna held up her hand. "I'm not through yet."

Riley huffed out a breath. "Fine."

"Do you think he's a good, decent man?"

"Of course he is."

"Do you think he cares for you?"

"I know he does."

"Then why the hell would you not want to be with someone that wonderful? Who, by the way, thinks you're wonderful, too?"

"It's not that simple."

"Yeah, sometimes it is that simple. Just because some very bad things happened to you doesn't mean some very good things can't happen. You've got your dream job. You're finally going to be able to make the people pay who tried to destroy you. And you've got a good, strong man in your life."

"It can't last."

"Just because something looks too good to be true, doesn't mean it is. You're the furthest thing from a coward I've ever known. Don't be afraid to be happy. Don't choose misery over happiness. It's a cold, lonely place."

Looking out over the untamed landscape before her, Riley absorbed Anna's words. Was that what she was doing? Choosing to be miserable because she feared happiness?

"Okay." Anna jumped to her feet. "Let's finish the trail, and then it's a double-fudge sundae. My treat."

"I thought the climb was in place of the sundae."

"That was the triple. I'll settle for a double."

Riley stood and eyed her friend. She'd been so immersed in her own misery that she hadn't recognized that her friend was hurting, too. And she knew the cause.

"Aidan didn't mean anything by what he said at the meeting. He's just concerned for you."

Anna shrugged and started up the hill again. "Aidan Thorne can go suck a raw rotten egg as far as I'm concerned."

The animosity between the tough-edged LCR operative and Anna was a surprise to everyone. Every woman at LCR had a slight crush on Aidan Thorne. He was charming, considerate, and gorgeous. But for some reason, he was the exact opposite with Anna.

What Noah had said at their meeting was true. He'd offered Anna an LCR position more than once, but she'd always turned him down. What most people didn't know was that Anna's rejection of Noah's job offer had less to do with not wanting to work for LCR and more to do with seeing Aidan Thorne.

Aidan and Anna had known each other for several years. He'd even helped rescue Anna when she'd been kidnapped years ago. But for some reason, every time the two got within a few yards of each other, one or the other ended up saying something or doing something stupid to rile the other one up.

Even though Anna would never admit it, Riley knew her friend had a crush on Aidan. So when he became surly with her, she took it to heart more than she would with anyone else.

Reading Aidan Thorne was the same as reading any other LCR operative—difficult to impossible most times. So the real reason Aidan Thorne couldn't seem to stand Anna Bradford was a mystery to everyone but Aidan. And she wasn't totally sure Aidan knew for certain himself.

"Come on, Riley," Anna called from above her. "That ice cream won't eat itself."

Standing, Riley pushed the sweaty strands of hair from her face and took in a deep breath. Anna had been right to suggest a hike. If she'd had her way, she would've holed up in her apartment and tried to hide from the world. That would have been the wrong thing to do.

Riley Ingram was through hiding.

Chapter Eighteen

Knoxville, Tennessee

The small accounting firm, housed in a small office off the interstate, was a cross between shabby chic and upscale contemporary. Designed to look like a moderately successful CPA office, it boasted two full-time accountants, three full-time assistants, and an administrative assistant. No one would suspect that five of the people in the small firm were better trained to annihilate an opponent than assist clients with their tax woes.

On one side of the building stood a bakery, on the other side a consignment store. Each business had recently acquired a new employee. If anyone noticed that the new hires spent more time standing at the window or walking the perimeter of the building, no one mentioned it.

All three businesses looked moderately successful but were in no way flashy. That was the name of the game for this op. Flashy would attract attention. No one would believe that a young woman hiding from her former life would risk exposure by working in any kind of business where she might be seen or noticed. Working in a small office with minimal exposure to the public was believable, and the cover was easy to set up.

Even though this was the perfect cover, Riley fought an unfamiliar panicky feeling. Not because she feared facing Dimitri or any of his goons. Since she had made up her mind to confront her past, she was ready to make this happen. No, her fear came from something more elemental and disturbing. She felt confined in the small office. Penned in. One of Dimitri's favorite punishments had been locking her in a small area. When he'd realized how much it freaked her out, he had commissioned a box to be built just for that purpose. And since the sadist believed in getting his money's worth, she had spent hours in that box. Twice he had left her in there for over twenty-four hours. When she'd been released, she'd been punished and mocked for soiling herself.

"You okay, Riley?"

Hearing her name, Riley jerked herself from the past. Standing before her, compassion in their eyes, were both Anna and McKenna.

"Sorry. I was—" *Was what? Torturing myself with memories?* One of the most important things she'd learned in her therapy was to never allow herself to go back in time and ruminate. The present and all the possibilities of the future should always be her focus. Those practices had sustained her, helped her heal. Damned if she would regress back into a victim.

"You don't have to explain anything to us." McKenna reached for her hand. "Been there, done that. Returning to hell, even if it's just in your mind, is never a pleasant journey."

With anyone else she might be embarrassed, but not with these two. These women knew her pain better than anyone.

She straightened her shoulders and turned to look around the room. "We should be hearing from Noah soon."

"He said it could take a few days before anything happens. Right?" Anna said. "He's just going to dangle the hook a bit?"

Taking a breath to center herself, she nodded. "Yes. Larson's not going to believe I was found so quickly. Plus, Noah wants to see if the man will reveal information about his...business."

"We're prepared for every scenario," McKenna said.

Yes, they were. Two days ago, Riley had endured the minimally painful but still unpleasant implantation of two tracking devices. One was beneath her right armpit, another on the outside of her left thigh. Though she barely felt them now, she was hyper-aware of them. Yes, they would help LCR track her if she was taken, but they also added to her feelings of confinement.

But acting normal was the name of the game until this op moved to the next phase. If that included staying cooped up inside an office, then so be it.

Maybe what was bothering her more than anything was that she and Justin hadn't had more than a casual conversation in days. Not really. They had both flown into Knoxville on the LCR plane with everyone else, and then he had disappeared. No one seemed to know where he had gone or why. She would have been totally frustrated if it weren't for the fact that he'd been sleeping beside her every night. They hadn't made love since that night in her apartment. She would have been worried that his feelings had changed if not for the fact that they fell asleep in each other's arms each night. But every morning, for the last three days, he had been gone before she woke up.

When she had questioned him, he'd given her one of his enigmatic smiles, told her not to worry, that he was making plans. He refused to elaborate on what those plans were.

Despite his lack of openness, she had total faith and trust in her partner. But as his lover, she was admittedly on thin ice. Could it be because the first and only time they'd been intimate she had pulled a gun on him afterward? What kind of freak did something like that?

The outside door opened, and the man himself walked in. Instead of greeting everyone, he zeroed in on Riley. She swallowed hard. If he had been avoiding talking with her, then that was apparently at an end.

She told herself that was a good thing. If he was having second thoughts about their new relationship, then they needed to have it out. End what never should have started in the first place. Finish this once and for all and go back to what they were before. LCR partners, nothing more.

Even as she told herself that, she knew it was a lie. She didn't want to have that conversation, because she didn't want it to end. That first night with him had been the best experience of her life. She had found fulfillment and happiness in the arms of Justin Kelly. He was her partner, then her friend, and now her lover. She didn't want to lose any of them. At the back of her mind, a fleeting, hopeful wisp of a dream was emerging. She wanted permanency, a commitment with this man. For a lifetime.

And despite her sensible brain telling her these things were impossible, she couldn't let go of the hope. She wanted to spend a thousand nights in his arms, exploring him, letting him explore her. She wanted to travel the world with him, rescuing victims. She wanted to share her hopes and dreams with him. She wanted to know what his dreams were. Oh dear heavens, she wanted it all.

His face was as stern as a general going into battle. "McCall just texted. He's making the first call now."

Riley's mind went blank. All breath left her body. This was what she wanted, what needed to be done, and now that it was in play, there was no going back. This was going to happen.

"Ingram."

Justin's hard tone pulled her out of her panic. Ashamed at her reaction, she glanced around, surprised to find that only she and Justin were in the room.

She took a breath and stood. "The sooner we get this started, the sooner we get it finished."

Not meeting his eyes, her gaze roamed the room. She was looking for something to do, trying to come up with something to talk about other than what she really wanted to know. What was going on with them? Where had he been the last few days? Why was there this new distance between them? Was it over?

She raised her gaze to his and caught her breath on a gasp. She saw tenderness, heat, and something else she could barely put a name to.

"Justin?"

He held out his hand. "Come with me."

She followed him into a smaller, private office. The instant the door closed, he pulled her around to face him.

"Before this goes down, you and I need to get a few things straight."

***

LCR Offices

East Tennessee Branch

Noah punched in the number he'd been given, sat back in his chair, and waited.

"Hello?"

"Mr. Larson? Noah McCall."

"Mr. McCall? Have you found her?"

"Uh, no. Not yet." He added a small amount of arrogant exasperation to his tone. "My people have just started on the case. I do, however, have a few follow-up questions."

There was a slight pause, and then Larson said rather cautiously, "Like what?"

"Has Jessica ever been to Greece?"

"Ah..." A slight sputter. "Um. Not that I'm aware of. Why?"

"Did she have any friends from there? Maybe someone who would have given her refuge?"

"I...uh. No. I don't remember any of her friends or acquaintances being from Greece."

"Hmm. Then this could be a dead end."

"What do you mean?"

"As you know, we have contacts all over the world. On an initial inquiry we made, we found a man who used to work on a cruise ship. He claimed a young woman stowed away on a ship that was docked in Greece."

Noah could just imagine Larson's consternation. His need to keep Dimitri's location out of the investigation was no doubt warring with the very real possibility that LCR had found a lead.

"The timeline fits. This was about eight years ago. The description fit Jessica, so he was shown the photograph you provided. He said that he remembers the girl as much thinner and very sad looking, but he thought it might be her."

"We'll just keep looking," Noah went on smoothly. "Knowing where not to look is almost as important as where to look. I'll—"

"Wait. Wait. Um, are you sure it was Greece?"

There was something in Larson's tone. Something not right. The man sounded genuinely surprised that Greece had been mentioned. Noah took a chance and threw out some more bait.

"The man thought it was Greece, but he also mentioned that the ship had several ports of call on that cruise. Perhaps this girl got on at another location, and he just thought it was Greece."

"Well now, come to think of it, I do believe Jessica had a friend from somewhere around there. I don't recall the girl's name, but I remember Jessica making mention of wanting to visit her. This definitely sounds like it's a lead worth pursuing, Mr. McCall."

"If you think that it's a possibility she visited her friend, then we'll definitely look harder in that direction. Are you sure you don't remember the exact location or the girl's name? Perhaps your wife might remember."

"I'm sorry. I don't remember. And Loretta? Well, her memory isn't what it used to be. I—Oh my, I just remembered something else. So tragic. The girl died in a car accident a few years ago."

So he didn't remember the girl's name, but he knew she'd been killed. The man's desperation was showing. He had not thought this through. There were more holes in his story than in a pound of Swiss cheese.

"That's too bad. Still, it gives us a more focused area to look at. I'll put my efforts into finding out more about this young woman who stowed away."

"It would be remarkable if it's her. I can't wait to tell Loretta."

"Don't get your hopes up too much. Again, this could just be a dead end."

"Any lead is better than nothing at all."

"I'll be in touch. Goodbye, Mr. Larson."

The moment the call ended, Noah slammed his fist on the desk. He'd played a small hunch, but now he had even more questions. Larson had sounded genuinely shocked at the mention of Greece. Was Dimitri not there after all? Had they been looking at the wrong damn country all this time?

CHAPTER NINETEEN

Justin looked down into Riley's wary eyes. He knew he probably looked like roadkill. Other than the few hours he spent with Riley each night, he had barely had any sleep since they'd left home.

After meeting with McCall that day and hearing how broken Riley had been when McCall took her in, how her ordeal had left her so damaged she couldn't even bring herself to speak, he'd been convinced of one elemental truth. Riley must be protected, no matter what. She had suffered too much. Allowing Larson or Dimitri to get their hands on her again, even now that she could protect herself and would have the best backup LCR had to offer, was just not acceptable.

He'd had a much-needed and brutal bout with Aidan and then started a plan of action. He had full faith in LCR in carrying off a successful mission, but they needed to use all of their resources.

He hadn't mentioned his idea to anyone until he had everything in place. Once he was ready, Justin had shared those plans with his boss, told him what he had done. McCall had listened without comment, nodding at all of Justin's carefully thought-out reasons.

The LCR leader had concurred that it was a good, solid strategy. He agreed that it should work and, most important, would ensure Riley's safety. Justin had been relieved to have him on board. McCall's assistance was integral to things going forward. Then McCall had put a kink in everything when he'd asked, "What does Riley think about this?"

When he had explained that he'd wanted to get everything in place before bringing her on board, McCall had shaken his head and delivered a final summation. "She'll never go for it."

Admittedly, Justin had squelched all the niggling doubts in the back of his mind that he should have talked with her before moving forward. But he had convinced himself that when he presented the plan, fait accompli, she would agree. McCall's statement had brought all those doubts back to the forefront.

Deciding the best defense was a good offense, Justin backed up against the edge of the desk and pulled Riley forward until she was standing in front of him. Keeping his hands on her shoulders, he locked his gaze with hers. "You need to know a few things, Ingram. First, I have a deep admiration for you. Not just for overcoming so much, but for what you've made of yourself. You have more courage and grit than anyone I've ever known.

"I've watched you dodge bullets, take down men three times your size, and rescue countless victims without showing the least amount of fear. Hell, the injury you received last year would've killed most people. You've got bigger balls than men ten times your size."

Riley's startled laughter was a welcome sound. He had said the last part intending for her to laugh, but the words were true. He'd kept his word to McCall that he would let her work through her emotions in her own way, but now that things were under way, he could wait no longer. They had to do this and soon.

"There is no doubt in my mind that you can destroy Dimitri, as well as William Larson and his disgusting band of human traffickers."

"Why do I hear a but in there somewhere?"

Instead of giving her a direct answer, he said, "You know Mia Ryker. Right?"

She frowned her confusion. "Of course I know Mia. She and her husband, Jared Livingston, are former LCR operatives, though they still work with LCR from time to time. Jared's the one who trailed Larson to LA."

"Jared is still there, but Mia is coming here."

"It'll be good to see her again. Did Noah ask her to help out with this part of the op?"

"In a way."

"In what way?"

Pushing aside all the doubts that were suddenly screaming for attention, he continued his explanation. "You and Mia have similar appearances."

"Yes," she said slowly. "I even switched places with her once on an op. We have the same build and coloring. No one even noticed. But what's that go to do with—"

Her eyes grew wide as comprehension hit. "You want her to pose as me for this op."

"I don't want you to have to see that bastard Dimitri again. Or Larson either. Neither man has seen you in years. Yours and Mia's physical similarities are close already. With a little extra makeup and enhancements, they'll never doubt that it's you.

"I've rented a place in upper East Tennessee, high up in the mountains. Used to belong to one of those doomsday preppers. The place is surrounded by a twelve-foot wall and an electric fence. It's a fortress. No one's around for miles. Most importantly, no one could get to you there. Anna can stay with you. We'll set up guards to patrol the grounds twenty-four seven until this is over. You'll be safe."

Her initial reaction was immense relief. She wouldn't have to see the monster again. Wouldn't have to hear his voice, smell his fetid breath, brace against the fear of his touch. And Larson. She wouldn't have to suffer through seeing the people responsible for putting her in hell.

She felt almost dizzy from the sense of freedom. Nothing extra would be required of her. The demons of her past would be destroyed, and she would…she would…

"Oh no. Oh, hell no." Jerking out of Justin's grasp, Riley jumped a foot away from him.

She had almost fallen for it. She couldn't decide whom she was more disappointed in—herself for being so damned naïve and weak, or Justin for his arrogance and lack of faith.

"Riley, think about it. You won't have—"

"I don't have to think about it." Hands on her hips, she glared at him. "This is my right. I deserve to bring these bastards down. No one has that right more than I do. I'll be damned if I'll let you treat me like a victim."

"I'm not treating you like a victim. I'm trying to protect you."

"As my partner, you protect me by having my back. Just like I have yours. You don't lock me away or hide me behind closed doors. You don't treat me like I'm some useless, untrained civilian, incapable of handling myself."

"That's not what I'm doing."

"Then what are you doing, Justin? Tell me. Because it sure as hell looks as though you don't think I can handle this op. If you don't, then we need to go to McCall and make some changes. I need a partner who believes in me."

"I do believe in you, dammit. And McCall already knows about this."

The betrayal hit her harder than she'd thought possible. She stumbled back, heard her numb lips whisper, "He doesn't think I can handle it either?"

"Of course he does. This has nothing to do with what you can handle. Hell, I just told you you're the strongest person I know."

"Words, Kelly. Actions speak louder than words."

She turned on her heel and started for the door.

"Where are you going?"

"I need to talk to Noah. If he doesn't think I'm strong enough to do this, then he can at least tell me to my face."

"Dammit, stop!"

A hand grabbed her shoulder. She whirled, and her fist zoomed to his face. A split second before it landed, she pulled it back.

Instead of ducking or blocking the punch, Justin twisted his mouth in a small smile. "That's what you call control, Ingram. Not slugging me when it's probably what you'd most like to do."

"What I'd most like to do is to never have had this conversation."

He closed his eyes, rubbed at a spot between them as if he had a headache. In all the years they'd known each other, she didn't think she'd ever seen Justin look so tired or frustrated.

She still seethed with anger, but she tamped it down and asked quietly, "Why, Justin?"

He shook his head. "I handled this badly. I was trying to protect you, and instead, you took it as an insult to your abilities."

"It's not my abilities you insulted. If that were in question, I'd laugh in your face because I know you don't question my skills.

You've seen what I can do. It's the fact that you don't think I'm mentally or emotionally stable enough to do the job."

"That's total bullshit!" he snapped. "That's not why at all."

"Then why?" she challenged.

"Because, the thought of anything happening to you, the thought of you being hurt in any way, of having to face those assholes again…it rips me to pieces."

Grabbing her hand, he pulled her into his arms. "This is why, dammit." Lowering his head, he covered her mouth with his, breathed in her gasp of surprise. She tasted more delicious than he remembered, better than anything ever had.

Justin controlled the kiss but made sure she knew she could pull away if she wanted to. He sent up a silent prayer of thanks that instead of pulling away, she moved into him with a small moan.

As tentative as he would be while diffusing a bomb, he slowly lowered his hands, caressing her lower back and then her sweet, firm ass. His control was being tested, because more than anything he wanted to dive into the need, the unbelievable heat that was now swamping him. He wanted to lay her on the desk, strip her naked, and devour every inch of her sweet body. But he reminded himself to be careful, gentle. Triggering any kind of horrific memory was the last thing he wanted.

She finally did ease away, slightly, her breath elevated. "I'm not fragile or breakable, you know."

"You're precious."

She snorted. "Poodles are precious."

He grinned and felt a loosening in his muscles. If she could joke and smile, he hadn't completely screwed everything up. "And Rileys are what? Rigid. Rambunctious?"

"Right," she whispered, pulling his head down to her again. "Rileys are right." Heat washed through her body, and she found herself wanting to rub up against him like a cat.

Justin drew her closer, slid his tongue into her mouth, thrusting deep. Riley gave herself up to these wondrous new feelings he aroused in her. She'd never believed it was even possible to have sexual desire after what she'd gone through. But she knew the reasons had more to do with the man than with her recovery. With any other man, she would have either pushed him away or been revolted. This man, her partner, the man she trusted with all her heart, had opened up a part of her she'd believed was closed forever.

She owed him her loyalty, and if he wanted it, she would give him her love. She would not, however, give up who she was. What she had become.

She told her erratic heart to slow down. There were things they needed to settle.

"I'm doing this job, Justin. It's my right."

"You have nothing to prove to anyone, Riley."

"Apparently, I do since you and Noah cooked up this scheme. Without consulting me, I might add."

"This wasn't McCall's idea. It was mine. He told me you wouldn't go for it."

Relief rushed through her. "At least he trusts me."

"Quit twisting my words, Ingram. This has nothing to do with trust. I just want—"

She held up her hand to stop his protest. "Fine. Whatever. No matter the reasons, here's the bottom line. I have to do this."

"No, you don't."

Her eyes glinting with determination, she put her hands on her hips in challenge. "Let me ask you this. If the men who kidnapped your sister were found to be alive and an op was put together to go after him, would you say, that's okay, I'll sit this one out because I'm too emotionally involved?"

"That's not the same thing."

"Oh yeah? Why isn't it the same thing? Because you're a man? Or because you're tougher than I am?"

"Because I wasn't held prisoner or brutalized by the bastards."

"No, but your sister was."

Justin began pacing around the office. Riley stayed silent, knowing he needed to work this out. She wouldn't back down, but she needed him to accept her decision and not continue to fight her.

Long moments later, he stopped and glared at her. "Fine. But if you deviate from the plan even a little, I don't care what you say, I'm hauling you to that safe house and you'll damn well stay there."

She could have challenged him, but she didn't. Dimitri had locked her up out of the need to control her. Justin wanted to protect her. There was a world of difference between the two. That didn't mean, however, that she would allow Justin to manipulate her. She'd worked too hard to become her own person. Yet, she also knew when to bend and be flexible.

"Fine."

"McCall is waiting for us at the apartments. He wants to run some things by you."

"Then let's go."

She put her hand on the doorknob, and Justin covered it with his. Pulling her back against him, he spoke against her ear. "Don't give up on us, Ingram."

Those words, more than any others he could have said, relieved her mind. He hadn't given up on her, on them. Then neither would she.

CHAPTER TWENTY

The apartment complex the operatives were staying in wasn't the most expensive, but the apartments were large. Each had its own washer and dryer and a surprisingly nice décor. Those weren't the reasons LCR had chosen these particular apartments, though. The biggest draw was the top floor of the apartment building. It boasted six apartments, each one connected to the other. This enabled operatives to move from one apartment to another without anyone seeing them.

Riley and Justin had been silent on the ride over, absorbed in their own thoughts. This was another reason she and Justin got along so well on an op. Neither of them ever felt the need to fill the silence with unnecessary banter. She was especially appreciative today, because her mind was running fast and furious.

William Larson had been contacted, told there was a possibility of a sighting. That she might be found soon. And there was no doubt in her mind that Dimitri now knew that as well. Even though it had just begun and neither man had been told where she might be, Riley felt her adrenaline surging. It would be only a few more days, and they would be in full operations mode. The serious stuff would begin.

On the elevator ride up, she glanced over at Justin. His jaw was clenched, his mouth a grim line. She knew he was worried about her. A part of her felt guilty for the hard time she'd given him before. The fact that he cared enough to want to hide her and make sure she came to no harm was sweet and romantic. For anyone else, it might have even been considered heroic. But for Riley Ingram, who fought everyday not to be seen as a victim, it hadn't been appreciated.

"McCall said he'd meet us in our apartment."

"I'll be glad when this is over and we can go back to my apartment in Virginia."

"You don't like where we're staying?"

She scrunched her nose. "Not enough windows."

"For a woman who needs to hide, you sure like to be out in the open."

He didn't know about her phobias, and she sure as hell wasn't going to get into them now. He knew more than anyone else, and as far as she was concerned, that was more than enough.

They reached their apartment door, but before she could unlock it, Noah opened it. He had the same worried look as Justin. That look made her even more determined to see this through. She knew they trusted her, but if there were doubts that she could handle this op, she needed to make sure she dispelled them.

She went to the living room and settled onto the sofa. First she would listen to what Noah wanted to say, then she would find the words to convince him that she could do this job.

"Justin told you I made the initial call," Noah stated.

"Yes. How did it go? Did you learn anything?"

Noah pulled his cellphone from his pocket and then clicked a key. "You tell me."

For the first time in eleven years, she heard the voice of the man she had believed was her father. His voice sounded a little older, gravelly, as if he might be a smoker. The excitement in his voice was over the top and unsettling. She could not recall a time when she'd ever heard emotion in his voice. When she was growing up, he had rarely raised his tone and oftentimes had sounded bored. In hindsight, it was hard to believe that she thought she had loved him as a parent. He had never shown her the least amount of affection. But she had admired him, believed he was such a hard worker, so dedicated to his employer.

Noah's conversation with Larson didn't last long. At the end, she heard a huskiness in his voice, as if he were so overcome with emotion he was trying not to cry.

There was silence in the room after the call ended. Finally, Justin broke it with a sardonic, "Laid it on a bit thick, didn't he?"

"That was my thought, too," Noah said. "The man has so little idea what real emotion is, he can't even fake it."

Two sets of eyes turned to Riley. "What did you think?"

What did she think? She thought if she had anything in her stomach, she might be throwing up about now. She drew in a breath. No. She knew how to compartmentalize. This was an op. He was nothing more than a sleazy human trafficker who was going to get his just deserts.

"He sounds older. And I agree. He was laying it on a bit thick. I doubt that he has to play the role of grieving father too often. Must be hard."

"Did you catch his surprise at the mention of Greece?" Noah asked. "That made me wonder if we've been looking in the right place."

"What do you mean?" she asked.

"We assumed you boarded that ship in Greece because of the language and the signs, but you might have merely been in an area heavily populated by Greek people."

"Crap." She shook her head. "All this time…"

"Don't beat yourself up. Dimitri is still too common of a name even in Greece, much less other countries."

She accepted the truth of that. Having nothing to go on but a first name and possible location had been their biggest impediment from the beginning. "We're still on target for another contact in a few days?"

"Yes. I'll wait three days and call him back. Let him know we may have found you. In the meantime, Livingston is still trailing him, trying to determine if he's got more than the three houses that we already know about."

"Good." She paused a beat, then gave both men a hard stare. "I know about the safe house. I won't go."

McCall's mouth twitched with a smile. Justin didn't bother to argue or defend himself. He believed in Riley, but that didn't mean he wouldn't try to protect her. He had, he now admitted, gone about it in a stupid-assed way, though.

"Justin said Mia's planning to come here, too."

"That's on hold for right now," Noah said. "We'll call her in if need be. Even if everything goes according to plan, it would be helpful to have a double in the wings, just in case."

"But you agree that I can handle this, right? You don't have doubts about my ability to cope?"

"Ingram," McCall said quietly, "do you remember what I told you when you first became an operative?"

"You said that if there was a time you didn't think I could handle an op, you would pull me off of it."

"And that hasn't changed. If I see you wavering in the least, I'll pull you out. Just like I would any other operative. Our priorities are and always will be the victims."

"And I'm no victim."

"No, you're sure as hell not. You're a survivor."

Justin not only felt like a third wheel, but also one that had rolled over a big pile of dog shit. Yeah, he'd screwed up royally. Riley thought he didn't believe she could handle this. She was wrong. But how the hell to convince her otherwise?

"Riley, I—"

McCall stood. "I'll leave you two to talk. I'm in the apartment on the other side of McKenna and Anna. See you at seven for a team meeting."

Justin waited until McCall walked out the door and then turned back to Riley. "What can I do to prove to you that I believe in you?"

The old Riley might have given him a snarky, sarcastic reply. But they had advanced far beyond her standard form of defense. Besides, she couldn't stand the worried, almost defeated expression on his face. His eyes were bloodshot, and his shoulders drooped with fatigue.

"Just tell me that you trust me to do my job."

"I trust you. Absolutely. I just wanted to protect you. I'm sorry."

This was a new thing for them. For so long, they'd been partners, trusting each other with their lives. But intimacy had added a new dimension. When it came to relationships, especially romantic ones, Riley knew she was a beginner.

Going on instinct alone, she went to him, leaned against his hard body, and softly kissed his mouth. "I believe you, and you're forgiven."

"Really?"

The grin on his face made her want to smile. He looked like a little boy who'd found out he wasn't going to be punished.

"With one condition."

"What's that?"

"Let me take care of you for a change."

"What do you mean?"

"Go take something for that headache I know you have. While you do that, I'm going to fix us something to eat."

He dropped a kiss on her head. "You've got yourself a deal."

She was about to enter the kitchen when Justin stopped at the bedroom door. "Hey, Ingram?"

"Yeah?"

"Thanks for not kicking my ass."

She grinned at him. "You're not out of the woods yet, Kelly."

"How so?"

She laughed softly as she walked away. "You've never eaten my cooking before."

CHAPTER
TWENTY-ONE

Three days later...

Noah closed the door to his office and locked it. He chose to make the call with no one around. Riley deserved to hear the conversation, but he'd give her the recording later, as he would the rest of the team. For right now, Noah wanted to fully concentrate on Larson's reaction to the news with the hope that it would give him an idea of how the man planned to proceed.

Hitting the call key, Noah waited for the man to answer.

"Yes? Mr. McCall? Tell me you have good news."

"We believe we've found her, Mr. Larson."

"Oh, thank God. Where is she? When can I see her?"

"We need to take this one step at a time, Mr. Larson."

"Oh. Of course. Of course. I just..." He blew out a ragged sigh. "Are you sure it's her, Mr. McCall? Over the years, my investigators reported sightings, but they all turned out to be wrong."

Lying to a client wasn't the norm for Noah. Yeah, he'd softened the truth occasionally. Even withheld information if he thought it could cause damage. But outright lying was a rarity. He'd created Last Chance Rescue out of the soul-deep need to rescue victims, bring loved ones home and closure to grieving families. Protecting victims had always been his number one priority, though, so in this case, lying was not only a necessity for the game they were playing, but also damn satisfying. The bastard was going to pay for the misery he had caused.

"I don't believe we're wrong, Mr. Larson. She's changed a little over the years, but we're almost certain this is your daughter Jessica."

"How did you find her so quickly?"

False modesty wasn't a natural position for him. Noah had no problem bragging about his organization. Without a doubt, he employed the best operatives in the world. In this instance, though, a modicum of modesty would go further.

He gave a short, abrupt laugh. "Actually, it was a lucky break. As I mentioned previously, we've got contacts all over the world in all lines of work. I sent Jessica's photograph to all of them. One of those contacts had just returned from getting his income taxes done and thought that one of the assistants in an accounting firm resembled the photograph. He got in touch with me, and we went from there."

"So she's actually working? Able to hold down a job?"

"Yes. She's quiet. Somewhat shy and awkward. Her employer mentioned that she's very intelligent."

"Yes, our Jessica was always a smart one. That's why when her delusions began, it just broke our hearts."

"She seemed quite sane and logical to me."

"You've talked to her?"

"Yes. I made the initial contact. She's agreed to talk with me again in a few days. As you can imagine, the news that you're trying to locate her was surprising."

"Yes…I'm sure it was. Mr. McCall…remember, Jessica is very ill. She may seem rational, but I assure you she's not. We need to see her as soon as possible. When can we arrange a meeting?"

"Soon."

"Is she in the States?"

"I won't reveal that information until I'm assured she wants to see you."

"I told you, Mr. McCall, Jessica is ill. I have doctors here in Los Angeles on stand-by, just waiting to give her the care she needs."

Larson's slip-up made Noah smile. "Los Angeles?"

"Oh…uh, yes. I should have mentioned before that we recently moved to Los Angeles. The, um, weather is better for Loretta's health."

"I see."

Obviously rattled, Larson hurried on, "You read the medical records I sent you. Jessica is delusional and needs psychiatric care."

Yes, he'd read the trumped-up medical records. Larson had probably paid a lot of money for them.

"Which is why we need to proceed slowly to avoid putting her health at risk. If she agrees to see you, I'll arrange a meeting. We'll assess how that goes and then go from there."

Steam was probably coming out of Larson's ears about now. After all this time, he seemed to want to barge in and take Jessica. There was something driving the man to get this done quickly.

"Very well, Mr. McCall. We'll play it your way. I couldn't bear it if we damaged Jessica. I'm just thrilled she's alive. With her mental health issues, I greatly feared she had harmed herself, perhaps committed suicide. We're just so grateful you've found her for us."

Larson must've been practicing his acting skills. He actually sounded like a loving father. But this man was as far removed from a loving father as Noah's own father had been. Both men belonged in hell. Thankfully, his old man had gone there years before.

"As soon as I can persuade Jessica to see you, I'll call you back."

"Thank you, Mr. McCall. I can't wait to tell Loretta that our little girl is coming home."

Noah rolled his eyes. The guy was laying it on thick again. Desperation made for bad acting. "We'll talk soon."

Noah ended the call and then sat back in his chair. Anticipating what evil people would do was part of his job. In earlier years, he had underestimated his opponents on more than one occasion, and it had cost him. They had to be prepared for anything.

***

Hera, Pavli

"Your pores look wonderful, sir. That new lotion is doing wonders for your skin."

His eyes closed, Dimitri didn't bother to respond to the technician's compliments. The man was here to give Dimitri his weekly facial. Pandering had its place, but this wasn't it. A successful procedure required peace and quiet.

"My, it was a beautiful day, wasn't it, sir?"

Did the imbecile not understand anything? Dimitri opened his eyes and gave him a hard stare. The technician paled and jumped a foot off the floor.

Satisfied he'd made his point, Dimitri closed his eyes again. The peaceful silence was a soothing balm.

A loud knock on the door almost brought him out of his chair.

"Who is it?" he shouted.

"Telephone call, sir."

The timid voice belonged to his assistant. The man knew not to interrupt his rejuvenating session. There was only one exception.

"Larson?" he asked.

"Yes, sir."

"Come in." He glared at the technician. "Get out of here now."

"But, sir...your mask!"

"I said get out!"

The technician nodded and ran for the door, passing Dimitri's assistant, who came rushing in, holding the phone. He placed the phone in Dimitri's outstretched hand, turned, and rushed out of the room.

At least some people knew their place.

He pressed the speaker key. "Larson? You have news?"

"Yes. She's been located."

"Where is she?"

"I don't know yet. She—"

"What do you mean you don't know?"

"The agency I hired, they have strict rules. They won't tell me anything until they make sure she agrees to see me."

"There's no way she's going to agree. She'll tell them things."

"I've got that covered. I've already explained to McCall that Jessica is mentally ill, that she's delusional. If she tells him anything, he won't believe her."

"Then how do you think that—"

"When he contacts me again, it will be to set up a meeting. If I can take her without bloodshed, I will. If not, I have no problem taking her by force. Either way, Jessica will be in my custody in a matter of days."

Dimitri thought about disagreeing. He had men who could wipe out a city block without blinking an eye. One little bitch and a man would be like swatting a gnat. Then again, it was Larson's failing that had caused all of this. If Jessica had been what Dimitri needed, none of this would have been necessary.

"Once you have her, how do you plan to proceed?"

"I can bring her to you. Or meet you somewhere. Whatever's most convenient for you."

"How accommodating," Dimitri said silkily.

"I want to make this right, Soukis."

It could never be right. The man was too stupid to realize that, though. The moment he had Jessica in his hands again, Dimitri had plans for Larson. Somebody had to pay for the heartache and loneliness Dimitri had suffered all these years. For all the disappointment he'd endured with those useless cows Larson had sent as replacements. Since killing Jessica would defeat his purposes, Larson could give his life in her stead. It was only fitting.

"As soon as you have her, let me know. I'll make arrangements for the transfer."

"Yes, that's fine. Whatever you want."

Dimitri heard the relief in the other man's voice and almost smiled. The imbecile believed that once this was over, and Jessica was returned to him, things could go back to normal.

Larson confirmed that with his next words. "And you'll tell others that I made good on my promise?"

Dimitri barely held back a snort. The man was finally doing something he should have done eight years ago. There would be no kind words from Dimitri. Not that he would say that.

"But of course I will," Dimitri assured him. "That was our agreement."

"I'll call you as soon as I have her."

"Very good," Dimitri said and ended the call.

Dimitri stood. He glanced at the mirror and grinned at himself. The blood-red goop on his face always yielded good results. However, he was impatient today. He took a wet cloth lying on the table and wiped at it his face. Not caring that much of it was still there, he walked out the door.

Pulling a set of keys from his pocket, Dimitri headed to one of his favorite places in the world. He had not played in his special room for years. Not since Jessica had left him. He'd used a smaller, less attractive room for the other girls. Lately, when he had the urge to indulge his desires, he went to a local facility that catered to his particular preferences. Allowing anyone into his home whom he didn't know or hadn't fully vetted would be absurd. No, he wasn't worried he would be caught. He owned enough law enforcement people to ensure no one could touch him. But the very idea of a stranger coming into his home was revolting. Only those he trusted, or was in complete control of, were allowed inside his domain.

He unlocked the door and allowed it to swing open. The lights came on immediately, illuminating the area. For the first time in a long time, a natural smile came to his lips. Those who knew him well would have been alarmed.

Since his servants kept the room clean, all the equipment and tools gleamed as if they were new. Everything was in place, as it should be, except for one thing. The one thing that would make the room complete was Jessica, down on her knees, or hanging from the hooks in the ceiling, or locked in the pretty little box in the corner he'd had designed especially for her.

Soon, very soon, she would be here again. A surge of lust swept through him, followed by a hearty laugh. This might be even better than before. She would be in complete fear, totally subjugated. Terrified of what he would do to her. Wondering if it could be worse than what she'd endured before. Wondering if this time he might actually kill her.

Oh yes, this would be so much more fun.

The bitch had eight years to make up for. He would make sure she paid for every single one of them.

***

Knoxville

The call came in the middle of the night. Just like most people, especially one who was away from his family, a slight panic surged through Noah as he grabbed the phone on the nightstand. When he checked the screen, he was only slightly less worried. A call from one of his research analysts at this hour was rarely a good thing.

"What's wrong?" Noah barked.

"We've got a problem."

As the analyst explained her findings, fury filled him. Vermin such as these did not deserve to breathe.

Pushing aside his anger, he said evenly, "Send me everything you have. And keep looking. There may be more. And good job, Lilly. You've saved several lives today."

He waited until he'd ended the call to let loose a string of vile curses. Rage made every muscle in his body rigid. The scumsuckers were not going to get away with this.

Punching in a speed-dial number, he barely waited for Riley to answer before he said, "Ingram, something's come up."

"What's wrong?"

"Kelly there with you?"

"Yes. Let me put you on speaker."

"I'm here, McCall. What's up?"

"We're going to have to move faster than we planned."

"What's happened?" Ingram asked.

"One of our analysts was trolling the dark web. She came upon a…if you can believe this…a coming-soon site."

"Oh shit," Kelly whispered.

"Yeah. The level of depravity defies description. As you know, we habitually search these kinds of sites, hoping we can stem the flow. We traced the IP address back to one of Larson's places, but this child isn't one of the ones we knew about. This one is a fifteen year old boy."

"So he does have more," Ingram said.

"Yes. We thought he might. It's good we waited, but dammit, we can't wait any longer. We've got to move now."

"When's the sale?" Kelly asked.

"The ad said he'll be ready for purchase in a couple of weeks."

"You're right," Ingram said. "We have to move now."

"When we get this piece of shit alone," Kelly snarled, "we better make damn sure he spills his guts on how many kids he's got now and how many he's sold over the years."

"Trust me," Noah said with lethal quietness, "the man will talk."

CHAPTER TWENTY-TWO

LCR Branch Office
East Tennessee

Things were moving fast. Tomorrow their team would leave for Los Angeles. Several operatives were already there, keeping eyes on Larson's houses. If one of the locations indicated something hinky, they would have to raid all the locations and rescue the kids immediately. Larson would go down, but Dimitri would probably stay free.

Riley had accepted that inevitability. It wasn't the ideal situation, but with so many different components, they had no choice but to stay loose. There were too many innocents riding on this to not allow for deviations.

Justin, Noah, Sabrina, Angela, Jake, Aidan, and Riley had reviewed the plan and each of their roles. Riley could have recited it in her sleep. If they were able to carry it out, she had no doubt they would be successful.

Even though the reason they'd had to move the mission up was a deplorable one, Riley couldn't help but be relieved. Carrying out a deep-cover operation was draining enough. Carrying one out that held such emotional impact was much more wearing. She wanted this over and done with. Kids saved and perverted, disgusting pieces of slime like Larson and Dimitri put out of business for good.

Very soon she would be in the presence of the people who had betrayed her in the worst way possible. Would she see both Larson and his wife? Or just Larson?

Though she had nothing but hatred and revulsion for both of them, she needed answers. Were these people really her parents, or had she, as Noah suspected, been abducted as a child? If so, did they know who her parents were? Was it possible that she had a blood family out there? One that might still be looking for her? Want her? Was it possible that the blood running through her veins didn't belong to vile human traffickers? She prayed that was so.

She told herself it didn't really matter. She knew who she was. Being related to evil didn't make one evil. And LCR was her family. She couldn't ask for a better one. But still, the fantasy that she had a mother and father who had once loved her was something she couldn't dismiss no matter how much she tried. What would it feel like?

She glanced over at Justin sitting at a desk a few feet away, staring intently at his laptop. Things still weren't right between them. There was awkwardness, an uneasiness, between them. It was similar to how they'd been with each other when they'd first become partners. Every word weighed, every sentence measured, every glance wary and questioning. She didn't like it but wasn't sure how to break the tension.

They slept side by side, in the same bed, each night. When nightmares woke her, she only had to turn to him. He immediately knew what had happened and would take her in his arms, hold her, whisper comforting words until she went back to sleep. It was beautiful, soothing, and comfortable.

She wanted more.

She wanted him to make love to her. She wanted those knee-melting kisses, his hands moving over her, his hard body surrounding her. But not once had he given the slightest indication that he wanted anything more to happen.

She refused to believe his feelings changed. No man could kiss a woman like he had, or make love to her as if he could never get enough of her, and not have a strong desire for her. So why didn't he ask for more?

Riley stifled an inward groan. She hated these squishy, girlie feelings. They made her feel vulnerable and alone. Having no experience with how romantic relationships were supposed to work, she struggled with the least little thing. Like, was she supposed to make an overture? Her heart was telling her to do what came naturally, what her instincts wanted her to do, which was touch him, kiss him, and tell him she wanted him.

A chair scraped across the floor, jerking Riley from her thoughts. Justin gave her what she could describe only as a fierce glare and growled, "I'm going out for a while."

Wordlessly, she watched him walk out the door, wanting so badly to call him back. Yet at the same time, if she did call him back, confront him with her questions, and he told her he no longer wanted her that way, she was pretty damn sure she would cry. And since she hadn't cried in over eight years, she feared tears almost as much as she feared him no longer wanting her.

"Okay, mopey girl. You're coming with us."

She looked up. Anna had spoken, but McKenna, who stood beside her, wore the same firm expression as Anna.

"What?"

"You need a girls' night," McKenna said. "We all need one."

"I'm not really in the mood to go out."

"Then we'll stay in and order takeout. Come on, it'll be fun. Just us girls."

Riley frowned. "We're not going to paint each other's nails and eat ice cream from the carton are we?"

Eden stuck her head in the open doorway. "Did I hear something about ice cream?"

"We're having a girls-only party in our apartment. Ice cream and takeout, not necessarily in that order. Are you in?"

"Definitely." Beautiful gray eyes sparkled with delight. "I haven't had a girls-only party since college. Jordan and I are just heading out. Need me to bring drinks?"

"Lucas flew in briefly last night" McKenna's golden skin blushed a bright pink. "He brought soda. No beer, though."

"I'll grab some beer and a bottle of wine. See you in a few."

Anna turned back to Riley. "You ready to go?"

"You never did answer me about the nail-painting part."

"No nail painting. I promise. We'll order Chinese from that place down the street. And if you're extra sweet, I might even let you use a bowl for your ice cream."

"What kind of ice cream?"

"Whatever kind you like. I polished off the last carton this morning for breakfast."

Anna cheerfully ignored both McKenna's and Riley's grimaces as she draped her purse strap over her shoulder. "We'll pick up more on the way." She held out her hand to Riley. "Let's go."

Grabbing her keys, Riley allowed Anna to pull her to the door. Gratitude flowed through her, and a strong surge of emotion built in her chest. Blood ties didn't matter. LCR was her family. The only one she would ever need.

***

Aidan Thorne flew through the air, landed with a thud on the mat, and let loose a cursing groan. Raising his head slightly, he glared at the sweaty, grim-faced man a few feet away.

"Hell, Kelly, when you said you wanted to spar, you might've mentioned somebody might die."

Rasping breaths heaving from overtaxed lungs, Justin looked down at the man. Frustration and fury made a lethal combination. He'd challenged Thorne to a spar, but he'd forgotten to mention that it would be like the ones they had at Bruce's in Virginia. Whenever they sparred at an LCR gym, they held themselves back. Today he hadn't been able to keep the anger inside and had let loose a flurry of punches that had Thorne battling to stay on his feet. The last one had sent him flying halfway across the room.

Grimacing an apology, Justin held out his hand to help his friend up. "Sorry. That shouldn't have happened."

Thorne accepted his hand and stood. Working his jaw to ease the ache, he shook his head. "Don't get me wrong. After sitting on our collective asses the entire week, working off some steam feels damn good. Thing is, I've got a date tonight. Hate to mess up this pretty mug of mine."

Justin snorted. "We've been working round the clock. How'd you have time to meet someone?"

"Didn't just meet her. I've known her a couple of years. We go out whenever I'm in her area or she's in mine."

"So nothing serious?"

His eyes went wide. "Serious? Hell no. Not my style."

At one time, Justin would have said the same thing. He'd had a few relationships over the years. Had even gotten semiserious a couple times. But none of them had lasted. But now? With Riley? He couldn't imagine wanting anyone else ever again. And, oh hell, did he want her. But since that one night together, she hadn't indicated she wanted more. Once this shit was over, though, he was planning some major time off. That place in the mountains might not look like a fairy-tale romantic castle, but it would definitely fulfill his privacy requirement.

"So you still want to beat the hell out of someone? If so, I'll go get my face gear and we'll go at it."

Oddly enough, he was over that need. He shook his head. "Come on. I'll buy you a beer. Take the sting out of your jaw."

Grabbing a towel, Thorne swiped it down his face and chest. "Might take something stronger." He worked his jaw again. "Something must've pissed you off mightily today."

Pissed him off? Yeah, but not just today. It happened every time he thought about Dimitri. "Ever wanted to rip a man apart with your bare hands?"

A hollow darkness flashed on Thorne's face. "Every. Damn. Day."

***

Ensconced on the sofa, Riley gazed around the room. A dozen half-empty Chinese carryout boxes, beer and soda bottles, and numerous fortune-cookie wrappers cluttered the coffee table. After stuffing themselves with half the menu from the Chinese restaurant down the road, they'd opened all the cookies and proceeded to try to outdo each other with their hilarious fortunes. So far Anna was winning with *Look before your behind.*

Anna giggled. "That's not even anatomically possible."

"Fortune cookies aren't what they used to be."

Eden shook her head. "They never have been. You make your own fortune."

The room went silent as each woman considered that profound statement. Riley glanced at each face and considered what she knew about them. Eden had endured a horrible event and had remade herself into someone else. Flawlessly beautiful, she had been with LCR for years and was the most seasoned operative. She and her husband, Jordan Montgomery, ran the LCR office in Paris.

Even though much of Eden's past was shrouded in mystery and intrigue, she had found the peace and happiness she sought, not only with LCR, but also with her very own hero. Riley didn't know a lot about Eden's personal life, other than she and Jordan had two adopted children, she could speak eight languages fluently, and she could assume a deep-cover alias in a matter of seconds.

When she'd first met Eden, Riley remembered being incredibly intimidated. Eden had a sophistication that seemed an innate part of her personality. After working on a couple of missions with her, Riley developed a less narrow view of the beautiful operative. Not only did she have a warm personality, she often went out of her way to encourage other operatives.

Turning her head slightly, Riley looked over at McKenna, the operative formerly known as Ghost. Unfortunately, much of McKenna's past was known. Her story had been splashed all over every tabloid. Though it was horrific and tragic, what McKenna had overcome was awe-inspiring. She looked as delicate as a flower, but beneath the façade was a backbone of steel. Married to Lucas Kane, one of the wealthiest men in the world, McKenna stayed deep undercover the majority of the time. No one would ever suspect that the same woman who hobnobbed with celebrities at world movie premieres and was a frequent guest of the royal family spent several days a week rescuing kidnap victims and taking down evil people.

Switching her gaze, Riley watched Anna nibble on a fortune cookie, a pensive look on her pretty face. She knew more about Anna than the other two women combined. Riley and Anna might be as different as night and day, but from their first meeting, they'd been fast friends. And considering she'd never been allowed friends and knew nothing about being one, she was surprised at how very easy it was to be Anna's friend.

All three women had survived horrendous events and come out on the other side, whole and healthy. And both Eden and McKenna had found the loves of their lives. It didn't take a psychic to read the soul-deep contentment in their eyes.

"How did you two do it?"

She hadn't meant to blurt the question out, but since all three women were looking questioningly at her, she forced herself to continue. She really wanted to know the answer.

"Eden, you and McKenna, you both found happiness. Found love. How did that happen?"

It was awkwardly worded, and she wasn't sure either of them could understand what she was getting at. Eden surprised her, though, and said, "You mean, how did I heal emotionally enough to find happiness with a man?"

Even though the question was an invasion of privacy, Riley was too anxious to know the answer to worry about being embarrassed. "Yes."

"I wish I could tell you it was a twelve-step program and that once I completed it I was there, but that's not how it went. Or at least for me it wasn't. Healing took years. It wasn't until I met Jordan again that I realized how far I'd come but also how far I still needed to go."

Her voice softened, and a smile curved her lips. "Jordan loved me for me. Not who I pretended to be or wanted to be. He saw the real me and loved me. That made all the difference in being able to move forward."

McKenna nodded. "I agree. Even though my past was out in the open, Lucas saw beyond all of that to love me. He took the time to know me and fell in love with the authentic McKenna. Not what the press or others had cooked up.

"But I think more than that, I was finally, for the first time ever, able to trust someone with everything. All of my secrets. All my pain. He knew everything I'd been through, everything I'd done. I spilled my guts to him, and in return he gave me unconditional love and acceptance."

"Exactly," Eden said. "Once I reopened my superficially healed wounds, spilled the poison that was still inside me, that's when I started real healing."

"Oh, that's a good word for it," McKenna said. "Poison. I didn't even know I still had it inside me. But once I shared it with the one person I trusted above all others, the dark hole I was always afraid I'd fall into and never get out of started to disappear. And then one day it was gone. Replaced by joy and happiness.

"Lucas didn't heal me, but his love and acceptance gave me the strength to heal myself."

There was silence again. It wasn't awkward or even maudlin. Just an easy, thoughtful quiet.

McKenna cleared her throat. "Since we're speaking of happy, Lucas and I are going to have a baby."

There were squeals of excitement and hugs all around. Then Anna brought out the ice cream, and in between creamy spoonfuls, they threw out baby names and then giggled as McKenna recounted how she told Lucas he was going to be a father.

A strong wave of affection flowed through Riley. These women had known exactly what she needed to get her mind off tomorrow. They knew her fear and her pain, but they'd made her focus on the joy that could be found after recovery.

Riley knew she still possessed the poison that Eden and McKenna mentioned. Though she had come a long way, healed so much, the poison would stay inside her until she shared it with someone. She wanted that someone to be Justin. Could she do it? Reveal the most horrendous moments of her life? Would saying the words really make a difference? And would Justin see her differently afterward? He said he trusted her, believed in her. So maybe the real question she should be asking herself was, just how much did she trust Justin? Enough to tell him everything?

CHAPTER
TWENTY-THREE

Justin crept into the apartment. Even though it was only a little after ten, he'd learned that Riley liked to go to bed early and get up just after dawn. Tomorrow would be hard enough. He didn't want to keep her from a much-needed good night's sleep.

His stomach rumbled. He and Thorne had downed a couple of beers and some wings a few hours ago. Thorne had gone off to meet with his date, and Justin had taken a long walk through downtown. The steep hills had been a good challenge for him, helping him work off some of the tenseness he felt about tomorrow. What he'd really wanted to do was come back to the apartment and be with Riley. Problem was, if he had, he wouldn't have been able to keep his hands off her.

Blowing out a silent breath, he opened the fridge and smiled. Looked like someone had cleaned out an entire Chinese restaurant. Apparently, Riley and several others had enjoyed a good meal. He told himself he wasn't bothered that he hadn't been invited.

Wrapping his arm around a half-dozen boxes, he closed the fridge and pulled out a drawer for a fork. Then, sitting down, Justin popped open boxes and enjoyed a cold but still tasty feast.

"The moo shu pork was the best."

His mouth full of noodles, he looked up to see Riley standing at the door. His partner had always amazed him at how silently she could sneak around.

Dressed in a pair of silky-looking dark blue shorts and a cropped white tank top, her long hair slightly mussed, she looked soft, warm, and sexy. Infinitely kissable.

Justin looked away from her, focused on the array of boxes before him. "Looks like you had quite the party tonight."

She walked over to the sink and filled a glass with water. "McKenna, Eden, and Anna came over, and we ordered out." She frowned at all the boxes on the table. "Guess we ordered too much."

"Glad you did. I was starving."

"You didn't eat?"

"Thorne and I had a couple of beers and some wings a few hours ago."

She sat down at the table across from him and, as if it was as natural as sunrise, reached out and touched his hand. "I missed you."

Having her touch him or admit she missed him almost stopped his breath. Spontaneity wasn't something Riley was known for. A lot of that had to do with the scumbags who raised her. Impulsiveness had most likely been discouraged.

"I missed you, too." He gave her a slight grin. "I was a little jealous when I saw all the takeout boxes. I thought you had a party and didn't invite me. Now that I know it was a girl thing, it's probably good I wasn't here."

"I don't know. I think you could've learned a thing or two."

"Oh yeah?" he drawled. "Like what?"

"Girl secrets," she said softly.

The instant she uttered those words, a hot flush swept through Riley, part desire, part embarrassment. She wasn't good at this flirting thing. Other than a few ops where she'd had to pretend an interest in a possible suspect to gain his trust, she had never tried to be coy. Was she coming on too strong or not strong enough? Did he even realize she was flirting?

"What's going on, Riley?"

Trust Justin to ask the hard question. And Riley, who didn't know how to be anything but direct, told him. "We haven't made love since that first time."

"Yes."

"Why?"

"I didn't want to put extra pressure on you." He squeezed her hand gently. "You're always straightforward about things. I figured you'd tell me when and if you wanted me again."

She gave a half smile. "I think you have too much faith in me."

His answer was surprisingly intense. "No, I don't."

"So…um." Now that he had made a statement about her straightforward manner, she felt the need to prove it. However, bluntly telling him she wanted to make love with him was just a little more than she felt capable of doing.

Justin, bless him, let her off the hook with, "You want me?"

"Yes." Her voice was so soft he had to lean forward to hear her. "I want you."

"And I want you so badly I'm dying with it."

Riley stood up quickly, her movement so abrupt she almost knocked over her chair. A fire had ignited at Justin's words. Her entire body felt flushed and feverish.

He gave her a slow, sexy grin. "Why don't you go on to bed? I'll put this stuff up and lock up for the night."

She nodded and headed back to the bedroom. It would take him a few minutes. Even though they were armed to the teeth, Justin never took any chances. Every night he made sure the doors were all bolted, and he set little sensors all through the apartment that would go off if an intruder passed by it.

At first she'd been amused by his caution, but now she thought it was incredibly sweet. He wanted to keep her safe and took his job very seriously.

Since she knew he'd be a few minutes, Riley took the time to brush her teeth again and comb her hair. Although she didn't own any perfume, Anna had given her some scented lotion for Christmas. Riley dabbed a little of it on her neck and at her wrists.

She stood back and stared at her reflection. She saw a hint of fear in her eyes, but more than anything, there was anticipation. Being in Justin's arms again, even for a few short hours, sounded wonderful to her.

She took in her appearance, wishing she had something pretty to wear other than her sensible pj's. Wishing even more that she had the courage to strip out of them and walk into the bedroom completely nude. She was brave in some things, but this wasn't one of them. If she were on an op, she'd slip into a role and walk nude through a large metropolitan city without a flicker of embarrassment. This wasn't a role. This was real life. And this was Justin, her partner, her friend. And so much more.

Frustrated with herself, Riley jerked the door open and walked out. The instant she walked into the bedroom, an amazing calmness washed over her. Justin stood at the edge of the bed, waiting for her. His shirt was already off, and he was in the process of toeing off his shoes. He looked up at her and grinned, and she knew everything would be all right. Because this *was* Justin. Her partner, her friend. The man she had been secretly dreaming about forever was standing at the bed, waiting for her. Wanting her.

Her heart pounding in anticipation…in need, she went to him.

He took her hand, pulled her against him, and just held her. Riley closed her eyes at the glorious feeling of his hard, naked chest warming her. She drew in a breath, delighting in his male scent, savoring this incredible moment.

His voice rumbled beneath her ear. "Are you as nervous as I am?"

She raised her head to look at him. Having guarded her emotions for so long, admitting vulnerability was difficult for her. But with Justin it felt so easy, so right. "A little. Even though we've done this once before, for some reason this feels different. Does it seem that way to you?"

"Yeah. Seems like I've been waiting forever for you."

Her heart glowed. Not just the words warmed her, but the emotion in his voice, the desire in his eyes.

"But it also feels like it's the most natural thing in the world."

"We've entrusted our lives to each other. This feels as natural as anything that's ever happened before."

Any remaining nerves dissolved. She pressed a kiss against his chest and hugged him hard. "Yes." She breathed the word against his skin.

"Can I undress you?"

She took a step back and gave him a look that told him everything he needed to know. She was his.

Instead of pulling the top quickly over her head, his big hands slid down her hips and then moved back up slowly, lifting material as he went. Warm and callused, gentle yet insistent, his hands awakened and sensitized her skin. Riley closed her eyes, moaned at the sensation.

Finally, the T-shirt came over her head. Then his hands moved in the other direction. Hooking his fingers in the waistband of her shorts, he tugged hard. She laughed softly, noting he was becoming much less patient now.

Once she was completely nude and standing before him, she watched as Justin's eyes roamed down her body. Riley told herself he wasn't judging her, but still she felt her spine stiffen as she waited for his next words.

"How could anyone so delicate-looking be so incredibly strong and brave?"

Tears sprang to her eyes, and her throat clogged with emotion. She took a step forward and lost herself in his embrace.

Justin groaned at the incredible woman in his arms. She felt small, delicate, so damn breakable. But that was window dressing. Beneath the façade of vulnerability was a resilient, determined, and courageous woman with a depth that he was just beginning to understand.

There was so much he wanted to say to her, so many things he wanted to ask her. But that would have to wait for later. For right now, he wanted to shower her entire body with kisses and show her with his hands, mouth, his entire body, how very special she was to him.

He led her to the bed. She sat down, and he took the time to unzip his jeans and drop them to the floor. He heard a gasp and grimaced. Hard as hell to hide that he was hard as hell.

Her hands reached out and touched him, holding him in her palms. The concern that he had frightened her dissolved, and a wave of intense heat flooded him. His body told him to push her onto her back, cover her, and mate with her. Show her she was his…only his. His mind and his heart said no way in hell. This was Riley's moment. If she wanted him to stand here all night while she explored his body, well, then, that's what he'd damn well do. Of course, he'd probably die from need, but that was okay. Dying with the memory of her soft hands all over his body wouldn't be a bad way to go.

"You're hard and soft at the same time."

Any kind of coherent word was impossible. He thought he managed a grunt but wasn't too sure. He looked down at her holding him and almost lost complete control. She looked both fascinated and turned on.

"Riley," he finally gritted out. "I need to—"

"Shh," she whispered. Leaning forward, she kissed him, and then her tongue came out to taste him. He pulled in a breath and held it, sure that he was going to explode.

She looked up at him then, her eyes dancing with humor and not a little bit of wickedness. "You have amazing control."

"And you have a mean streak."

Laughing softly, she released him and scooted back on the bed. "Yes, I do. Want to find it?"

His lungs exploded with air, and he followed her down on the bed. Having Riley tease and laugh was a delight. She wasn't nervous or afraid of him. This was joyous loving, and he wanted to show her how damn good he could make her feel. His hands began their own exploration.

Riley closed her eyes at the glorious feel of Justin's hands. She was burning from the inside out, incinerating. He was everywhere at once, leaving a blazing trail of need as his hands moved over her. His mouth followed his hands, kissing, sipping, licking. Riley was squirming on the bed, stretching sensuously. Never had she felt more desirable, more feminine. More needed. Justin's groans and words of adoration and praise made her feel cherished and wanted.

He kissed her everywhere, from her mouth, to her chin, to the hollow of her throat. And with every kiss, her body responded with answering zings of heat and need. When he stopped to pay homage to each breast, his tongue encircling a nipple, she gasped at the sensations. But when his mouth covered her nipple and suckled, her entire body arched off the bed.

"Justin...please."

"I'm just getting started," he growled. And proved his words with actions as his hands and mouth continued their fiery exploration. He kissed her stomach, swirled his tongue in her belly button, and then moved down and stopped. She looked down at him. His eyes were glittering like hot coals, the heat in them amazing her. And then she saw the question, saw what he wanted. Without a hint of embarrassment, Riley opened her legs. The heated approval in his eyes brought tears to her own.

And then all coherent thought dissolved into a tornadic, mind-altering experience beyond her imagination. He licked, kissed, suckled her into a need she had never imagined. An unfathomable vortex of heat and want whirled inside her, taking her to a place she'd never known existed. She was flung into the stars.

Justin could wait no longer. He had to be inside her now, this second. Coming over her damp, heaving body, he propped himself above her and looked into her face. Even though she'd been incredibly responsive, he wanted to make sure this was still what she wanted. If he had to stop, he figured he'd die, but damned if he would scare her. What he saw in her face reassured him, and turned his heart over, too. Never had he seen such satisfaction or acceptance.

His entire body rigid with need, he slid slowly, carefully into her heat and groaned at the fire consuming him. He told himself to go slow, easy…to be careful. This was just their second time together. He wanted her lost in passion, overwhelmed with need. Frightening her in anyway was something he could not bear.

Riley demolished his concern. The instant he buried himself inside her, she wrapped her legs around his waist, settled her hands on his ass, and pulled him in even deeper. Even if a freight train had crashed into the bedroom, he couldn't have stopped. Plunging, retreating, and plunging again, he gave her everything he had. In return, she gave him her all.

And with a shout, perhaps of victory, but mostly surrender, Justin exploded into bliss.

Chapter Twenty-Four

Hours later, Riley woke. The feel of strong arms holding her didn't scare her. The sound of shallow breathing was a comfort, the soft snore in her ear a surprising delight. The man in her bed was Justin Kelly. Never had she felt so safe, so treasured. So whole.

"Everything okay?"

His gruff, sleep-filled voice caused all sorts of delicious shivers throughout her system.

"Everything's wonderful. Didn't mean to wake you."

His arms tightened around her. "Having trouble sleeping?"

"Not really."

She bit her lip as she remembered what Eden and McKenna had told her hours earlier. Could she get the poison out of her once and for all? Could Justin handle it? Was he ready to learn things she'd never told another living soul? Things that kept her awake, cringing with mortification and soul-wrenching pain? Could she handle him knowing?

She took a breath, let it out slowly, and said, "He made me bark like a dog." The whispered confession took every bit of her strength.

She knew he was awake, that he had heard her. His body was rigid, and he seemed to have stopped breathing. His single strangled, "Fuck," conveyed both rage and pain.

She closed her eyes for a brief second. Lance it like a sore. That's what they told her. Be quick but get all the poison out.

"That was for his amusement. Bark, meow, other animal sounds. He made me crawl. A lot at first, but when I started developing blisters and scabs on my knees, he told me to stop. Said they marred my beauty.

"I don't know how many times he raped me. I was a virgin, of course. Had never even been kissed. My *parents*, or whatever the hell they were, forbade me from having any kind of friends, much less boyfriends.

"I knew about sex, of course. Human anatomy was part of my learning curriculum. That included reproduction. But I never knew more than that. Until him."

"That was probably part of the plan."

"How so?"

"The bastard wanted you as innocent as possible."

"Well, he got his money's worth."

She forced herself to continue. "He's, I guess, what you'd call a classic sadist. Hurting me turned him on. Whippings with belts and canes were his favorites. He said he didn't want to mar me, though—spoil my beauty. So he never went beyond bruising me.

"When he punished me, he never used his hands to beat or whip me. I think he knew he would go too far. His punishments were physical discomfort and humiliation. He'd lock me up for days in my room. Keep the electricity off so the only light came from sunlight. Sometimes, he'd starve me with a bread-and-water diet. Occasionally, a protein milkshake, if he thought I was getting too skinny."

She swallowed hard. "The box was the worst."

"Box?"

"It was his most severe punishment. Infractions like not saying 'yes, sir' or not answering quickly enough. It was four-by-four-by-four."

"So you weren't able to stand."

"No. At first, there was only a small air hole. I passed out once. Maybe even stopped breathing. He had three more holes drilled."

"How considerate."

The bitter sarcasm made her smile. Which seemed totally incongruent with what she was telling him. She realized Eden and McKenna were so right. Getting the poison out was freeing.

"The scars?"

"I said he never punished me in anger. But he did once." She laughed, though it was a thick, awkward sound, almost unrecognizable as humor. "I was so very stupid. So incredibly naïve. I had convinced myself that my parents didn't realize they'd given me to a monster. I lied to myself that they cared about me, that if they knew how horribly I was being treated, they would do something. Come for me. Rescue me." She shook her head. "Sometimes it amazes me how very stupid and ignorant I was."

"What happened?"

"I swiped a cellphone from one of the guard's pockets. Ran to a closet, shut myself in, and called my mother. She sounded genuinely shocked when I told her what Dimitri had been doing to me. It was only later that I realized the shock came from me calling her, not because of his treatment."

"What did she say?"

"That she was horrified. That she'd believed that because Dimitri was so wealthy, I would have everything they couldn't afford to give me." She sat up in bed and covered her face with her hands. "Can you believe I fell for that? How stupid can one girl be?"

"Not stupid. Innocent."

"Yeah, well, not after that I wasn't."

"What happened?"

"She told me to go to my room, that she would tell my father, and they would come for me. I didn't question how she would get me away, how she knew where I was. I knew I was living on borrowed time. People would soon notice I was missing.

"I was smart enough to mute the ringer of the cellphone and hide it beneath a potted plant in the foyer. I thought if something didn't work out, I'd go back for it.

"I went to my room and waited. Dimitri arrived within the hour."

"She called him."

"Of course she did. And he was livid. I'd never seen him so angry. He told me my punishment would be beyond anything I'd ever experienced. He was right.

"He carried me to the punishment room, tied me to the whipping post. I'd been there before. Even though I dreaded what came next, I thought I knew what to expect. Turns out, I didn't.

"He left me alone. The lights went off. It was silent, quiet for a long time. Then the sounds started. The first ones were rats. At least I think they were. It sounded like there were hundreds of them. That lasted for I don't know how long. Then there was total silence. A little while later, it was snakes. I could hear them slithering around, hissing and spitting. That lasted awhile, and then the rats returned. I finally realized they were just sound effects. But there was always that horror that at some point I'd feel that first bite.

"I don't know how long I hung there. A long time. By the time he returned, I'd urinated, defecated, and thrown up. The stench was hideous. My eyes were swollen shut from crying.

"The lights came on suddenly. Blinding me. When I was finally able to focus, he stood before me with a whip. He'd never beat me with one before. I was barely conscious, but I remember feeling vaguely relieved, thinking the total darkness and sounds were the worst part. I knew the pain would be horrific, but he had never drawn blood before. That changed that night.

"I don't know how many lashes he gave me. I passed out long before he finished. When I woke up, I was in bed, and my entire body was on fire. I was covered in bandages."

She swallowed hard, suddenly realizing her throat was parched.

As usual, as if he could read her mind, Justin said, "Hold on." He jumped out of bed and seconds later returned with a chilled bottle of water.

"Thanks." She took a long swallow.

"What happened after that?"

"I didn't see him for weeks. I figured he decided he no longer wanted me. I was scarred, no longer his beautiful doll."

"But he did come back, didn't he?"

"Unfortunately, yes. He told me the scars were a good reminder that there were worse things than our everyday encounters. He said if I ever tried to contact anyone again, I might not survive the punishment. I knew he was telling the truth.

"After that, we went on as if it had never happened. I submitted to whatever he wanted. I learned to go someplace else in my mind. I convinced myself there was no hope. No way out. That this was my life."

"But you did escape."

"Yes. On my twenty-first birthday, I gave myself a present and finally left."

"Why then?"

"He held a special dinner party. I had attended a few in the past." Her voice quivered, but she found her control and continued, her voice harder. "For entertainment purposes.

"But I wasn't asked to do anything other than sit and look properly submissive. When dessert arrived, bottles of champagne were opened. Dimitri raised a glass and announced that I was to be his bride. I had apparently passed some sort of test for him, and he'd decided he was going to keep me. He also announced that he would make sure that by the time my next birthday rolled around, I would be...heavy with his child."

"Oh hell no."

"I could not let that happen. I might not have had the courage to escape just for me, but I was not going to expose a baby, an innocent child, to that fiend. So I took a chance. Hid in a dinner cart that the servants pushed into the kitchen. And that was that."

She shrugged. "I don't know how I did it, really. Never thought I'd find the courage to escape. I was weak, scared. I'm not sure how long I walked, and of course, I had no idea where I was going. I only knew that if I didn't leave, I would have to kill myself. No way in hell was I going to be his wife or have his child. I thought maybe at some point I'd just find a place, curl up, and die. That sounded so incredibly peaceful. A release."

"You stowed away on a ship. How'd you get on it?"

"It was a cruise ship. I'd spotted a ferry and thought that would've been my best bet. But it started backing away from the pier. I thought I was doomed. Then I saw the cruise ship and headed that way. It was enormous and I thought surely one little person could hide in it and not get caught.

"This large family…there must've been a dozen of them, half of them teenagers, were boarding the ship. There was a man standing at the entrance, waiting for passports. The man, the father I guess, was so harried and frazzled, he just shoved a dozen passports at the guy, and then, all at once, everyone swarmed onto the walkway. No one noticed that I was in the middle of them."

"Did anyone ever see you on the ship?"

"I'm sure they did. I didn't have a room, so I'd sleep in the lounge chairs during the day. At night, I'd roam around. Sneak food out of the kitchen when I could. Occasionally, I'd act like I was a regular guest, but since acting normal wasn't easy for me, I tried to stay out of everyone's way. I borrowed some clothes from dryers in the laundry room. I returned them every couple of days. Borrowed more.

"I thought about jumping overboard a couple of times. That just seemed to be the easiest route to peace. Couldn't do it, though. Too chicken, I guess." She blew out a ragged breath. "Guess I wanted to live after all."

Dropping back down onto the pillows, Riley realized she was so tired she could barely hold her eyes open. Justin's arms came around her, and she snuggled against his shoulder. "They were right," she mumbled against his chest.

"Who was right, baby?"

"Eden and McKenna. They said getting the poison out would help. It did."

Hard arms tightened around her. "I'm glad. Sleep now. Okay?"

"'Kay."

Justin waited until she fell asleep before he let loose an explosive, vile—albeit very quiet—curse. If Dimitri had been standing in front of him, he would have torn him limb from limb with his bare hands without a shred of remorse or guilt.

Tears slid down his face, and he did nothing to stop the flow. What she had endured. What she had survived. God in heaven, he'd never known anyone braver. And she actually believed she was a coward, a weakling. She was the strongest person he'd ever known, bar none.

In a few hours, she would be facing the people who had betrayed her in the worst possible way. He knew she wanted answers almost as much as she wanted retribution. He would get all of it for her, one way or another.

And then he would find the monster named Dimitri and give him a taste of his own medicine.

CHAPTER
TWENTY-FIVE

The next time Riley woke, it was daylight and she was alone. She lay quiet for a few moments, absorbing what had happened last night. She'd found a deeper connection with Justin than she could have ever imagined having with anyone. The shared intimacy had been profound and more real than anything she'd ever experienced. So profound that she had opened herself up afterward and shared with him what she'd believed she'd never be able to tell anyone. And then she'd fallen into the most dreamless but peaceful sleep of her life.

Would things change now that he knew everything? How would it affect their relationship, their partnership? She prayed it wouldn't change things but couldn't help but worry.

Knowing there was nothing to do but get up and face whatever she had to, Riley bounded out of bed. She rushed through a shower, quickly braided her hair, slapped on a minimum of makeup, and slid into a pair of jeans and T-shirt.

She walked into the kitchen and found Justin there, dressed and in the midst of making breakfast. He turned from the stove, spatula in hand, and grinned. "Hope you're hungry. I'm making enough to feed an army."

Relief flooded through her. He was acting normal, natural. She saw affection and warmth in his expression. Not a hint of judgment.

"I'm starving."

Surprising her, he swiftly picked her up, set her on the counter, and dropped a kiss on her head. "Watch and learn from a culinary genius."

"We've been partners for years and I'm just now learning you can cook?"

Instead of answering, he sent her a wink. And then she watched, stunned, as he showed her he wasn't all talk. His hands diced and chopped so fast she could barely see the knife. In less than a minute, he had a mound of tomatoes, mushrooms, onions, and peppers.

She watched in awe as he briskly whisked eggs and then made what had to be the biggest omelet she'd ever seen. A few minutes later, she was sitting down to the most delectable-smelling meal she'd had in ages. She took one bite of the omelet and exclaimed, "My gosh, you are a genius!"

He grinned. "Just wait till you taste my pasta calabrese."

They ate in companionable silence for the next few minutes. With each bite, Riley could feel her energy build.

She sat back in her chair and shook her head at her empty plate. "I can't believe I ate all of that. I feel like I could take on the world."

"Like my mama always said, breakfast is the most important meal of the day." He pushed their plates aside and then took both her hands. Kissing each one, he held them gently. "Hard to believe these small, slender hands belong to the strongest person I've ever known."

Embarrassed by his praise, she tried to pull away, but he wouldn't let her go. Shrugging, she said lightly, "I don't think I'm strong so much as stubborn. It took me years of therapy and training before I could get to being halfway normal."

He placed her hands on the table and then covered them with his. "What you endured...what you conquered. Believe me, that's strength."

"You know I told you that LCR rescued my sister years ago?" There was pain in his voice, a dark hollowness in his eyes.

"Yes. From a human trafficker."

"I didn't tell you the rest of the story, though. We got my sister back home, but she had a tough time coping with what happened to her. Looking back on it now, I don't think we handled things very well."

"What do you mean?"

"We babied her, coddled her. Treated her with kid gloves. She went to counseling sessions but quit after a few weeks, said they weren't doing any good. My mom and dad are what we in Ohio call salt-of-the-earth people. Good and decent. They just didn't know how to handle her. Lara was the baby of the family, and instead of expecting her to be strong, they made excuses for her bad behavior. The responsibility fell on everyone else's shoulders, never hers."

His voice thickened. "She turned to drugs and alcohol. We had interventions, family counseling. Nothing helped. When she was nineteen, she jumped from a bridge about five miles from my parents' farm."

"Oh, Justin, I'm so sorry."

"The family never really recovered. Each one of us asked what we could have done differently. And though I know we enabled her, letting her remain a victim, I look back on it now and realize one very important issue. Lara never wanted to be saved…rescued. She never tried to save herself.

"That's the difference between you and her, Riley. You helped rescue yourself. You became your own hero. Do you know how phenomenal you are?"

"I had a lot of help."

"All the help in the world is worth nothing unless you're willing to help yourself."

The lump in her throat was now the size of a bowling ball. She felt the sting of tears and almost panicked. Crying, today of all days, was strictly prohibited.

She was saved from breaking her no-tears policy by the buzz of her cellphone. She'd laid the phone on the table beside her. "It's Noah."

Kissing each hand once more, he let her go so she could answer. She answered and put the call on speaker so Justin could hear. Noah, as usual, was to the point. "Meet us in the hallway in half an hour."

"Will do," Riley answered.

She ended the call and then looked up at Justin. "Guess we'd better get ready."

"I'll clean up in here."

"It'll be faster if we do it together."

Five minutes later, the dishwasher was running and everything was set to rights again. They went into the bedroom and continued to get ready to leave. Just as they were about to exit, Justin stopped at the door and took her in his arms again. "When this is over, let's take a trip. Just you and me. Together. No phones. No bad guys. Just us."

"Where to?"

He grinned. "That safe house in the mountains is paid up through next month."

"Sounds perfect."

He pressed a gentle kiss to her forehead, her nose, and then a soft, thorough one on her mouth. "Thank you, Riley."

"For what?"

He dropped a hard, quick kiss on her mouth. "Just thank you."

Taking him at his word, she smiled and then opened the door.

The instant they were in the hallway, all gentleness disappeared and Justin became her implacable, grim-faced LCR partner. His eyes coldly determined, he growled, "Let's go rescue some kids and kick some asses, Ingram."

Riley realized something profound. Justin had done that deliberately, to make a statement. When they were alone, sharing their lives, themselves, they were Riley and Justin. Friends, lovers, confidants. Their intimacy was hot, affectionate, fun.

In their LCR world of danger and high-risk stakes, they were Ingram and Kelly, full-fledged partners, their trust in each other complete, total.

This realization, more than any other, gave Riley hope for the future. Their future.

CHAPTER
TWENTY-SIX

Los Angeles, California

The instant he saw the caller ID, William's heart gave a hopeful lurch. He grabbed the phone, his anticipation so great it took almost no effort to act like the excited, hopeful parent of a missing child. "Mr. McCall? You have news?"

"Yes, Mr. Larson. Very good news. Jessica has agreed to meet with you. We'll be landing in Los Angeles in just a few minutes."

"What? She's with you? But I—I wasn't expecting this. I assumed you would tell me where she is and let me meet with her there. I'm…uh—"

"I thought you would be pleased, Larson."

The concerned surprise in McCall's voice jerked him upright. *Play it cool, idiot! Remember you're anxious to see your little girl.* "Yes. Yes. Of course I'm pleased, Mr. McCall. I was just caught off-guard. But I'm overwhelmed with joy and delight. I never expected it would be so soon or turn out this way."

"I told you from the beginning, Mr. Larson. We set up the meet. We need total control in case things go wrong. Jessica is wary of seeing you. Like you feared she would, she's made some outrageous claims. She claims you gave her to a man who beat and raped her."

William kept the anger out of his voice. That little bitch would not spoil things now. "I'm not surprised. That was one of her most frequent delusions."

"It's apparent that Jessica is a deeply disturbed young woman. Very unstable. However, she has asked to see you. If things go well, and she agrees, I'll release her to you. I trust that you'll get her the help she needs."

"Oh, most certainly I will, Mr. McCall. You can definitely trust me on that. The instant she's with Loretta and me again, back where she belongs, she'll get exactly what she needs."

"Excellent. I'll meet you at 1201 Sheffield Avenue. There's a small office complex there. Suite 1001. One hour."

"One hour? Oh, but I—"

"Larson, are you sure this is what you want?"

"Of course it is. I'll be there, Mr. McCall. Thank you so much for all your hard work."

The instant the call ended, William let loose a long string of curses and then made another call.

"Jessica is on her way to Los Angeles."

"What? I thought you were going to grab her."

"That was my plan until a few moments ago. The jerk that found her is on his way here, bringing her to me. What was I supposed to do? Tell him I'm not ready to see the daughter I've been searching for the last eight years? I had no choice."

"Very well. You take possession. This actually works better for me. I'm in the States and can be there in a matter of hours."

William decided his day was looking up. This would all be a bad memory soon. "I'll text you the address. While we're waiting for you, I'll make sure Jessica understands that disobedience will never be allowed again."

"Do whatever you like, but if I see one bruise on her when I get there, you will pay."

"Understood," William said stiffly.

Ending the call, William surged to his feet. Dammit, this wasn't the way it should have played out. McCall was supposed to tell him where she was. He would've had her taken, then Dimitri would have taken over, and William would have been out of it. Now he was going to have to continue to play the joyful, grateful father.

Growling his frustration, he went inside the house. Loretta was out for the day, which was a blessing. Having her tag along was the last thing he wanted. She was much less skilled at acting the caring parent than he was. The woman didn't have a caring bone in her body.

He'd get the girl and take her to the new house he was getting ready to set up for some new merchandise. It would be the perfect place to store her until Dimitri arrived.

And even though he'd been warned not to leave any bruises, he'd make damn sure the bitch knew what he thought of her. After all the frustration and expense he'd gone through to get her back, she owed him that.

***

Riley's transformation from kick-ass Elite operative to sad, defeated Jessica King was something Justin would not have believed if he hadn't seen it with his own eyes. It also hurt his heart in ways he could barely comprehend.

Is this what Jessica had looked like when McCall found her? Limp, lank hair, pale face, slumped shoulders, unable to meet anyone's eyes. Nervous hands that couldn't keep still. Her thin body jumping at every loud noise.

His gut told him she had probably looked much worse.

He remembered what she'd looked like when Eden and McKenna had taken her into the back room of the plane a couple of hours before they landed. She had walked back there with her head held high, posture straight, and a glint in her eye that said she was ready to take on the vermin and win. Now, she looked as though she'd been beaten to the ground and would never rise again.

Her thick hair was still long but they'd done something to make it look greasy and lifeless. Her skin had a dull, sallow cast. She wore jeans and a button down cotton shirt but he could swear she looked as though she'd lost twenty pounds. Her clothes hung from her body as if they were two sizes too large.

Riley's eyes were always gleaming with life, sometimes with anger, occasionally with humor. But absolutely, totally alive. Jessica's eyes were dull, lifeless...defeated.

Even though Justin tried to remind himself that this was an act, that Riley was one of the best at assuming an assigned role, he had to clench his hands to prevent himself from going to her. He wanted to make her look at him so he could be reassured that behind the façade of defeat and anguish was the strength and determination he knew she possessed in spades.

"We're set," McCall said. "Larson sounded both surprised and panicked at first. And then predictably arrogant."

The room was filled to capacity with operatives. Each one had their individual assignment. By the time Larson arrived, the room would be empty save for McCall and Riley. They all knew each other's jobs and roles. Before McCall had even tried to assign him a role, Justin had done it himself. Fortunately, McCall was in total agreement. Justin's job was to protect Riley at all cost.

McCall zeroed his gaze in on Riley. "He may have to hold you for a while, maybe a couple of days, until Dimitri arrives. Since he never physically harmed you before he turned you over to Dimitri the first time, I'm hopeful he won't harm you now. Regardless, I want no heroics from you, Ingram. Do not put up with abuse in the hope of gathering more information. We'll get it later, once we have him in custody. If things get rough, we're getting you out."

She gave a solemn nod, but Justin saw the customary stubborn set to her mouth. He knew his partner. She'd put up with a lot to get what she needed. And Justin would be close by in case that happened. Sacrificing Riley was not part of the plan.

"Any questions?" McCall said.

When no one spoke, he continued, "Even with light traffic, it should take Larson another half hour or so to get here. Still, let's get in place and be ready." He glanced over at Riley. "Ingram, I'd like to talk to you for a minute."

All the other operatives filed out. Justin was the last one to leave. He gave Riley a nod of encouragement before walking out the door.

Riley smiled slightly at Justin's nod. That was a deviation from their normal thumbs-up acknowledgment, and she found she liked the change.

"Doing okay?" Noah said.

"Yes. I feel like I've been preparing for this for a long time. Glad it's finally happening."

"We've come a long way."

She caught a glimpse of what looked like worry in his dark eyes. "I'll be fine, Noah. I can do this."

"If I didn't think you could handle it, you wouldn't be here. That's not an issue. But I meant what I said earlier. Do not take any abuse from these bastards. We'll bring them in and do what we have to do to get the information we need. You don't have to—"

"I know that, Noah. I promise I won't take anything I don't think I can handle. I've suffered enough abuse at their hands. I won't take more. Trust me."

"I do." He suddenly smiled, and Riley couldn't help but smile back. If not for Noah, she would be dead. She had no doubt about that. She owed this man so much. "I won't let you down."

"You never have. You've exceeded every expectation every single time."

"I don't plan to change."

Noah laughed, as she'd intended.

A buzzer on Noah's phone gave the alert. Larson was within five miles of their location.

Riley met Noah's eyes, and they both grinned. This was it. Justice was at last here.

CHAPTER
TWENTY-SEVEN

"When we get there, I'll go in alone. Try to stay out of sight. I don't want McCall to know I brought you with me."

Frederick Finch, or the man William had secretly nicknamed Dumbass, nodded, his thick neck creasing like an accordion. The guy was a behemoth, and William had learned that just because his head was the size of a gorilla's didn't mean it held a large brain. The stupid baseball cap only made him look more stupid. But what the man lacked in intelligence, he more than made up for in obedience and brute strength. William had more than enough smarts for both of them. Finch's only job was to protect William if something went wrong.

With the short notice that McCall had given him, he hadn't been able to bring in more men. His intention had been to find out Jessica's location and have some of his guys grab her. William had had no idea he'd have to do the dirty work. Even though it didn't sit well with him, he had no concerns that this would work. He'd play the grateful, loving father, overjoyed to see his long-lost daughter returned him, for the few minutes it would take to convince McCall that things were copacetic. Then, when he got her into the van, he'd lay down the law.

254 | CHRISTY REECE

"I'll make nice for a little while," William explained. "Hopefully, I can get close enough to the bitch to put this on her." He held up a tiny, skin-colored patch. "Best invention ever for subduing a woman. Ever try one?"

Frederick shook his head. "Don't need drugs to handle a woman. Got my own method of making them do what I want." He smiled, revealing a giant space between his front teeth. William wasn't sure if the man's tooth had been knocked out or if that was just how his teeth were. Hard to believe anyone had gotten close enough to the giant to sock him in the mouth.

"I don't use drugs all the time, but they come in handy. They're especially good for mellowing out kids."

"I hate kids," Frederick muttered.

William thought that was probably best, since Frederick's ugly mug would scare most of them out of a year's growth. He'd definitely never take the brute on a hunting trip. Idiot would scare off any perspective candidates.

William pulled into the large parking lot. He spotted an empty space at the very end and made a beeline for it. Should be out of the way enough. McCall might wonder why he'd driven a van, but it wasn't that unusual a vehicle. Asking him why he'd brought along a giant would definitely raise some suspicions.

He parked and then turned to Frederick. "Get in the back until I come back."

The man's ugly scowl would've halted a normal person's heart. William was made of sterner stuff.

"Don't give me that look. I can't risk you being seen."

One giant shoulder shrug and an inhuman-like grunt was Frederick's only reply. William took that as agreement.

"I shouldn't be more than an hour, hopefully less. When I come back with the girl, you can drive. I'll be busy in the back with her."

Beady eyes perked up. "Can I have a go at her when you're done?"

"I'm not going to do her, idiot. We're just going to talk. Set a few things straight."

Finch's glare could've melted iron, but he thankfully seemed to accept William's explanation. The last thing William wanted to do was have to kill the idiot for trying to play with the merchandise. Getting rid of that big of a body would be a nightmare.

Pulling down the sun visor, he checked his reflection in the attached mirror. There were worry lines in his forehead. He'd rubbed his eyes hard for several minutes. Now they were slightly swollen and red. Caused by the grateful tears a loving father would shed, of course. He played with several expressions, settling on a hopeful but somewhat frightened demeanor. After all, he didn't know if his dear, precious Jessica would even remember her loving father.

He smiled at the perfection of his expression. Damn, he could've made millions as an actor.

William gave Dumbass one last warning. "You see anything or anyone suspicious, call me on my cell. I have it on vibrate, but it'll give me a heads-up that something's wrong."

William watched Frederick crawl into the back. He then got out of the van and headed across the parking lot. The strip mall held a variety of businesses including a furniture store, mattress outlet, and barbershop. The suite he was to meet McCall and the girl was apparently vacant. A good thing for him if this didn't go down as he planned.

Smoothing down his hair, William plastered his practiced expression on his face as he drew closer to the building. His beloved, precious Jessie was waiting inside, and he couldn't wait to see her again!

***

The notification that Larson had arrived came from Jake, who was on the third floor of the building, keeping lookout. "Subject has arrived in a white van. He has a male passenger." He snorted and added, "Subject appears to be practicing several expressions in the visor mirror. Apparently, he's picked one. He's getting out of the van, headed your way. Passenger is getting into the back. One hell of a brute, too. Looks like he can pack a punch."

They had expected this. Riley knew she wouldn't get out of the op without a few bumps and bruises. That was an acceptable risk. As long as the end result was the apprehension of Larson and all his hired perverts, as well as Dimitri, she'd take whatever hits came her way. She'd lived through much worse.

"I've got your back, partner." The earbud in Riley's ear was of the best quality. Justin's voice was as clear as if he were standing beside her. His words made her glow. He knew what she'd been through and had full faith that she could handle this. His confidence gave her a boost. She could do this!

Riley heard footsteps coming closer. She drew in a breath, let it out slowly, and then once again became Jessica King.

Noah watched Larson come through the doors, his expression of hope firmly fixed on his face. The instant he spotted Riley sitting in a chair across the room, Noah saw a flash of the real man—the predator behind the façade.

"Jessica...darling! It is you!"

He took a running leap toward her, and Noah caught his arm, jerking him to a stop.

"What the hell? Mr. McCall, it's my Jessie."

"I'm glad to hear that, but our agreement still stands. This reunion is not only for your benefit but also for Jessica's."

"I—" Larson's effort to hide his anger wouldn't have convinced a three-year-old. Noah had a fleeting thought that the man had obviously never used the money he'd made in human trafficking for acting lessons.

Larson backed away and sighed. "You're right, Mr. McCall. The excitement of seeing my daughter again is almost overwhelming."

"I understand. We'll just start out with some small talk and go from there."

Noah pulled up a chair, placed it in front of Riley, and gestured at Larson. "Have a seat."

***

The fire-engine red Lamborghini parked two spaces away from the white van. The driver, a tall, beautiful woman with long, auburn hair and creamy magnolia skin, opened the car door. Since her target couldn't yet see her, she scrunched her toes in the tight shoes and grimaced in pain. Dammit, if you pay five hundred dollars for a pair of shoes, shouldn't they be at least a little comfortable?

Swinging her mile-long legs out of the car, she stood and lightly stretched, the sexy, black lace minidress going tight in all the right places. If she already had an audience, she wanted him to get the full effect. Deeming she'd preened long enough, she lowered her head and addressed the woman on the passenger side. "I don't care what you say, Tawny. This is the address Harold told me to come to."

A tall, beautiful brunette with long, black hair and dark, exotic eyes got out of the car, her deep-red halter dress with its plunging neckline a perfect complement to her light olive skin tone. "This can't be right, Sissy." She spoke in a soft, sultry voice. "There's not a house anywhere. These are all businesses."

When nothing happened, the two women locked eyes. They knew they were going to have to be a little more creative.

"Maybe we shouldn't go to the party," Sissy said. "Standing around looking beautiful doesn't sound like a lot of fun to me."

"As long as we don't have to take our clothes off like we did last time, I'm okay with just standing around," Tawny said. "Parading around in a G-string and nothing else gets chilly."

That did the trick. A head and then giant shoulders appeared at the window of the van. "You ladies sound like you could use some help."

Both women looked around and smiled brilliantly at him. Frederick Finch didn't think he'd ever been so dazzled in his entire life. Two women, both about six feet tall, built like Amazons, with faces like angels, were looking at him as if he'd hung the moon. Today was definitely his lucky day.

***

Aidan Thorne shook his head. Men were so damned predictable sometimes. He waited until Sabrina and Angela had the big brute facing away from the van. He half listened to their chatter about Hollywood parties, naked swimming, and all-day orgies as he slid under the back of the van and placed the GPS device. He flipped the switch and nodded his satisfaction as the light beamed red. The van shouldn't get away from them, but just in case, they'd be able to locate it up to one hundred and twenty miles away.

A minute later, he slipped from underneath the van and then peered around the corner just in time to see Sabrina placing her hand on the guy's back. The man probably thought he was about to get lucky. What he didn't know was Sabrina had just placed a small bug beneath his collar. Now, wherever the big guy went wearing that shirt, they'd be able to hear everything he or anyone close to him said.

Pleased with the smoothness of their operation so far, Aidan disappeared through a door at the side of the building. If everything else would go as smoothly as that had, this would be a piece of cake.

***

William settled into a chair across from Jessica. So what if he had to play the doting father for a few more minutes? He'd spent a lot of time practicing, might well have some fun with it.

"Jessie, darling, do you remember me? I'm your father."

The girl raised her head and looked blankly at him for a few minutes. He immediately nixed the idea of drugging her. She already looked half stoned. No wonder McCall bought his story of mental illness. This was going to be easier than he thought. The bitch looked crazed.

When he'd sold her, she was young, fresh, and very pretty. Even though this was definitely the same girl, she was a pale imitation of what she'd once been. He'd fix that, though. Her clothes would have to do. He didn't have time to go shopping. But no way in hell was he giving her over to Dimitri looking like death warmed over. The jerk would probably demand his money back the instant he saw her.

"Sweetheart? Do you remember me at all? Your mama, Loretta, and I have been looking for you for years. I'm so happy to see you."

"Her name's Lorraine."

William put on a tragic expression and gazed up at McCall. "That was one of her delusions, too. She gave us different names. I was Lloyd and Loretta was Lorraine. She even gave us a different last name." He furrowed his brow as if trying to remember. "What was it?"

"King," McCall provided. "She told me her name was Jessica King. And you're right. She said you were Lloyd and her mother Lorraine."

As if she wasn't aware that they were talking about her, Jessica asked dully, "Where's Mama?"

"She's not feeling well. She's at home waiting to see you."

"Home?"

William almost laughed. At last, a light gleamed in her eyes. The girl almost sounded hopeful. "Yes. You remember home, don't you, sweetie? Our house hasn't been the same since you left us."

Her mouth twitched slightly, as if she wanted to smile but didn't quite know how. "I would like to go home."

Triumph surged through William. At last, he was going to get the bitch back.

"Are you sure, Jessica?" McCall asked, a concerned frown on his face. "You don't have to make the decision today. We can—"

"Mr. McCall, please. She says she wants to come home. You agreed that—"

"Yes." Jessica looked up at McCall and said softly, "I do want to go home." She looked back at William and added, "You won't let that man…Dimitri…near me, will you?"

Keeping his happy expression firmly in place, he said soothingly, "Of course not, Jessica. You don't have to see anyone you don't want to see."

William glanced over at McCall, making sure his expression had just the right amount of tragic sadness. Hell, after what Dimitri did to her, the bitch might really be a head case. Didn't matter to him, though. Dimitri wanted the girl back, and that was all William cared about. Once she was under lock and key again, and Dimitri had made good on his promise to repair his reputation, William could proceed with the sales of his other merchandise. He never had to worry about the bitch ever again.

Things were working out just as he'd planned.

McCall stood. "Larson, can I speak with you in private for a moment?"

"Of course." He reached out and gently patted Jessica's clenched hands. "I'll be right back, sweetie."

Riley watched as Noah walked with Larson across the room to a corner. She knew her boss was giving the man some instructions and warnings in case anything went wrong, as well as some psychiatric recommendations.

Noah's expression was intense and sincere, as if the father-and-daughter reunion was the most important thing on his mind. As they spoke in low voices, Riley took a moment to observe William Larson and compare him to the man she'd known as Lloyd King.

The man was short in stature, maybe about five-six and probably weighed around one hundred forty. His hair was now salt-and-pepper gray. Other than that, he looked about the same.

At one time, she remembered thinking he was handsome. Little had she known that this was what evil looked like.

Even though she was confident she could do this job, she had wondered how she would feel when she saw him again. If she'd become nauseated or have to hold herself back from scratching his eyes out. She was pleased that neither was the case. She felt absolutely nothing. She had a gut-deep knowledge that this man was not in any way related to her. That was a freeing feeling. This man was no different than any other human trafficker she'd helped bring down. It didn't matter that she had once been his victim. She was one no longer, and she intended to make sure the bastard never victimized a child again.

Noah slapped Larson on the back in a friendly, manly way, and Riley had to swallow the laughter that bubbled inside her. Her boss was almost a foot taller and weighed at least eighty pounds more, all muscle. Larson almost went flying across the room.

Recovering his equilibrium, Larson returned to Riley and gave her what he probably thought was a loving smile. To her, it was smarmy and slick.

"Shall we go, sweetie? I know your mama is going to feel so much better when she sees you."

Riley stood and allowed Larson to take her hand and lead her to the door. Before going out, she stopped and gave Noah a quick nod and a timid whisper of, "Thank you, Mr. McCall, for your kindness."

"My pleasure, Jessica. Please be sure to check in when you can and let me know how you're doing."

She nodded again and then allowed Larson to pull her through the doorway.

CHAPTER
TWENTY-EIGHT

Justin sat in an SUV across the parking lot. His heart was in his throat as Larson and Riley walked out of the building. Apparently concerned that McCall might be watching, Larson was solicitous as he held Riley's arm and led her to the van.

The side door slid open, and he helped her inside. The door shut, and there was silence for all of thirty seconds. Then there was a loud clap, and he heard Riley's gasp. The son of a bitch had slapped her.

His hands gripped the steering wheel, and it took every bit of his strength not to race over there, rip the door off the van, and get her out of there. Not only would it completely destroy the op, but Riley would be infuriated. And rightly so. He had to trust that she could handle this. He did trust her. But still... Damn, this was hard.

"Oh, get up and stop your sniveling. Do you know what you've cost me, you little bitch? I can't make another damn sale because of your owner. Dimitri has spread lies and half-truths all around about my business practices. I had to get you back to fix my reputation.

"I don't care that I promised him no bruises. You both owed me that."

"No, Daddy. You said you wouldn't make me see him."

Larson laughed. "You're still the same dumb, clueless bitch you always were. No wonder Dimitri beat the shit out of you all the time.

"Frederick, let's get going. I've got a phone call to make."

"Why do I have to be tied up?"

Riley, using Jessica's voice, was difficult to hear. She sounded as if she were crying and gasping for breath. Justin told himself it was an act. He'd seen his partner play many different roles, and she'd been convincing in each one. Even though Larson had slapped her, Riley Ingram would not shed a tear. But the beaten-down, helpless Jessica King would. That was the only reason for the tears.

The van pulled out of the parking lot, the giant named Frederick driving. For right now, Justin was the only one following. In about ten minutes, three other LCR team members would be on Larson's tail. The man would not know until it was too late that he had been played.

Larson started talking again, apparently on the phone call he'd said he had to make. "Yes, I need to get in immediately. She needs the works, hair, face, nails, all over body treatment."

He was calling a spa? What the hell?

"Yes, that's right." He barked out a laugh. "A fashion emergency. I'll pay double. Good. Thank you. We'll be there in about half an hour."

"Frederick, go to 1440 Rodeo Drive. The Sparkling Swan."

"What's that?" Frederick asked.

"It's a day spa. There's no way in hell I'm going to give her back to Dimitri looking like this. She's so dammed ugly, he'll demand his money back. She's going to look like a million bucks before the day's out." He gave a harsh chuckle and then added, "Rather, five million."

Riley watched through the strands of hair that had fallen into her face when Larson slapped her. He had just revealed an interesting tidbit. Apparently, the price Dimitri had paid for her was five million. Quite a lot for a human-trafficking sale, but with all the money, time and effort he'd put into her, Larson must've felt the asking price was worth it.

That Dimitri would pay such an amount was the confounding part. Why pay that much for someone he was just going to beat, rape, and torture? Not that the reason mattered, but it was still odd.

What else could she get out of Larson? She knew she couldn't ask too many questions without running the risk of making him either suspicious or angry. An angry Larson would haul off and hit her again. A suspicious Larson would be much worse. She would not blow her cover, no matter what.

"Are you my real father?"

He didn't answer her. Just gave her a glare and looked down at a text message on his phone. She couldn't make anything out from where she was and couldn't take the risk of leaning forward.

She tried again. "Is Lorraine really my mother?"

Larson blew out an explosive sigh. "When did you get so mouthy? I swear, Dimitri's going to beat you and skin you alive if you talk this much to him. You'd better start practicing silence, girl."

Knowing it would do no good to ask him anything else, Riley bowed her head and did what she was told. She became silent. And in that silence, she heard the most wonderful thing of all. Justin's voice in her ear.

"You're doing good, Ingram. Not too many questions, though. Asshole's not in a confiding mood right now. We'll get you answers. Don't worry."

She closed her eyes and drew in a silent, calming breath. The throb in her cheek from the slap to her face, the ache in her wrists and ankles from being tied too tight, all disappeared. With a couple of deviations, this was what they were expecting. Things were going just as they'd planned.

***

Five hours later, Riley allowed Larson to shove her into a house. At no point in their planning had they ever considered that she'd spend half a day at a spa getting her hair cut and styled, her entire body buffed, and a facial. Hell, she was more exhausted now than she'd ever been on an op.

Larson had walked away from her for a time, putting Riley more on edge. She wanted the bastard in her sight at all times. According to Justin, who chatted with her during her harrowing beauty ordeal, Noah and the other operatives knew exactly where he was at all times.

The only tense moment came when the stylist asked about the earbud. It was clear plastic, almost invisible. Larson had heard the question and had looked at her, puzzled. Riley calmly explained that she had a slight hearing impairment in that ear and the earbud was merely a hearing aid. Larson didn't question her, but she had a feeling it might come up again.

Losing Justin's voice in her ear would be a big loss, but it was a luxury, not a necessity. She needed to be prepared.

The house was small, but elegantly decorated. It smelled like new construction. Riley wondered if this was a house where

Larson kept another of his fake families. That was one of the many questions she had for the man. How many times had he done this before? How many children had he sold? How many were being readied to be sold? How many young women and men were in the midst of hell thanks to Larson's total lack of conscience and morals?

Shoving her into a chair in the living room, Larson growled at Frederick. "Tie her up."

Frederick, for all his strength and seeming lack of intelligence, wasn't cruel. Though he did tie her to the chair using duct tape, he kept asking if it was too tight and if she was uncomfortable. When she complained that her wrists were hurting, he loosened the binding and then looked up at her for approval. She couldn't help but smile at him. Poor guy was in way over his head.

Figuring it would be odd for her not to ask his identity, she said, "Are you a friend of my daddy's. Why are you tying me up?"

Frederick sent a panicked look over at Larson. Before he could say anything, Larson snapped, "Keep your mouth shut."

She wasn't sure which one Larson meant, she or Frederick. Didn't really matter. Being tied up without having any explanation went against every independent molecule in her body. Until he told her specifically to shut up, she was going to keep asking questions.

"Daddy, why do I have to be tied up? You told Mr. McCall you were happy to have me back. Where's Mama? Will she be here soon? I thought you would take me home."

Larson marched toward her. Frederick scrambled to get out of his way. Even though Riley couldn't glare at him with anger burning in her eyes, she refused to shut up. "Why are you being mean to me?"

Grabbing her face in his hands, his palms pressed hard into her cheeks. "Shut your damn mouth before I slap you into next year. Do you hear me, bitch?"

Figuring she'd made her anxiety and fear look realistic enough, Riley gave a rapid nod of her head and tightly compressed her lips.

Apparently satisfied, both Larson and Frederick left the room. Riley sat alone, wondering just how long she'd have to wait until Dimitri came for her. They couldn't take Larson down until they knew when, how, and where. In the meantime, she had questions she wanted answered.

She had to wait longer than she'd anticipated. Three hours later, Larson finally returned to the room. By that time Riley needed more than answers—she was in desperate need of the bathroom.

Larson never questioned her about the earbud, for which she was grateful. So while she waited, Justin had been telling her corny jokes to keep her entertained. But there was no getting her mind off her need. If Larson didn't release her soon, he'd have a large puddle to clean up. The image of that cheered her somewhat.

Behaving like a traumatized victim when all she wanted to do was rip Larson's ugly face off wasn't easy. She didn't have a choice, so she tamped down her anger and said, "Would it be okay if I went to the bathroom?"

Larson had sprawled in a recliner across from her. When Riley took a close look at him, she understood what he had been doing for the past three hours. His eyes were glazed, so she figured he was either drunk or high. Or both.

Was Larson a mean drunk or a friendly one? If his guard was down, maybe she could get some answers. But first, she had to go to the bathroom.

"Daddy, could I please go to the bathroom?"

He huffed out a breath that sounded like a sick horse and said, "Sure. Why the hell not? Don't want you smelling like piss when Dimitri arrives." He went to his feet, swayed a little, and then drew a knife from his pocket.

Riley didn't have to pretend to act afraid. Knives made her wary. One wielded by a drunk, even more so. While on an op last year, she'd been stabbed in the stomach and had almost died. Her gut cringed at the memory.

Larson staggered over and, with surprising steadiness, cut the binding at her wrists and then her ankles. He reeked of bourbon. When she stood, he stumbled back, and then belched in her face.

Ignoring the stench and hiding her disgust, she turned to leave the room. Asking him where to go would be pointless. The man was plastered.

She found the bathroom down the hallway, used it quickly, and then drank down gulps of cool water from the faucet. The jerk hadn't even bothered to provide water for his prisoner.

She looked up and caught her reflection in the mirror, barely recognizing herself. The overly made-up face and too-styled hair was so not her thing.

She made a quick perusal through the drawers and cabinets. They were disappointingly empty, which was no surprise. This must be a new rental for Larson. Or maybe it was a place he only brought his wayward fake children when they had the audacity to run away.

A fist pounded on the door. "Get out here, girl!" Larson shouted.

Manipulating her tired shoulders to get the kinks out, Riley opened the door and walked out. Larson jerked his head toward the living room.

Riley returned to her chair and sat quietly while Larson wrapped duct tape around her wrists, securing her to the arms of the chair and then binding her ankles together. When she complained that the tape cut into her wrists, he looked up at her and grinned. "Good."

Refusing to allow her anger to distract her, she waited until Larson was back in the recliner. This time he was sipping something. More bourbon probably.

As soon as he took another sip, she asked, "Did you kidnap me from my real parents?"

Larson snorted into his drink. "You still under the misguided notion that somebody out there gives a damn about you? Wants you? Hell, what I provided for you was a million times better than what you would have had."

So he had abducted her. A lump developed in her throat. Riley swallowed hard.

"Easy, Ingram," Justin murmured in her ear. "Don't let him see how much knowing this means to you. He'll shut up just to torture you."

Even without being able to see her face, her partner knew Larson's words had affected her. The man knew her so well. And he was right. If Larson knew how very badly she wanted the truth, he'd refuse to answer anything.

She waited until he had almost finished his drink, then said, "How old was I when you found me?"

He drained his glass, shrugged. "Four, maybe five. You were a cute baby. Got ugly for a while when you got older. Thought I was going to have to offer you at a bargain discount. Then you got better looking. Blossomed, you might say. Soon as Dimitri saw your profile, he had to have you." He belched and added,

"Paid top dollar, too. Most money I ever made on a sale." He glared and added, "Then you had to ruin it, you selfish bitch."

Refusing to allow him to get sidetracked, she tried to appeal to his ego. "Abducting a child must be difficult. How did you carry it off?"

He stared at her and then let loose a loud guffaw. "I didn't kidnap you, you clueless idiot. Lorraine is your real mother."

Justin cursed vehemently. He remembered the mic and covered it for the rest of his explosion. Riley sure as hell didn't need to hear him lose it. But dammit. How could a mother do that to her own daughter? What kind of pond scum was she?

Or was Larson really telling the truth? Maybe this was just another way to torture Riley. He had a sick feeling that this was one time Larson was telling the truth.

Shit. Shit. Shit.

"Kelly, get hold of yourself."

McCall's harsh reprimand told him he hadn't hidden his fury as he'd hoped. Hell, he was doing Riley no good. Best he could do was continue to encourage her, and when he finally had her back in his arms, he would remind her what a remarkable person she was. And how very much she was loved by a lot of people, including him.

He listened as Riley softly asked Larson question after question. Her calm, unemotional tone, her pointed, specific questions regarding her upbringing amazed him. Justin knew she was suffering. Knew that finding out the bitch who'd raised her really was her mother was devastating. But not once did her pain come through. She was out for answers, and nothing would prevent her from knowing the truth.

And what a gold mine she was uncovering. Larson, his tongue loosened from both alcohol and arrogance, began a litany of his accomplishments over the years. Not only had the bastard been trafficking humans for over two decades, he named places where he conducted business, described procedures he used to find the perfect victims, and outlined how he arranged for the sales of his "merchandise."

McCall would take this information to the FBI. Kids who had been missing for years might be found. Families could be reunited. Lives could be saved. And Riley Ingram, once a broken, abused young woman, now a warrior, would be responsible for it all.

"Company just arrived."

Thorne's gruff voice pulled his attention away from the conversation. Justin had positioned himself in the backyard, behind a clump of shrubbery. He had wanted to be as close to the house as he could be in case he needed to get inside pronto. Thorne, Fox, and McCall were parked out front in an SUV about twenty yards from the house.

Thorne continued to report, "Big-assed Hummer. Two men getting out. One's about six-two, two-twenty. Other guy's about five-five, two hundred. Both carrying concealed under their shirts. They're heading to the front door. Once they're inside, I'll mosey over to the Hummer and take a peek inside."

Adrenaline surged through Justin, but he forced himself to stay put. Was one of the men Dimitri? Neither of the men fit the description Riley had given them of the bastard.

How'd they get here so fast? All signs had pointed to him living in Greece, or a nearby country. He probably had contacts all over the world. Maybe these guys were hired goons Dimitri had called in for the job.

Or were these men here for a different reason? Maybe they weren't related to the business with Dimitri at all. Could Larson have something else going on? Something they hadn't anticipated?

The doorbell chimed. Larson cut off mid-brag and said in an almost gleeful voice, "Jessica! Daddy's home!"

CHAPTER THIRTY

Riley was glad for her ability to compartmentalize. While one corner of her brain was still reeling from the disappointing and revolting knowledge that the woman who had raised her really was her biological mother, another part absorbed the wealth of information Larson was spilling. She would deal with the rotten truth of her parentage on her own time. For now, she let Larson spill his guts and hang himself at the same time. What a pleasure it was going to be taking this disgusting piece of humanity down.

When Aidan's low voice said, "We've got company," her senses went on alert. Dimitri was here already? How was that possible?

She mentally shook away her disquiet. It didn't matter how he'd gotten here so fast. She needed to be ready. After all these years, she was finally going to see the devil again. Her stomach roiled, and she was suddenly grateful that Larson hadn't bothered to feed her. The small amount of water she had consumed was churning in her stomach like an angry ocean.

A doorbell sounded, and Larson stopped in the middle of bragging about his sale last year of teenage twin boys to a Russian politician. He jumped to his feet as a grin split his face in two. "Jessica! Daddy's home!"

Larson came toward her, and Riley couldn't prevent the instinctive need to shrink away from him. Instead of hurting her, though, he fluffed her hair, then stood back and eyed her critically. "Good. The makeup hides the bruise on your cheek."

Seconds later, Frederick walked into the room. Two men followed behind him. Riley held her breath. One was tall and broad-shouldered, with olive skin and emotionless black eyes. The other was much shorter and thicker, with a jagged scar running down the side of his face. Both men had expressions so blank and cold, they could pass as cyborgs. Disappointment and relief created an odd mishmash of emotions inside her. Neither man was Dimitri.

"We're here for the girl." The bigger man's accent reminded her a little of Dimitri's, though this man's was much thicker.

"She's here." Larson waved a hand at her. "But where's Dimitri?"

"He's too important to trouble himself with something so trivial. We're here to take her to him."

Even though they had known this was a possibility and had planned for this scenario, Dimitri's absence made things a little more difficult. She waited to see if Larson would ask questions. That was a useless hope. Larson's only objective was to get rid of her. He was about to accomplish that goal.

"Take her, then. Tell him I expect him to keep his end of the bargain."

"That's between you and Mr. Dimitri," the shorter man intoned. "We are here for the girl. Nothing more."

Knowing there was no other choice, Riley whispered into the mic embedded in the pendant hanging around her neck, "Now."

Only seconds later, the house exploded with action. The front door burst open, and Noah, Sabrina, and Aidan rushed into the room, shouting, "Drop your weapons!"

The larger of Dimitri's men did as he was told, but the shorter one looked as though he was going to refuse, until Justin growled behind him, "Weapons on the floor. Now!"

Larson, his reaction time slowed by alcohol, took longer to take in what was going on. When it finally clicked, he whirled toward Riley, snarling a curse. It was too late. Riley had already pulled the blade hidden in her belt and cut the tape on her wrists and ankles. The minute she was free, she lunged for Larson. She couldn't rip his face off, as she wanted, but she allowed herself one solid hit to his jaw. His eyes rolled back in his head, and he went down like a felled tree.

Grabbing the duct tape from the shelf, she was quick and efficient in tying his wrists and ankles together. She thought she was being very generous, because she didn't bind him nearly as tightly as he had tied her.

She looked up to find both of Dimitri's men lying on the floor, hands and feet secured. And poor Frederick was sitting in a corner. Hands tied behind his back, he was sobbing like an infant.

Justin stalked over to Riley, his eyes roaming her from head to foot as if making sure she wasn't injured. When his eyes darkened, she knew he'd spotted the bruise on her cheek.

"It's nothing," she said softly. "I'm fine."

He held her gaze for several more seconds, and she saw in them what she was feeling herself. They were on a mission, they were partners, not lovers. Still, the warmth in his expression felt like a hug.

"Hungry?"

She nodded. "And thirsty."

He held out a bottle of water and a PowerBar. Gladly accepting the sustenance, she took a giant gulp of water and followed it with a man-sized bite of the bar.

Things hadn't gone perfectly, but as she looked around the room, she couldn't help but be pleased. All in all, this part of the op was a success. Now to get to the questioning. Between Dimitri's two men and Larson, they would get what they needed to find the devil.

Stretching her stiff muscles and enjoying her small meal, Riley walked closer to where Aidan was questioning Dimitri's men so she could listen. With every moment that passed, she was getting more frustrated. They refused to talk. Even Aidan, LCR's best interrogator, was getting nowhere. The only information either man condescended to reveal was that Dimitri had sent them. A plane was waiting at a small airstrip about twenty miles away. It was to fly them to Dimitri's home. That was it. No location. No last name. Nothing that would tell them how to get to the bastard.

Larson regained consciousness but wasn't any more helpful than Dimitri's men, although he did put on a better show. He assured them that he realized how much trouble he was in and was willing to share everything he knew. Unfortunately, he claimed, he knew nothing about Dimitri. When he'd sold Jessica to him, the funds had been transferred to an offshore account in the Cayman Islands. Larson swore he knew only Dimitri's first name.

No one believed a thing he said.

Riley swallowed a frustrated groan. Time was running out. The longer it took for the men to return to the plane with her, the more likely it was that Dimitri would find out there were problems. The men might eventually talk, but if Dimitri was as wealthy as they suspected, he could easily disappear. Perhaps forever.

Riley couldn't take that chance.

"Noah, can I talk to you?"

She walked into the hallway, aware that Justin's eyes followed her. She knew he would be furious once he heard her plan. But she had to try.

Since she knew she had only a limited amount of time before her partner arrived, and she wanted to get her argument in first, she said quickly, "Let me get on Dimitri's plane."

Noah cocked his head. "And do what?"

She had to give him credit. He didn't immediately say no.

"Once we land, they'll take me to him. He won't be expecting me to fight. I can take him down."

"What about Dimitri's men? The pilot will be expecting them to return with you."

"I'll hold a gun on them until we get there. Then I'll force them off the plane and make the pilot fly me to Dimitri."

"And when you land and he has an army of men at his disposal? What about then? You plan to take on an entire army?"

Okay, admittedly that would be harder for one person to handle. "You can track me, follow with the LCR plane. I still have the implants in me. Even if he takes me to his home, LCR can come in and rescue me. He won't kill me. I know he won't. This isn't that different from what we originally planned. I'll be fine until you guys arrive. We can take Dimitri and all of his—"

"Oh, hell no, Ingram. Hell no!"

She turned and faced a livid Justin. She'd seen him angry before, but this went beyond mere anger. He was looking at her as if she'd betrayed him.

"You are not, do you hear me, *not* going to do this. We will get the son of a bitch, but not at the expense of your life."

"He's not going to kill me. I cost him too much money."

"No, he'll just beat the shit out of you and rape you again."

"That's enough, Kelly," Noah said.

"Hell no, it's not enough, McCall. You cannot seriously be considering letting her do this."

"This isn't your fight, Kelly," Riley snapped. "It's mine."

"The hell it isn't. We're partners. We face danger together."

She took a breath, struggling for the right words that wouldn't make him implode. He had to see reason!

"I can do this."

"You don't have to do this. We'll get the bastard another way."

"And what if we don't? Tell me that. When his men don't deliver me, he'll know something's wrong. Then he'll hear about Larson's arrest, and he'll be in the wind. He'll disappear. And we'll never know where he went. What happens then?"

His glittering eyes narrowed as they glared down at her. "What happens then? You live. That's what happens. Is your life…your sanity worth the chance at revenge?"

"This has nothing to do with revenge. And my sanity is fully intact. How many others do you think Dimitri has abused? Will continue to abuse? I can stop him."

Giving her a fury-filled look, he turned to Noah. "You can't let her do this, McCall."

Noah was looking at her, his dark eyes searching. She faced him unflinchingly, her expression both fierce and resolute.

Finally, he nodded. "Very well, Ingram. I'll give you this chance. With one condition. If necessary, you take him down. No heroics."

Uttering a vile curse, Justin walked way. She watched him murmur something to Aidan, who gave her a surprised look. Aidan then turned to Sabrina and said something to her. Together they started jerking the clothes from the larger of Dimitri's men.

Then, to her astonishment, Justin began to strip.

She ran forward, grabbing his arm. "What are you doing?"

As if standing in nothing but boxer briefs was an everyday occurrence, Justin pulled away from her. "I'll take this guy's place. We're about the same size."

"You're blond. He's not."

"It's dark and…" He walked over to Frederick, who was still whimpering in the corner. "Mind if I borrow your cap?" Justin helped himself, adjusted it, and then slapped it on his own head. "Problem solved."

"This can't work. You know it can't."

Ignoring her, Justin slid into the black jeans and black shirt. As he buttoned the shirt, he turned around and eyed her coldly. "I'll wing it, Ingram. Isn't that what you're doing?"

She grabbed his arm again, tried to pull him around to face her. "This is my fight."

"So you keep saying."

"Dammit, Justin. No. Listen to me. This is my—"

Justin whirled and glared at her. "Ingram, if you say this is your fight one more time, we're going to have it out. Right here. Right now. Get your head out of your ass and listen up. This is an LCR op. We are partners. We watch each other's backs. End of discussion. Get it through your head. I'm going with you."

She turned to her boss, hoping he'd make Justin see reason. "Noah, I should go in alone."

His expression as implacable as her partner's, Noah gave her a hard, uncompromising look. "That's not your choice to make, Ingram. You want my support, you follow LCR protocol."

They were on their way to the airport within five minutes. Just before they walked out the door, Justin watched Riley go over to Larson. The man was still tied to a chair, his eyes glazed from shock. She stopped in front of him and whispered something in his ear. His eyes went wide and then narrowed with fury.

She gave him a small smile and then sauntered away.

Though still furious with her, Justin couldn't help but ask, "What'd you say to him?"

"I thanked him for hiring LCR to find me. I told him I'm one of LCR's best operatives, and I enjoyed rescuing myself."

He gave a small jerk of his head, barely acknowledging what she'd told him. A part of him wanted to grab her, kiss her, and tell her how damn proud he was of her. He would later, when this was over. Now his only concern was making sure she stayed alive.

To say he was pissed would be an understatement. She didn't think he understood her need for revenge. He sure as shit understood it. And he wanted it for her. If anyone deserved payback, Riley did. But putting her life at risk like this? Hellfire no.

And she'd gone behind his back with McCall. Maybe that was what enraged him more than anything else. They were partners. No, they were a hell of a lot more than partners. And by her actions, she'd relegated him to just another LCR operative. Like hell he was.

This wasn't the time to get into a discussion about loyalty and trust. That would be later after this was over and she was safe. For right now, they had to figure out how to take down a demon in his own backyard.

They'd brought the shorter of Dimitri's men with them. He remained silent as he drove them toward the airport. Justin sat in the front passenger seat. Riley was in the back. They both had guns on the man. Once they arrived at their destination, they'd have to play it by ear. Having no real plan of action was a piss-poor way to handle an op. This time they had no choice. Until they knew what they faced, they couldn't know how to go on.

Though both of Dimitri's men spoke English quite well, neither of them had been the talkative sort. The minuscule information they'd provided, very grudgingly, was of little help.

Yeah, this had *shit-storm disaster* plastered all over it.

Justin used his gun to poke the man beside him. "What's your name? Can't keep calling you asshole."

Moving his gaze from the road in front of him, he glared at Justin. "My name is Ari. I tell you this because it's good to know the name of the man who will soon kill you."

"Oh yeah?" Justin grinned. "If that's the case, you might want to know my name. It's Justin. And since I have a gun pressed against your kidney, I'd say your chances of dying are a whole lot better than mine."

Ari moved his eyes back to the road, a small smile on his face. "We shall see."

"Now that we're on a first-name basis, here's what we'll do, Ari. When we get to the plane, you will get out and open the back door." He didn't glance behind him when he said, "Ingram, you get out and do your act. We'll walk up the steps, with Ari in front. You're between us. I'll be right behind you.

"Ari, if you make any kind of sudden moves or open your mouth to warn anyone, a bullet will go into your brain a half second later." For emphasis, he pressed the gun deeper into the man's side.

"I am not a fool," Ari stated. "However, you will pay dearly for your insolence. And you." He glanced in the rearview mirror at Riley. "I was there when Mr. Dimitri owned you. It will be a pleasure to watch him make you crawl and beg again. You—"

"You shut your foul mouth before I put my gun in it," Justin snarled.

"It's all right, Justin," Riley said. "Nothing these bastards say can hurt me anymore."

He didn't look back at her. She could read him too well. It would hurt her if she saw doubt in his expression. Because he did have doubts. What if Dimitri did or said something that triggered a memory she couldn't handle?

Willingly returning to hell might well be the most courageous act he'd ever seen, but it was also one of the most foolish things he could imagine. Revenge was a damned hollow victory if you died in the process.

They drove through the gates of the small airstrip. A large private jet waited on the tarmac. Every instinct on high alert, Justin gave Ari one more warning. "Do anything at all to alert anyone, and you'll be burning in hell one second later. Got that?"

Ari parked several yards from the plane and then glared. "I am not an imbecile, Mr. Justin. Nor am I hearing impaired."

"Good to know, Ari," he responded cheerfully.

Justin dared one glance back at Riley. She had that indomitable look in her eyes, and her chin was set at an angle he knew all too well.

Ari behaved himself. He got out of the Hummer and then opened the back door for Riley. Justin held his gun beneath his shirt but kept it pointed at the man. The slightest error and Ari was history.

They single-filed it up the steps to the plane. Every instinct Justin possessed told him to grab Riley and get the hell out of there. But it was too late for that. They would play the game and pray to God that they would win.

Ari stepped into the plane, Riley right behind him. The instant Justin walked in, Ari shouted, "It's a trap!"

In one swift movement, Justin shoved Riley out of the way, grabbed Ari by his collar, whirled, and threw him down the stairs. He turned back and faced his worst nightmare. Riley was lying face down on the floor, her body twitching as if in spasms. A man stood over her. His smile was both evil and smug. Though Riley had told them that her eight-year-old memories might be too vague to describe him accurately, Justin could see she had been right on target. This was Dimitri.

Swinging his gun up, Justin took a step toward him. The sick freak would die today, right now.

Piercing pain exploded in the back of his head. He wavered and wobbled. His vision blurred. An urgent voice in his head told him to shoot. He squeezed the trigger, heard a shrill scream of pain. Knew a second of satisfaction.

Darkness washed over him.

CHAPTER
THIRTY-ONE

Noah paced up and down the length of the LCR jet. Telling his pilot to fly faster wasn't possible. Not only were they heading into a severe thunderstorm, but they had yet to receive permission to land.

He and his team were a day behind but were armed with a helluva lot of information. They now knew who and where. Question was, would Riley and Justin be alive when they arrived?

Noah had talked with every government official he could think of from the US and Greece. He had called in favors, negotiated deals, and made numerous threats. But now he had almost everything he needed to destroy the devil.

The bastard's name was Dimitri Soukis. Wealthy beyond belief—a net worth of over thirty billion—he was one of the top twenty richest people in the world. He had the kind of power most people could only dream about. The Greek government hated the man with a passion and would have loved to see his ass locked behind bars for the rest of his life. There was only one catch. Dimitri was not a Greek citizen.

Soukis resided in his home country of Pavli. Located between Greece and Malta, Pavli was a small sovereign nation of about three million people. Noah had talked at length with Andrew

Kopsas, the president of Pavli. Kopsas knew all about Soukis. He also knew the man could buy himself out of any kind of trouble and had done so frequently. Soukis had numerous politicians in his back pocket, and though Kopsas claimed he wasn't one of them, Noah had his doubts.

The Pavlian president refused to assist in taking down Soukis. He claimed his people would rebel if they heard his government helped Americans in the arrest of a Pavli citizen. He did promise, however, that there would be no interference if LCR managed to apprehend the man. And Kopsas coolly added that if the operation resulted in the death of Dimitri Soukis, there would be no repercussions from his government.

In other words, the president had given LCR license to kill one of Pavli's own citizens.

Noah had never gone into a mission with the intent to kill anyone. He'd dealt with some of the lowest forms of human filth, and not once had he ever set out to end a life. The only time anyone died was when it was unavoidable. This mission was no different. However, if it came down to choosing between an LCR life and Soukis's, Noah wouldn't hesitate.

"This is the captain," a hard masculine voice boomed overhead. "Buckle up and hang on, young'uns. It's about to get bumpy."

Noah grudgingly went to his seat and buckled in. Sitting still when adrenaline was pumping like a geyser was not easy. He had two operatives in danger, and the knowledge that there wasn't a damn thing he could do right now was eating a hole in his gut.

As if reading his mind, Fox said, "At least one part of the operation went off without a hitch."

Noah nodded. That was true. Larson and his people had been taken into custody. When they'd realized Riley and Justin had been outed, Noah had given the order. All of Larson's houses had been raided. The children were safe and the squalor that was Larson and his scum-sucking employees was now in jail facing a ton of charges.

When Riley returned to the States, she'd have to decide whether or not she wanted to see her mother. And even though Larson had claimed that Lorraine King aka Loretta Larson was her biological mother, Noah would suggest a DNA test to confirm. Larson would have done and said anything to hurt Riley. Lying about her parentage would have been entertainment for him.

"You think anyone in the Pavli government will tip off Soukis that we're coming?" Thorne asked.

"Wouldn't surprise me one damn bit. We'll go in with the assumption that they know and are prepared for war."

Thorne glanced around the plane. Because they'd needed to move fast, they hadn't been able to bring in any more operatives. Only four operatives had been able to board the plane. Thorne, Fox, Mallory, and Delvecchio. They were seasoned and able to handle anything that came their way. Still, he couldn't help but wish he had a half-dozen more.

"Tell me again why she's here."

Noah looked at Thorne and then the object of his apparent wrath. The additional person he'd invited along was not an LCR operative or employee. Anna Bradford was here for another reason entirely.

Thorne definitely had a burr up his butt when it came to Anna. Before Noah could respond, Anna answered for him.

"For support, Thorne. Riley may need me. It's called being a friend. You should try it sometime."

"As long as you don't get in the way, you're welcome to go wherever you like."

"Oh, thank you so much for your permission, Mr. Thorne. You stay out of my way, and I'll stay out of yours."

"You don't—"

"That's enough from both of you," Noah snapped. "Thorne, Anna is here as moral support for Riley. She will stay with the plane and will be safe."

Thorne gave Anna one last hard look and turned away. Noah knew what Aidan Thorne's problem was, and there wasn't a damn thing he could do to help him with it. He was going to have to work it out for himself. And considering the anger boiling inside the man, Noah didn't see that happening any time soon.

That was a worry for another day.

His cellphone buzzed, and he frowned at the unfamiliar number. "McCall."

"Mr. McCall? My name is Aletha Villas. I understand we have a mutual enemy."

"And who would that be, Ms. Villas?"

"Dimitri Soukis."

Noah was already texting Deidre for her to do research on Aletha Villas as he said, "You have my full attention, Ms. Villas."

"I'd like to help you."

"Help me, how?"

"As you will soon find out when your research comes through, I head an opposition party against my country's current president, Andrew Kopsas. He and Soukis are like brothers."

"I see. And what do you propose to do to help me?"

"I know you will soon be landing at the airport in our capital city. I have a small but loyal team of well-trained men and women who can assist you."

"I'm not interested in your politics, Ms. Villas. And unless I have no choice, I don't plan on any bloodshed."

"Believe me, Mr. McCall. I don't want you involved in my politics either. And I do not want Dimitri Soukis killed. He is a blight on our beautiful country and belongs in prison. I am merely suggesting that my people assist you in saving the young man and woman Soukis has stolen from you."

"And what do you get in return? If Pavli's president is indeed friends with Soukis, won't he intervene and try to prevent prosecution?"

"No. It will be made public what Soukis has been doing. The people will not allow the president to take sides. President Kopsas will turn on his friend without a second moment of thought."

As she talked, Noah read the information Deidre had been able to provide. From what he could tell, Aletha Villas was telling the truth. And even though she had her own agenda, Noah would gladly accept her help to achieve his own.

"Very well, Ms. Villas. This is how you can help."

***

Hera, Pavli
Dimitri Soukis's mansion

She woke in the box. Naked.

It was pitch dark, but Riley had no problem recognizing her location. The instant she realized, all breath left her body. Harsh gasping sounds echoed in the small area, pounding her ears.

Can't breathe. Can't breathe.

No. No. No!

A harsh voice screamed inside her head. She would not succumb to the terror. She was no longer the helpless victim she'd once been. She was Riley Freaking Ingram. LCR Elite operative. She could kick ass. She was a defender of the weak and no longer weak herself.

The self-lecture did the job. Air returned to her lungs, and though she continued to tremble, she forced herself to take slow, deep breaths. Calm flooded her senses, and at last she was able to concentrate.

What did she remember? Dimitri had been on the plane after all. The instant she had walked onto the plane, she had been Tasered. And then—

Horror swamped her once more. Justin! Where was Justin? What had happened?

Think, Ingram, think!

She had woken once. She'd been tied to a seat, the drone of a jet engine beneath her feet. She had raised her head, barely conscious of her surroundings. But she remembered one important thing. Justin had been sitting across from her, hands and feet bound, his head bent forward, unconscious. But he had been alive. She remembered focusing on his chest moving as he breathed. Yes, he was still alive. But for how long?

She had to get out of here. Fists clenched, her entire body stiff with tension, she licked her dry lips.

Think, Ingram. Think!

There had been occasions that Dimitri hadn't locked the box. It had been a ruse to trick her. She had made the mistake of trying to open it once and had found him standing above her, waiting for her to try to escape. Her punishment had been swift, and she had learned her lesson. She had never tried to open the box again.

Could he be doing the same thing this time? Was he waiting nearby, hoping she would open the box? She hoped so.

As she was curled up in a fetal position, Riley raised one hand and tried to force the box open. It was locked.

She swallowed a frustrated sob. Of course it wouldn't be that easy.

From what she could remember, the lid of the box was about two inches thick. The lock he'd used back then had been an old-fashioned padlock. Could she break through? Maybe split the wood? She never had tried before, simply because she'd been too scared of what he would do to her. Her fear for Justin far outweighed any other horror she'd ever felt. If anything happened to him...

Pushing that gut-wrenching thought away, Riley maneuvered herself onto her back. Her legs were bent, her knees touching her breasts. Raising her hands and knees, she shoved hard against the lid. No give at all. She shoved harder. Nothing.

Refusing to let up, she shoved again and again. Over and over. The heat was unbearable, and for the first time she thought she might be grateful to be nude. If she had been wearing clothes, she was sure she would suffocate. She drew in a deep breath, gathering strength, and shoved again. Was that the sound of wood splintering? She shoved again and again. She had to get out of here and find Justin. She had to!

***

His head pounding, Justin woke with a splitting headache and smelling the stench of his own vomit. His eyes were bleary. He blinked to clear them and groaned. Hell, even his eyelids hurt.

Where was he? What the hell had happened? He remembered a plane, someone screaming. And then...

Riley!

Reality crashed down upon him as he tried to sit up. Three things hit him instantly. There was no need to sit up, because he was hanging from the ceiling, his wrists locked in leather cuffs. The equipment on the wall indicated he was inside some sort of torture chamber. And he was naked.

Well, shit.

He told himself he'd been in tighter spots, but he wasn't sure that was helpful. Worry for Riley overwhelmed everything else. What had that bastard done to her? Fury engulfed him, overwhelming the agony in his head. They'd made a crucial mistake. Their trap had backfired on them, and instead of capturing the asshole, they'd walked into his lair.

He searched the room for an escape route. From what he could see, there was only one way out, and that was the door across the room. Now for the biggest problem—getting out of the cuffs. At least his feet were firmly on the floor. That made things a little easier.

He pulled down hard. There was little give, but since there was no other option he could see, he didn't let that stop him. He jerked repeatedly. At some point, the ceiling would give way. Patience wasn't easy when all he wanted to do was rip the ceiling down and go find Riley. Since that wasn't going to happen quickly, he put everything he had into his efforts.

The door flew open, and he glanced over. A man came into the room, and though Justin wasn't a big believer in supernatural demons walking the earth, he could swear the room dropped ten degrees as the man came closer.

He got his first up-close look at Dimitri. This was the man who had purchased Riley, raped and beaten her, treated her like garbage. He looked as common as a housefly. Standing maybe five-ten, Dimitri had a wealth of curly black-and-silver hair. Thick, shaggy brows hovered like giant black caterpillars over eerie coal-black eyes. He probably weighed one-seventy soaking wet, and much of that weight looked as though it had settled into his middle. Justin figured the man to be in his early-sixties.

All in all, he was a disgusting piece of human excrement.

"Who are you?"

Apparently, Dimitri wasn't one to waste time on idle chitchat.

Justin remained silent. The ice-cold look of a killer gleamed in Dimitri's eyes. This was a man who preyed on the weak and helpless. He not only lacked the slightest amount of human decency but also courage.

"What were you doing with my Jessica? Are you her friend? Her protector?" His voice went shrill. "Have you touched my Jessica? Put your hands on my beautiful girl?"

Silence.

"Answer me, you cretin! Who are you?"

Justin maintained his blank expression.

The longer Dimitri waited without getting a response the more incensed he became. How dare this imbecile, this filthy interloper, act so arrogant, so unafraid? Did he not know who he was?

Perhaps that was it. He didn't realize the power and influence of Dimitri Soukis. After all, Jessica didn't know that much about him. She didn't know that he had enough wealth to buy anything and everything, including governments.

Yes, this man had no idea who he was dealing with. He would enlighten him, then he would be suitably impressed and frightened.

"Do you know who I am?" He swaggered toward the giant, feeling quite safe. The man was naked as the day he was born and hanging from the rafters. All that muscle and sinew was worthless now. He was at the mercy of Dimitri Soukis. Before he had the man killed, he would have him begging for his life.

The thought made him smile.

Like a powerful gymnast, Justin grabbed hold of the chains securing him and pulled himself up. Raising his legs, he kicked out with all his might. Dimitri's eyes barely showed shocked comprehension before he went flying across the room, landing in a heap in the corner.

A small smile cracked Justin's face. Now that had been fun.

CHAPTER
THIRTY-TWO

Sweat covered her entire body, and Riley knew that if she didn't break out of the box soon, she would pass out. She had pushed, shoved, and hit the lid so many times, her hands and knees were ripped to pieces, drenched with blood. A sob built in her chest and tried to break free. The feeling pissed her off. She was not going to cry like a weakling, like some kind of sniveling coward. She was going to get out of this freaking box and go rescue her partner!

With one final shove, giving it her last ounce of adrenaline, she splintered the box apart. Riley drew a giant gulp of fresh air into her starved lungs. Gasping, she crawled out of the box and landed on her hands and knees. Standing wasn't quite as simple. Thousands of tiny needles held her limbs hostage, and she had no choice but to allow her circulation to return. The instant she felt her legs would hold her, she stood. The pain was still there, but as long as she could run and fight, she was good to go.

She didn't bother to look around the room for weapons. This was her former bedroom and would hold nothing that could help. She raced to the door, opened it, and peeked out. The hallway was empty. Dimitri had not lost his arrogance. He'd never expected that she would dare try to escape the box.

She crept down the hallway. The mansion was huge, and though she had only been allowed inside a few rooms, she had no real problem determining where she should look first. The torture chamber was on the first floor, at the back of the mansion. She had been there numerous times.

Knowing Dimitri as she did, he would need to feel in control. There was nowhere that he felt more superior than in the place where he considered himself master of everything and everyone.

She stopped at the landing and looked down at the giant marble foyer. A guard stood at the bottom, facing the stairway. He would see her the moment she started down the stairs. She needed a diversion.

Turning, she quickly took in her options. Up and down the long, carpeted landing were paintings that were probably supposed to be erotic art but looked violent and evil to her. Looking farther, she spotted a long, narrow table holding a sculpture, the perfect size for what she needed. Creeping down the landing, she lifted the statue. It was heavier than it looked but would do the job.

Returning to the top of the stairway, Riley hefted the statue over her head and threw with all her might. The sculpture landed with a crash behind the guard. The man rushed over to it, and Riley zoomed down the stairway. She made it to the bottom without detection. The guard was now looking up at the stairway, apparently trying to figure out how the statue had fallen. When she was inches away from him, he turned around. His eyes and mouth opened in shock. A naked, bloody woman was one thing he was not expecting to see.

He never knew what hit him. With swift precision, she delivered multiple punches to his face. He managed one swipe at her head, which she was able to duck. She then finished off with a one-two kick, first to his stomach and then his groin. His eyes rolled back in his head, and he collapsed at her feet.

She took precious moments to take off his heavy shirt and confiscate his weapons. Even though it was dangerous to leave him lying out in plain sight, she couldn't spare the time to hide him.

Now to find Justin and get the hell out of here.

***

Dimitri crawled out of the corner, his ears ringing. What had happened? He shook his head to clear it and looked around. When he spotted the man hanging from the ceiling, he roared with fury. He dared to attack him? The stranger would pay dearly!

Stomping to a long, narrow cabinet hanging from the wall, he swung the doors open and viewed his selection. He had started collecting swords a few years ago. He'd wanted to learn how to fence, but taking on an opponent who had the same weapon and possibly better skills than his own wasn't something he enjoyed. He preferred having an advantage in everything. He did, however, love the weapons themselves.

Withdrawing one of his favorites from its sheath, he swung the sword in an intricate, artistic pattern he'd seen in a movie once. Mocking male laughter from the other side of the room stopped him in the middle of his swing. Stumbling, he glared, stupefied, at the man who dared laugh at him. He was hanging from the ceiling without a stitch of clothing, and he dared laugh?

Dimitri stalked over to the insolent man, raised his sword, and slashed a long, bloody slice across the man's broad chest. Instead of screaming, the man never changed his expression. There was still amusement in his eyes. And something else. Something that made Dimitri shiver.

His unease increasing, Dimitri swiped the blade down the man's shoulder and then across his belly. Bloody lines appeared and oozed in streams down his body, dripping to the floor. And still the man continued to stare, his expression unchanged.

"Who are you?" Dimitri bellowed.

Amusement flashed on the man's face. "Your man Ari told me it's good to know the name of the man who's going to kill you. My name is Justin Kelly, and I'm going to rip your dick off and make you eat it. Then I'll use your sword to disembowel you. And if you happen to still be breathing after all that, I might be generous and tear your head from your body."

Dimitri almost stumbled back but caught himself in time. Showing any kind of weakness would be an abomination. He was Dimitri Soukis. He had people like this giant maggot killed all the time.

"You're very arrogant for a man hanging from the ceiling with no weapons but your mouth."

The man said nothing more. Just continued to look at him, almost as if he were bored.

"Not that a weapon would be helpful. You can't even shoot straight. You shot at me and injured one of my men instead. Perhaps I should use your weapon against you. Shoot you straight through your heart."

The taunt had no effect whatsoever. The man, Justin Kelly, never blinked. It was infuriating!

With a loud curse, Dimitri lifted the sword. One hard swipe, and the insolent bastard's head would be rolling on the floor.

"Dimitri!"

He was so surprised, he almost dropped his sword. Turning, he gawked at the vision in front of him. His Jessica, his beautiful girl, was standing before him with an M16 she'd obviously stolen from one of his men. The rifle was almost as large as she was, but she held it with a confidence he found stupefying. She was also wearing a thick, long-sleeved, olive green shirt, the kind his men wore.

Had one of the guards given in to her charms? That was the only explanation he could come up with. One of his men had betrayed him by letting the girl out and, adding insult to injury, had provided her with the shirt from his back and a weapon.

"Jessica, what are you doing? Put the gun down before you hurt someone."

"Drop the sword, Dimitri."

He waved the sword at her for extra emphasis and said in an imperious tone, "You do not call me Dimitri. Do you understand? You know the punishment for such familiarity and rudeness. Put that gun down, take off that ridiculous shirt, and get on your knees. You will beg for forgiveness. Then you will service me to show your remorse."

The man hanging beside him gave a roar of protest and jerked on his chains. Dimitri smiled. That was more like it.

"It's your turn to get on your knees, asshole," Jessica snarled. "You have three seconds to drop your sword before I put a bullet in your brain."

Dimitri shook his head, bewildered. It was like he was in some kind of parallel universe where everything was the opposite of normal. This was surely a nightmare that he would wake from soon. His Jessica, his pretty, little slave, who hadn't an ounce of gumption or bravery in her body, was ordering him about. She was like some kind of parody of a macho woman. It was unattractive and disgustingly unfeminine.

His eyes narrowed as he noticed something else. Her gaze kept skittering over to the man hanging from the ceiling. The anxious look she was giving him told Dimitri that this man meant something to her. The very idea that she had given her affections to someone besides him steeled his resolve.

Dimitri nodded. "Very well. If you insist. I'll lower my weapon if you lower yours."

"Think again, shithead," Jessica snarled. "I'll put sixteen holes in your body before you can take another breath. Now drop the damn sword!"

She would pay for every single insult she had uttered today. This he swore. Taking a bold chance, Dimitri moved in front of the hanging man. If she shot him, the bullets were powerful enough to go through him and into the man behind him. Feeling quite smug, Dimitri swung the sword up, bringing the blade against the man's thick neck, right over his artery. And then he smiled.

"You twisted piece of garbage, I *will* kill you," Jessica growled.

"Perhaps, but if you shoot me, you'll kill him, too. Now drop the gun and do as you're told." He gave a jerk of his head. She would recognize the gesture. It was a command to go to her knees in supplication.

When she hesitated, he pressed the sword deeper into the man's neck. "Do it now, or he bleeds out in seconds."

Justin saw the indecision in Riley's eyes. She was considering doing what the asshole ordered. "No, Ingram. Don't do it."

Dimitri jerked at Justin's words, and the sword cut into his skin. Any deeper, and the dirtbag would get his wish to see him bleed to death. But damned if he'd let Riley subjugate herself to this monster to save him.

"Do it now, Jessica. I'm not going to tell you again."

She placed the rifle on the floor.

"Now take off that ridiculous garment and get on your knees."

She went to her knees but didn't take off the shirt. And because he knew his partner, knew what made her tick and how she thought, Justin knew Riley had a backup plan.

"Crawl to me, Jessica, and I might consider allowing him to live. I've never had a male slave before. It might be fun."

Justin snorted. "And you won't ever have one, dirtwad."

"Your insults are becoming tiresome."

Justin kept his gaze on his partner. She had something up her sleeve. As she crawled toward them, he watched the way she moved and wanted to shout his triumph. Yeah, she did indeed have something up her sleeve.

She stopped about a foot away from Dimitri and kept her head bowed.

"Very good. I'm glad you're finally minding your manners. Now sit up and take that hideous shirt off."

She sat back on her heels and started slowly sliding the shirt off, the left sleeve first.

Dimitri was so sure he had her cowed that he barely jerked in reaction when the shirt fell free of her right hand and she quickly shifted up on her knees, positioning her own blade mere centimeters from his crotch.

"Drop the sword, Dimitri. Now!"

The sword clattered to the floor.

"Now hand me the key to the cuffs."

Still arrogant, even with a knife at his groin, Dimitri snapped, "This is unacceptable and inexcusable behavior, Jessica. You will be punished severely."

"Don't test me, asshole." She pressed the blade harder against him. "I go any deeper and your tiny dick gets sliced off. Give me a reason, bastard, because there's nothing I'd like better."

He glared down at her for another second and then said, "Very well."

His hand slid into his pocket.

She and Justin saw the gun at the same time.

As if choreographed, Justin wrapped his legs around Dimitri's neck in the same instance that Riley sprang up and plunged the knife deep into Dimitri's gut.

Riley backed away, and Justin loosened his legs. Like a broken marionette, Dimitri collapsed to the floor, his eyes wide with shocked horror.

"Your flare for drama never fails to impress me, Ingram."

She didn't react to his words. Just stared down at the lifeless man.

"Ingram. Look at me."

She raised her head. The expression on her face was a mixture of shock, triumph, and grief.

He wanted to hold her, tell her how proud he was of her. He also wanted to shake her until her teeth rattled. Since he was still hanging from the damn ceiling, all he could do was say, "How about letting me down from here?"

Riley pulled the keys from Dimitri's pocket. Grabbing a chair, she stood on it so she could unlock the cuffs around Justin's wrists. He noted she didn't meet his eyes. He figured she was in shock, and he wanted to do nothing more than hold her, reassure both of them that she was alive.

The instant he was loose, Justin bent down and checked Dimitri for a pulse. "He's dead. I wish I'd been the one to do the deed, but if anyone had the right, it was yours."

"I didn't want him to die." Her voice was dull, unemotional as she continued to stare down at the body of her abuser.

"Why?"

"He turned me into so many things. I didn't want him to make me a killer, too."

Her answer didn't surprise him, but it did break his heart. And it pissed him off.

"Bullshit, Ingram. A killer has a choice. You didn't. Do you doubt he would have shot you or me if given the chance?"

"No, I know he would have. I saw it in his eyes. He would have killed both of us."

"And if this had been any other op, would you have made a different decision?"

"No."

"Remember that. It was either him or us. You made the only choice you could have."

"You're right."

As if she were coming out of a trance, she shook her head swiftly and went into action. Grabbing the shirt she'd taken off, she held it out to him. "This probably fits you better than it does me. There are clothes in the bedroom closet I can wear."

No way in hell was she going to wear anything that piece of shit had bought for her. "You wear the shirt. I'll find something else."

Without a word, she shrugged into the shirt, and then her eyes swept over him. "We need to get you to a doctor."

"The cuts aren't deep." He nodded at the blood on her hands and knees. "How'd you get so bloody?"

A fleeting look of pain entered her haunted eyes. "It doesn't matter."

"Yes, it does, Ingram."

"I broke out of the box."

He closed his eyes briefly. "I'm sorry. I should have—"

306 | CHRISTY REECE

Holding up a bloody hand, she backed away from him, her head shaking in denial. "Don't you dare apologize to me. I'm the one who brought us here. I'm responsible for all of this."

He moved toward her, held out his hand. "Come here."

"No. He's got more guards. We need to get out of here."

"And we will. But right now, we both need this more."

She took his hand, allowing him to draw her into his arms. Yeah, they were both bloody. He was naked, she was barely clothed. And they had a dead maniac lying only a few feet away. But he couldn't think of anything more important than this right now.

She pressed her head against his chest. "I was so frightened. I was prepared to deal with him on my own. Putting you in danger..." She shook her head. "I'm so very sorry."

"I'm not. And you need to start putting the guilt where it belongs."

"You're right."

She pulled out of his arms and looked up at him, his blood now on her face. Using the shirt she wore, he swiped at it, making it look worse. "We're both a mess."

The smile she tried for barely lifted her lips, didn't reach her eyes. "Let's get this over with and get out of here."

"We make a good team, Ingram."

"Yes, we did."

Before it registered with him that she had used past tense, the door burst open. McCall, along with Fox and Thorne, rushed inside.

McCall skidded to a halt. "You guys okay?"

"Yeah," Justin said. He looked down at his bloody, naked self. "Anybody bring an extra pair of underwear?"

Fox grinned. "I did."

Justin barked out a laugh. "Thanks. I'll pass."

McCall nodded at the body on the floor. "He dead?"

"Yes," Justin answered.

"Well, hell," Thorne drawled. "Didn't you guys leave us anything to do?"

"There are probably a dozen guards or more who need their asses kicked."

"Not anymore," Fox said. "We had a little help from some new friends."

McCall's gaze went from Riley's to Justin's, his eyes full of questions. He had obviously picked up on the tension, said only, "Fox, see if you can find Kelly and Ingram some clothes. Thorne, see to their injuries and then get them on the plane."

"Where are you going?" Justin asked.

Giving a grim smile, McCall muttered as he walked away, "To play politics."

***

An hour later, they were sitting on the LCR jet, waiting for Noah to arrive. Riley had been cleaned up and bandaged, none the worse for wear. A doctor had to be called for Justin, as he'd needed more than two dozen stitches. Aidan had offered to do the deed, but laughingly admitted his sewing skills were a little rusty.

Even though Justin had acted like every stitch the doctor made was no big deal, Riley had winced in shared pain. It felt like the needle was going through her own skin. This was all her fault. She had put her own selfish needs above the safety of others. If there was one concrete rule at LCR, it was that revenge had no place in their work. Beyond their goal of rescuing, they always sought justice. However, it could never get in the way of their real purpose. For the first time in her career, she had put herself before others.

Anna sat down beside her and put her head on Riley's shoulder for a quick hug. "You're sure you're okay? You look kind of shell-shocked."

"I'm fine." She considered trying for a smile but was too tired to make the effort. "Just exhausted. Can't believe it's over. The bastard is really dead."

"How do you feel about that?"

How did she feel? Beneath the guilt she felt for almost getting her partner killed as well as the exhaustion, she recognized an immense relief. An evil had been eliminated. She couldn't say she was happy that she had ended a life but neither did she feel guilt. Justin was right. Dimitri had given her no choice.

"Relieved. Angry." She searched through her emotions, shrugged, and said, "Tired."

"You've been through a lot these past few weeks."

"I'll be fine. Just need some sleep."

"Why don't you and Justin lie down in the bedroom? When Noah arrives, I'll let you know."

Riley shifted her gaze to Justin, and then her eyes skittered away when he looked at her. "I'm fine here. Besides, I doubt that Justin wants to be near me right now."

"Why would you think that?"

"He's angry with me. Rightfully so."

"Hmm. Doesn't seem angry to me. In fact, he looks pretty doggone happy."

"If he isn't angry, he should be. I put his life in jeopardy."

"He's a big boy," Anna said dryly. "I think Justin can make his own decisions."

"But I'm responsible for—"

She cut off when Noah walked onto the plane. The grim set to his mouth and his weary, bloodshot eyes told her he'd had a rough few hours. "Let's get the hell out of here."

"How'd it go?" Justin asked.

"The official news story is Dimitri Soukis's estate was attacked. His security guards were disabled, and Soukis was abducted. His body was discovered in a ravine ten miles from his mansion. A former business rival, already in prison, apparently ordered the hit."

"Sounds quite slick," Justin said. "Who came up with the story?"

"As the saying goes, politics make for strange bedfellows. President Kopsas and his rival, Aletha Villas, arrived at this together. I don't know what promises were made between them. I don't want to know. But as far as they're concerned, LCR was never even here."

Riley received the information with immense relief. At least her screw-up wouldn't cause Noah or LCR any problems. And now she felt hollow, empty. A huge chapter in her life had ended. As she looked around at the faces of the people she worked with and admired, she accepted that another chapter needed to close as well.

CHAPTER THIRTY-THREE

LCR Headquarters
Alexandria, Virginia

Riley sat across from Noah. She figured he'd been waiting for her to rest and recover before calling her in. She had decided to save him the trouble and came in on her own. If there was one thing she'd learned in her life, being proactive saved not only time but also heartache.

"It's only been a day. You're sure you're fully recovered?" Noah asked.

"Yes. Feeling fine."

His dark eyes searched hers, concern in their depths.

"I was going to wait until both you and Kelly recovered before we did an official debrief. Especially since things are still happening."

She gave a nod of acknowledgment. Arrests were still being made throughout the country. Larson and his people were still being questioned. The man had been in the human-trafficking business for decades. There were victims going back twenty years or more. It would take the authorities months, if not years, to uncover the garbage that had been William Larson aka Lloyd King's life.

"Lorraine King is being transferred to a jail in Anaheim tomorrow."

Noah left it at that. Riley knew he wouldn't ask her if she would go see Lorraine. He would leave that up to her. He had been kind enough to rush through DNA testing. Confirming that the woman had been her birth mother had been vital for her to know. Once the results came, she accepted it as fact. What more could she do?

She had thought about and rejected going to see the woman who had given her life and then betrayed her, to ask her why she had done something so heinous. Then she had decided it didn't matter. Whatever the woman's reason, it would never be enough. There could be no justification for her actions, so what was the point in hearing what she had to say?

"Larson is singing like the proverbial bird. When this is over, it's going to bring families together again and closure to those looking for answers."

He seemed to expect an answer, so she gave him one. "Good."

"Really? You don't look too happy about it. I've seen you get more satisfaction out of a practice session with a dummy than you're exhibiting right now." He waited a beat and then added, "It was a successful mission, Ingram."

"We both know it wasn't perfect."

"No mission is. But when we save lives, then we damn well call it successful."

No longer able to sit here and listen to his praise, she blurted out, "I screwed up."

"How so?"

She stared at him as if he'd lost his mind. "You know how, Noah. I put my need for revenge over the safety of my team.

Over the safety of my partner. It was only by sheer luck that Justin wasn't killed."

"Luck? Divine intervention maybe. I'm not a big believer in luck. The reason you and Kelly weren't killed was because you're both trained professionals."

"A trained professional who put her own self-interest ahead of her team."

"Ingram, if you're looking for censure, you've come to the wrong person. There's not a person on this earth who would blame you for wanting to punish the man who repeatedly brutalized you for three years."

"Maybe not, but I should have waited."

"Waited for what?"

"To see if Larson would talk. Or his bodyguards."

"You think this would have had a better outcome?"

"I don't know."

"We do what we can. Using our best judgment. That's what you did."

"Is it?"

"Does the fact that you had to take Dimitri out bother you?"

She'd thought long and hard about this last night. "It bothers me, but not in the way you might think. I didn't have a choice. Dimitri would have killed both Justin and me if I hadn't taken him down.

"If this had been any other op, I would have made the same decision. Dimitri is dead because of his actions, not because of anything I did wrong."

"I'm glad you understand that." His eyes narrowing, he said, "So what is this meeting really about, Ingram?"

She took a breath, expelled it, and said, "I'm resigning my position as an LCR Elite operative. Effective immediately."

***

Justin pounded on the door, fury and worry creating a morass of emotions. For the last three days, he'd been trying to get her to answer her door or her phone. She had told him she needed time to herself. He had agreed to that at first, sure that she just needed to sort out some things. Instead, what did she do? She quit her freaking job. And did she bother to tell him? Hell no. McCall was the one who'd given him the news.

"Ingram, I know you're in there. Now open the damn door before I knock it down and your neighbors call the police."

Nothing but silence.

He raised his hand, about to pound again, when a quivery voice called out, "Are you looking for Riley?"

Turning, he saw a weathered-faced elderly man with a head full of white and gray hair standing at the door of an apartment down the hallway.

"Yes. Do you know Riley?"

"I do. Not well, though. She's a little shy, but she picks up my medicine from the pharmacy sometimes and feeds my cat when I'm visiting my daughter. She's a good girl."

"Yes, she is. Have you seen her lately?"

"She came by yesterday evening. Wanted to know if I needed anything. Said she was going away awhile and—"

His heart stuttering, he barked, "Away? Where?"

Thankfully, the old man didn't seem to take exception to Justin's lack of diplomacy. "She wouldn't say. Just that she needed to go away. When I asked her how long she would be gone, she said she wasn't sure."

Justin wanted to roar with anger and frustration. Where would she have gone? And why had she left? Why hadn't she talked to him since they'd gotten back? Why had she resigned from LCR? What the hell was going on?

"She looked kind of peaked to me."

"How do you mean?"

"She had shadows under her eyes, and she was pale and sickly looking. I asked if she was okay. She said eventually she would be." He gave Justin a stern look. "Did you break her heart, young man?"

"No, sir."

"Did she break yours?"

Justin didn't answer. He thanked the man for the information and walked away, the answer to that question reverberating through his brain. Had Riley broken his heart? Yeah, he thought she might just have.

***

Aidan hobbled over to the sofa and collapsed. Propping his leg on the stack of pillows, he winced with more aggravation than real pain. He was in a piss-poor mood. He had dodged bullets, survived knife fights, lived through a plane crash, plus a brief imprisonment when he was in the military. But today, he'd almost lost his life because he wasn't paying attention. If his partner hadn't pulled him out of the way of a speeding car at the last second, he'd be dealing with something a hell of a lot worse than a broken leg. Sabrina had literally saved his life.

Now he was out of commission for at least a month, leaving McCall even more shorthanded. Ingram had up and resigned. With both their partners gone, Fox and Kelly would team up for the next few weeks. Aidan didn't like it. When things went out of whack, the universe responded in kind. He considered himself a realist more than a pessimist. He didn't automatically expect the worst, but he did his dead level best not to mess with what worked. When shit changed, other shit didn't work right. That was just life.

He had a gnawing feeling in his gut that this was just the beginning of shit not working right.

The cellphone he'd dropped on the coffee table in front of him buzzed. He glared at the thing. He didn't want to talk to anyone but was too responsible not to check the display in case he was needed. Swallowing a groan as the movement shifted his leg on the pillow, he grabbed the phone and then sat back. He frowned at the unfamiliar number but answered anyway. "Yeah?"

"Aidan?"

He stiffened in denial. The soft, husky, female voice was one he recognized immediately. And the last one he wanted to hear. Dammit, why was she calling?

"Aidan, are you there?"

"I'm here. What do you want?" He winced the moment the words were out of his mouth. Why did he have to be such an asshole with her?

Her response was a small, humorless laugh. "Your phone skills aren't any better than your people skills."

"How can I help you, Anna?"

Her voice went softer. "I heard about your injury. Are you okay?"

Hell on wheels. Why'd she have to be so nice? Especially when he was such a jerk to her?

"I'm fine. Just a minor inconvenience."

"That's good, then."

When she didn't say anything else, he asked, "Was that all you wanted?"

"What? Um. No. I…uh."

"Spit it out, Bradford. You don't usually have trouble telling me what's on your mind."

"Fine," she snapped. "I was just trying to be sensitive since I'm sure you're in pain."

"The only pain I'm experiencing is because of this conversation."

She went silent again, and he figured she'd just hang up on him. It was nothing less than he deserved.

Her voice now icy cold, she said, "If I didn't need your help, I wouldn't be calling you. Believe me, I know you despise me, so I'll try to make this quick."

Jerking upright, he barked out, "What's wrong? Are you in trouble?"

"No, I'm not in any trouble. I…" She took an audible breath and gushed out, "I want to arrange a meeting between Riley and Justin."

"What kind of meeting?"

"They're both miserable."

"You've seen Ingram?"

"Yes. She's totally devastated."

"From my understanding, it was her decision to leave. McCall didn't fire her."

"I'm not just talking about that. I'm talking about her relationship with Justin."

Oh hellfire no. He did not get involved in other people's personal lives. Having done a bang-up job on his own, he sure as shit didn't interfere with anyone else's life. Especially a friend's.

"Sorry, sugar. You're barking up the wrong tree. If Ingram and Kelly are having difficulties, they'll have to work it out themselves."

"They can't. Not while they're apart. I just want to bring them to the same place and let it go from there. If they decide to leave each other after that, it's up to them."

Aidan was shaking his head. Lord save him from romantic fools. Before he could tell her no again and end this ridiculous discussion, she dropped a bombshell.

"If you do this for me, Aidan, I promise to leave you alone."

"What do you mean you'll leave me alone?"

"You'll never have to see me again. If Noah asks me to work on an LCR case you're attached to, I'll make sure to meet with him only when I know you won't be there. You never have to suffer my presence again."

Shit. He really had convinced her he didn't like her.

"Listen, Anna. That's not why—"

"It doesn't matter, Aidan. If you'll just help me with this, I'll get out of your life for good. Promise."

Even though he was sorry he had damaged her feelings, he couldn't help but ask, "What if I don't agree to do this? What would you do?"

"Well, Noah keeps asking me if I'd like to work full time for LCR. He believes I'd make a good operative. Maybe at some point I could work for LCR Elite. We could work together on ops. We'd—"

"I'll do it." The thought of the beautiful, innocent Anna Bradford in the trenches of LCR, exposed to the underbelly of the scum they dealt with on a daily basis was as disgusting a thought as he'd ever had.

"Thank you."

If she wondered about his quick agreement, she didn't say. He was sure she believed it was because he couldn't stand to be around her.

"How do you propose we do this? Justin Kelly isn't exactly an easy man to fool. And Ingram is no pushover either."

"I thought I'd arrange a vacation for Riley. Tell her she needs to get away, get some sun. You could tell Justin the same thing."

That sounded about as easy to him as dismantling an M24 sniper rifle with his toes. Justin Kelly would see through the ruse in seconds. But it was workable.

"Do you have a place in mind?"

"No, not yet. I wanted to get your agreement first."

"Let me get the place. My folks have a house in the Caribbean. No one uses it much anymore."

"Oh, that would be wonderful. How do—"

"I'll send you the details."

"Thank you, Aidan. I'll just…um—" She stopped abruptly, and the following silence was awkward.

"I'll be in touch once I set it up."

"Okay."

"And Anna?"

"Yes?"

Knowing he shouldn't, but unable to allow her to believe he despised her, he said, "I don't hate being around you."

He heard a hitch of breath and then, "But why—"

He ended the call before he could say any other stupid, nonsensical, useless words. Having her believe he hated her would have been so much wiser and more convenient. She didn't need to know that his feelings for her had nothing to do with hate. It was safer for both of them if it stayed that way.

CHAPTER THIRTY-FOUR

The Caribbean

The speedboat puttered to the beach and then bumped gently against the small dock. The boat driver turned around and grinned at her. "We are here."

For some reason, Riley wanted to laugh. And how weird was that? Riley Ingram was not the laughing sort. Especially not lately.

"Thank you, Nico."

"Are you sure you do not want me to help you with your luggage?"

"No. I only have this one bag, and it's not heavy."

"I will be back for you one week from today. If you need anything before then, please do not hesitate to send word through the housekeeper."

"I'll do that." And even though she had been told not to do so, Riley dug into the pocket of her jeans and pulled out several bills. "Please. Take this. And thank you for your help."

His grin almost as bright as the sun, he accepted her gift with a wink. "We will keep this between us. Yes?"

"Yes, we will."

She grabbed her duffle bag and stepped onto the pier. Nico backed the boat away, gave her a final salute, and then sped away. Riley waited until he was several yards away before she turned around and took in her surroundings. What a beautiful, magical-looking place.

When Anna had told her about the small island with only one house in the middle of the Caribbean, she had thought it sounded like heaven on earth. Since she had left LCR, she had been in limbo. She had visited briefly with Anna and then had traveled to various cities, wondering where she could go and what she could do. She felt so lost and unfocused.

And in the back of her mind, there was the constant drone of her conscience reminding her how very badly she had treated Justin. Her partner deserved so much better. And Justin Kelly hadn't just been her partner. He'd also been her friend, her lover. The one man who understood her better than anyone else. She had treated him as if he didn't matter to her at all.

She knew he would never forgive her. She couldn't blame him. If anyone had done the same to her, treated her so poorly, she was sure she would feel the same way.

Stepping onto the beach, she took a moment to take everything in. This was no doubt paradise. A half mile of white sandy beach, palm trees swaying gently in the wind. Interspersed between the vivid green of bushes and trees was a profusion of **bougainvillea**, orchids, and hibiscus blooming with wild abandon. The house was a glorious two-story colonial with a wraparound porch and lots of windows. Oh yes. Lots and lots of windows.

Something inside her settled, a feeling of rightness she hadn't experienced since before she had confronted Dimitri. She would stay here and figure out who Riley Ingram was and how she fit in this world. And then she would return home, ask Justin for forgiveness, and see if he still wanted her in his life.

She just prayed she wouldn't be too late.

Justin had seen her get off the boat. He'd been here for a few hours, trying to figure out if this was a good idea or not, and knowing that even if it wasn't, he wouldn't leave here without confronting her.

When Thorne had told him about Anna's plan, his first reaction had been an absolute no. If Riley didn't want to see him or be with him, he sure as hell wasn't going to trick her. Then he'd gotten his head on straight and thought about things. About all that they had shared. All that they'd been through.

Riley was hurting. He had no doubt about that. And it wasn't in her nature to hurt anyone she cared about. So with those two things firmly in his mind, he realized he had to see this through. Because if there was one thing he knew for sure, if he could prevent Riley hurting, then he was damn well going to do everything within his power to do just that. Bottom line, he loved her.

He watched as she came toward the house. She was thinner, and the set of her shoulders told him she had a huge weight of worry holding her down. He hoped she would let him help her deal with whatever was hurting her.

Turning, he headed to the back of the house. The veranda was in the shade, and he'd already mixed up a pitcher of lemonade. She would eventually come out here to explore, and he would be waiting. If she was angry for being tricked and wanted to leave, well, that would be just too damn bad. The boat wouldn't return for a week. He would use those days to convince her that she couldn't live without him. Because he sure as hell didn't want to live without her.

The décor was understated elegance, pretty but without a hint of formality or pretension. The colors ranged from pale yellow to bold splashes of reds and blues. It was restful without being boring. Riley felt instantly at home. Deciding to wait until later to unpack, she dropped her bag on the floor and went exploring.

It was an open floor plan with so much natural light that Riley felt as though she were outside. Everywhere she went, from the modern kitchen to the media room to the three spacious bedrooms, she fell in love with what she saw. How on earth anyone could stand to leave this place was beyond her.

As she headed back down the stairs, an overwhelming feeling of sadness washed through her. This was a place for a family or a honeymooning couple. A lone woman with more baggage in her head than she'd brought with her on vacation didn't belong here. Still, she would use this time as promised and try to get her head on straight.

Wanting to see what she imagined was going to be a spectacular veranda and backyard, Riley pushed the glass door open and stepped out. And there he stood.

"Hello, Ingram."

She had the thought that if he'd called her by her first name, she would have run. Where to, she didn't know. She couldn't think beyond the fact that Justin was here, in front of her. All she had to do was reach out, and her fingers would be on him. She could touch him the way she'd dreamed of a thousand times since the last time she saw him.

"I guess it's pointless to ask who set this up."

She was proud of herself. Her voice didn't waver or quiver. She was matter-of-fact. Calm. Rational. Odd, but inside she was anything but. Emotions like fireworks were exploding inside her. She wanted to run. To stay. To leap into his arms and beg for his forgiveness. To tell him to leave, that they had nothing to say to each other. That she knew she had screwed up beyond all hope and didn't deserve an ounce of forgiveness.

Instead, she stood there. Waiting. Hoping.

There were a thousand things Justin wanted to say to her. None of them seemed the right thing, though. She wore that wary, closed expression he knew all too well. At one time he'd thought it was because she was emotionless and cold. Then he'd learned it was a shield. A protection. Because beneath that façade were the emotions and feelings of a warm, gentle, compassionate soul. Riley had been so hurt, so damaged, that her only way to survive was to shut herself off from people, feelings. Things that could hurt her.

"Are you angry?"

She shook her head. "I should have guessed Anna would do something like this. She's been urging me to call you. Talk to you."

"I wish you had."

She shook her head again. "I didn't know what to say. How to say it."

The sadness in her midnight blue eyes tore at him. It lightened his heart a little to see she no longer wore colored lenses. She had no reason to hide herself anymore. But she was still hurting and dammit he wanted to fix it.

Resisting the urge to go to her, hold her, he turned to the table and chairs behind him. "Let's sit down. Want some lemonade?"

She sat down, watched in solemn silence as he poured two glasses of lemonade and handed her one. After taking a long swallow, she placed the glass on the table and looked around. "It's beautiful here." She frowned. "Anna told me this island belongs to a friend of hers. She never said who, though."

"I think it belongs to someone in Thorne's family."

She nodded, seemingly out of ideas on small talk.

"Why did you run away?"

"I thought it was the right thing to do."

"Tell me why."

Her eyes took on a distant look, and she spoke in a slow, reflective tone. "Do you know why I wanted to work for LCR? For Noah?"

"To save lives. Rescue victims. Prevent what happened to you from happening to someone else."

"Those reasons came later. Once I realized I could make a difference, my goals…" She frowned. "They didn't change, really. I guess they developed, expanded."

"Then why?"

She faced him then, and he thought it might be the bravest thing he'd ever seen her do. The longing in her eyes sliced into his heart.

"I wanted to see if I could be worth something. Be someone. I had been Lorraine and Lloyd's good, obedient daughter. Trained to do as I was told. Never questioning. Never being anyone other than what they wanted to create. Then I became Dimitri's trained pet. After that?" She lifted her shoulder in a small shrug. "Then I was nothing. Just an empty shell. I didn't know who or what I was because I had no one to tell me what I should be. I was taking up space without any redeeming attributes."

"That may be how you felt, but that's not who you were. The abuse you suffered—"

"Yes, I know. I was taught to feel worthless and helpless, to have no mind or will of my own. That was how they controlled me.

"But don't you see? Just because I realized that was wrong thinking, that no one should be treated that way, didn't mean that I was suddenly filled with self-worth, that my life had meaning.

I had to prove to myself that I was something besides a victim. That I was actually somebody.

"Noah didn't believe I'd make it as an operative. He never said those words, but I knew what he thought. But you know what I absolutely loved?" Her voice thickened. "He gave me a chance. No one had ever expected anything of me before, other than blind obedience. Noah gave me a chance to prove myself. To be something.

"That, more than anything, made me determined to succeed."

"And you succeeded beyond anyone's expectations."

"Yes, I did. LCR gave me purpose. I finally had a reason to get up in the morning. I was needed. Not only needed, I was damn good at what I did. I made a difference."

"So why did you quit?"

She gave him an *are you kidding me?* look. "How could I not? I almost got you killed. Almost ruined the entire op. I put myself above others. The victims became secondary to my need for revenge."

"No one begrudged you that. I sure as hell didn't."

"You were furious with me. And you had every right to be."

"I was furious with the situation, not you. Though, when you kept saying it was your fight, like I wasn't personally involved, too, that pissed me off. Believe me, it was very personal to me. I wanted to rip Dimitri's head off for what he did to you. I understood why you felt you had to do it."

"It was wrong of me."

"It was human."

"But I—"

"What do you want me to say? That it was a bone-headed thing to do? Okay, yeah. It was. And you know what? If I were in the same position, I probably would've done the same thing."

"No, you wouldn't. You're too noble. Too—"

Justin gave a disgusted snort. "Bullshit, Ingram. Where'd you get the idea that I'm anything but human just like you? I'm fallible. Imperfect."

She gave a little smile. "I never said you were perfect."

"Good. Perfect is not only boring, it's impossible. Besides, that's the thing about families, Ingram. You don't have to be perfect. They love you just the way you are."

A glowing warmth suffused her entire body. LCR was her family. And she had left them as if they didn't matter, when the truth was, they meant the world to her.

Swallowing hard, she looked away from him again, chewed on her lip. "So where do we go from here? You and I?"

"What do you want?"

"I want…" She shook her head, swallowed hard. "I want—"

"Hell," Justin whispered. Unable to have her so close and not touch her, he held out his hand. "Come here."

"What?"

"I can't sit here any longer and not hold you. Come here. Please, sweetheart?"

She stood and allowed him to pull her down onto his lap. He wrapped his arms around her and just held her for a few seconds. Riley closed her eyes, absorbing his warmth, his strength. She never thought she'd be this close to him again.

"Tell me what you want, Riley."

What did she want? She had been so focused on what she needed to do, what she should do, she had rarely given thought to what she wanted. But now, now she knew there was something she wanted more than anything.

She buried her face against his neck. "You. Oh please, Justin, I want you so very much."

He squeezed her tighter, dropped a kiss on her head. "Good, baby," he said, his voice a husky whisper. "Because I'm not going anywhere."

Happiness like she'd never believed possible flooded through her. He still wanted her, despite all the stupid things she'd done.

"What else do you want?"

"I know Noah is disappointed in me, but I want to work for LCR again. If he'll let me."

"McCall knew I was coming here. Told me to tell you your resignation was never accepted."

"And we'll still be partners?"

"That's never going to change."

"Justin?"

"Yeah?"

She opened her eyes, then sat up in his lap. This was too important to cower or hide from. Holding his gaze with hers, she said the words she'd never said to anyone before. "I love you."

With a groan, he took her mouth with his, the kiss sweet, gentle. And then it became something else as his lips moved over hers. Riley opened her mouth, and his tongue delved inside, tangling with hers. Within seconds, they were panting, caressing each other as if they'd never let the other go.

Pulling away slightly, he looked down at her. "I love you, too, Riley Ingram. So damn much."

She reached up, trapped his mouth with hers, playing, wanting, needing.

They parted again, both breathless and needy.

"You asked what I wanted. Tell me what you want." She scooted around on his lap, straddling him. "What do you, Justin Kelly, want?"

A beautiful smile curved his mouth, and she knew from the way he answered that he'd given this a lot of thought. "I want to have fun with you. Take you places you've never been. Hear you laugh. I want to dance with you. Make love to you till we can barely move or speak from exhaustion. I want to see happiness in your eyes. A smile on your luscious mouth. I want to hear you giggle at a corny joke. See you roll your eyes at the ridiculous things in life. I want to see you happy."

"What if I don't know how to be happy?"

"Baby, you've got so much love and goodness stored up inside you. There's no doubt in my mind that you can be happy."

"Teach me?"

He spoke against her lips. "We'll teach each other." And then he swept her away on a tidal wave of love and acceptance that she'd never believed was possible.

Riley Ingram, the girl who had never belonged to anyone, had finally found her way home.

Thank you for reading Running Scared, An LCR Elite Novel

If you enjoyed RUNNING SCARED, please consider rating the book at the online retailer of your choice. Your ratings and reviews help other readers find new favorites, and of course, there is no better or more appreciated support for an author than word of mouth recommendations from happy readers. Thanks again for reading my books!

OTHER BOOKS BY CHRISTY REECE

LCR Elite Series

Running On Empty, An LCR Elite Novel

Chance Encounter, An LCR Elite Novel

Last Chance Rescue Series

Rescue Me, A Last Chance Rescue Novel

Return To Me, A Last Chance Rescue Novel

Run To Me, A Last Chance Rescue Novel

No Chance, A Last Chance Rescue Novel

Second Chance, A Last Chance Rescue Novel

Last Chance, A Last Chance Rescue Novel

Sweet Justice, A Last Chance Rescue Novel

Sweet Revenge, A Last Chance Rescue Novel

Sweet Reward, A Last Chance Rescue Novel

Chances Are, A Last Chance Rescue Novel

Grey Justice Series

Nothing To Lose, A Grey Justice Novel

Whatever It Takes, A Grey Justice Novel

Wildefire Series
Writing as Ella Grace

Midnight Secrets, A Wildefire Novel

Midnight Lies, A Wildefire Novel

Midnight Shadows, A Wildefire Novel

ACKNOWLEDGEMENTS

Special thanks to the following people for helping make this book possible:

My husband, for his love, support, numerous moments of comic relief, and respecting my chocolate stash.

Joyce Lamb, for her copyediting, fabulous advice, and for helping to make Riley and Justin's story shine.

Marie Force's eBook Formatting Fairies, who always answers my endless questions with endless patience.

Tricia Schmitt (Pickyme) for her awesomely beautiful cover art.

The Reece's Readers Facebook street team, for all your support and encouragement.

Anne Woodall, my first reader, who always goes above and beyond, and then goes the extra mile, too. You're awesome!

My beta readers, for reading so quickly, all the catches you guys made, and your great advice.

Linda Clarkson, proofreader extraordinaire, who did an amazing job, in an unbelievably tight timeframe. So appreciate your eagle eye, Linda!

And to all my readers, a very special thank you! Without you, this book and all the others, past and future, would not be possible.

About the Author

Christy Reece is the award winning and New York Times Best-selling author of dark romantic suspense. She lives in Alabama with her husband, three precocious canines, two incredibly spoiled cats, one very shy turtle, and a super cute flying squirrel.

Christy also writes steamy, southern suspense under the pen name Ella Grace.

Praise for Christy Reece Novels

"The type of book you will pick up and NEVER want to put down again." Coffee Time Romance and More

"Romantic suspense has a major new star!" *Romantic Times Magazine*

"Sizzling romance and fraught suspense fill the pages as the novel races toward its intensely riveting conclusion." *Publishers Weekly, Starred Review*

Have you met Grey Justice?

Justice isn't always swift or fair and only those who have felt the excruciating pain of denied justice can truly understand its bitter taste. But justice delayed doesn't have to be justice denied. Enter the Grey Justice Group, ordinary citizens swept up in extraordinary circumstances. Led by billionaire philanthropist, Grey Justice, this small group of operatives gain justice for victims who have been let down by the law.

Turn the page for excerpts from the first two books in Christy Reece's Grey Justice series, **NOTHING TO LOSE** and **WHATEVER IT TAKES**.

Nothing To Lose
A Grey Justice Novel

Choices Are Easy When You Have Nothing Left To Lose

Kennedy O'Connell had all the happiness she'd ever dreamed—until someone stole it away. Now on the run for her life, she has a choice to make—disappear forever or make those responsible pay. Her choice is easy.

Two men want to help her, each with their own agenda.

Detective Nick Gallagher is accustomed to pursuing killers within the law. Targeted for death, his life turned inside out, Nick vows to bring down those responsible, no matter the cost. But the beautiful and innocent Kennedy O'Connell brings out every protective instinct. Putting aside his own need for vengeance, he'll do whatever is necessary to keep her safe and help her achieve her goals.

Billionaire philanthropist Grey Justice has a mission, too. Dubbed the 'White Knight' of those in need of a champion, few people are aware of his dark side. Having seen and experienced injustice—Grey knows its bitter taste. Gaining justice for those who have been wronged is a small price to pay for a man's humanity.

With the help of a surprising accomplice, the three embark on a dangerous game of cat and mouse. The stage is set, the players are ready…the game is on. But someone is playing with another set of rules and survivors are not an option.

CHAPTER ONE

Houston, Texas

Kennedy O'Connell stepped back to admire her work and released a contented sigh. *Yes.* Even though she'd painted only a quarter of a wall with one coat, she was almost sure this color was the right one.

"Oh holy hell, you changed your mind again."

Grinning, she glanced over her shoulder at her husband. "Eighth time's the charm."

His arms wrapped around her and pulled her against his hard body. As he nuzzled her neck, she could feel his smile against her skin. Kennedy knew if she looked at his face, his eyes would be dancing with good humor. Thomas O'Connell was a patient, even-keeled man, but her indecisiveness about the color for the nursery had put him to the test.

Snuggling back into his arms, she asked, "So do you like this color better than the last one?"

Without raising his head, Thomas growled, "It's perfect."

She snorted softly. "That's what you said about the first seven."

"That's because they were perfect, too. Anything you pick is going to look great."

She appreciated his faith in her. Having grown up in various foster homes, her priorities had been getting enough food to fill her belly and staying out of trouble. Surviving her childhood hadn't involved learning about colors, textures, and fabrics.

When she and Thomas had married, almost everything she owned was secondhand and ragged. Since then, she'd been learning little by little, mostly by experimenting, what she liked. She had delighted in setting up their home, creating a beautiful environment she and Thomas could enjoy together. Now that their first child was on the way, she wanted everything to be just right, so she had taken experimentation to a whole new level.

She was on winter break from her first year of law school. In her spare time, she freelanced as a researcher for several law firms. She had considered taking on some jobs to earn a little extra money while on break, but Thomas had encouraged her to take her time off seriously by doing nothing at all. Never one to be idle, she couldn't stop herself from working on the nursery. This wasn't dry contracts, torts, or mind-numbing procedure. This was relaxing and fun.

Thomas's big hands covered her protruding belly and caressed. At just over twenty-two weeks, she was all baby. The weight she had gained—thirteen pounds so far—had gone straight to her stomach.

"How's Sweet Pea doing today?"

Smiling at the nickname Thomas had taken to calling their baby, Kennedy covered his hands with her own. "Sweet Pea is doing wonderful." She tilted her head to look up at him. "But you know, if it's a boy, you cannot call him Sweet Pea, right?"

"It's a girl," he assured her. "As sweet and beautiful as her mother."

"I hope you're right, if only because everything I've bought so far is pink."

"I'm right." He kissed the nape of her neck. "So. No queasiness?"

"Nope. I think she's decided to take the day off."

Warm breath caressed her ear as Thomas gently bit her lobe. "I'd say that calls for a celebration."

Heat licked up her spine. Morning sickness that lasted long past morning had put a damper on their lovemaking lately. When she wasn't in the bathroom throwing up, she was concentrating on staying still to keep from getting sick. But today, for whatever reason, the baby had decided to give her a break.

Turning in his arms, she whispered against his mouth. "I've missed you."

His mouth covered hers, and Kennedy gave herself up to the delicious and familiar taste of the man she adored. Two years of marriage had only increased her love for him.

He raised his head and dropped a quick kiss on her nose. "Think that'll hold you till tonight?"

Her smile teasing, she winked at him. "Yes, but don't blame me if I get started early."

His gruff laughter was cut off abruptly as he kissed her once more. Before she could pull him in for a deeper connection, he backed away. "Save some for me."

Already tingling in anticipation of the coming night, Kennedy watched him walk away, loving how his swagger denoted confidence without a hint of conceit.

Thomas stopped at the door and looked over his shoulder. "I'll call you before I head home to see what you need."

Blowing him a kiss in thanks, Kennedy turned back to her project, blissfully unaware that it would be the last time she would see her husband alive.

***

Detective Nick Gallagher slid into the front seat of his car, started the engine and flipped on his headlights. Damn, it was already dark. He pulled out of the parking lot and headed in the opposite direction of his apartment, pushing the vision of going home for a quick shower out of his mind. In fact, he'd be lucky to make his date on time. This was the first time today he'd had a few minutes to himself. This morning he'd been tied up in court, waiting to testify in a murder trial. The minute he'd walked out of the courtroom after his testimony, he'd been called in on a double homicide.

He took all of that in stride. He had played this dice when he'd chosen his career path. Sometimes, though, a little downtime to handle personal issues would have been nice.

With that thought in mind, he grabbed his cellphone and punched the speed dial for Thomas. His best friend was a detective in the Narcotics Division. Lately, the only way they'd communicated was through text messages and emails. Yesterday, Nick had gotten an oddly obscure text from him that had put his cop instincts on high alert.

Thomas answered on the first ring. "You forget something?"

"How's that?" Nick asked.

Thomas chuckled. "Hey, Nick. Sorry. I was just talking to Kennedy. She's been having some wild cravings lately, and I figured she'd thought of something else she wanted."

"So you're headed home for the night?"

"After I make a stop at Bailey's grocery."

"Where's that?"

"Corner of Kendrick and Mulberry."

"That's on the other side of town. Why so far?"

"I'm on a mango run. I was in the area last week and picked up some fruit at the store. Kennedy went crazy over the mangoes and asked me to pick up some more. I think she's got some sort of special dessert in mind for tonight."

Nick didn't question his friend's need to please his wife. He'd seen Thomas's devotion to Kennedy firsthand...there was almost nothing he wouldn't do for her. And Kennedy was the same way about her husband. If anyone had the perfect marriage, it was the O'Connells.

"Sounds like you guys have plans for the evening."

"Yeah, something like that. Why? What's up?"

"I thought we might meet later and talk about that text you sent me yesterday. You know...about the Slaters."

The slight pause before Thomas answered told Nick that plans or not, his friend didn't want to discuss the subject. "It's nothing, really. I made a couple of calls, thinking I'd found something interesting, but nothing panned out. Forget about it."

Thomas O'Connell was the finest man Nick knew, but he couldn't lie for shit. Something was definitely going on. "What do you mean you made a couple of calls? To who?"

"No one...really. Just forget I mentioned anything, okay?"

"Look, I'll be the first to admit there's no way the Slaters are as squeaky clean as they pretend. But if you are right, they'll screw up big-time one day and get what's coming to them."

"Yeah, I know that. Like I said, it was just an idea that didn't pan out. I'm over it now. So who's the hottie of the night?"

The less-than-smooth effort to change the subject made Nick even more suspicious. Letting him off the hook for the time being, he said, "Louisa something or other."

"Where'd you meet this one?"

"Belden's party last week."

"Where're you taking her before you take her to bed?"

Nick snorted his disgust. His reputation of being a lady's man was mostly fictional. Yeah, he dated a lot of different women, because he enjoyed their company. Somehow, even Thomas was under the impression that it also meant he had a lot of sex.

"I don't sleep with all of them."

Thomas gave his own snort, this one of disbelief. "Yeah. Right."

Knowing whatever protests he made would only be construed as modest, Nick decided to go back to their original discussion. "Seriously, let's talk about the Slaters tomorrow. If you've got something on your mind, I want to hear about it. Want to meet for lunch at Barney's?"

"Um…yeah…sure, lunch sounds good. But I promise there's nothing to talk about. Gotta go. Catch you later."

Nick cursed softly at the abrupt end to the call. Thomas was definitely keeping something from him. Tomorrow he'd get in his face and make him talk. Screwing around with the Slaters wasn't a good career move. With their kind of influence, they could end a career with a phone call. On the other hand, if Thomas did have something significant on the family, then Nick wanted to know about it.

Mathias Slater and his clan were Texas royalty. Few people in America, much less Texas, hadn't heard of the Slaters. They were one of the oldest and wealthiest families in the country with descendants dating back to the first American settlers. Nothing seemed to tarnish their good image. Even the arrest and conviction of the youngest Slater, Jonah, on a major drug-smuggling charge had done nothing more than elicit sympathy. Shit bounced off of them like they had some kind of protective shield.

Nick knew almost nothing personally about the family—just what he'd seen on the news or read in the paper. One thing he did know was they had major connections. Hell, last week he'd seen a photo of Mathias Slater shaking hands with the president. The family had the kind of influence that most people could only dream of having.

A few months back, Thomas had handled the investigation of Jonah Slater and had given Nick the lowdown. Slater had been caught red-handed with a boatload of illegal drugs. In fact, he'd looked so stinking guilty that Thomas had said he would have suspected the guy had been framed if he hadn't been a Slater. According to Thomas, it'd taken almost no investigation or effort to put Jonah away. He was now serving a hefty sentence in Brownsville.

Mathias Slater had made the most of the publicity. He'd held a press conference, stating that he still loved his son and offered his full support. He'd even donated millions to a drug-rehab facility. Nick had caught the press conference on television and had seen more than a few people wipe away tears.

Thomas had described an incident the day Jonah Slater was sentenced. Said it had given him several sleepless nights. Jonah had been about to walk from the courtroom, his hands and ankles shackled, but he'd stopped in front of Thomas and said, "Hell of an investigation, O'Connell. Hope you didn't break a nail."

Nick agreed it was strange but had encouraged Thomas to let it go. Cryptic remarks from convicted criminals weren't exactly unusual. And prisons were filled with criminals who swore they were innocent. Few freely admitted their guilt.

As Nick pulled in front of Louisa's apartment complex, he glanced at the dashboard clock. Yeah, seven minutes late. Jerking the car door open, Nick strode up the sidewalk. Before he got to Louisa's front door, she had it open for him. Long-legged, honey blond hair, full pouty lips, and exotic eyes. She looked exactly like her magazine photo that had been splashed all over the country last month. Many men would have given their eyeteeth to talk with a cover model much less date one. So why did he want to turn around and walk the other way? Since he already knew the answer to that, he kept moving forward.

Giving her one of his stock smiles in greeting, Nick listened to her chatter with half an ear as he led her to the car. Had she been this talkative last week?

Thankfully, the restaurant wasn't far away. Within minutes of leaving her apartment, they were seated and had ordered their meal.

They were almost through with their appetizer when Nick had to stifle a giant yawn. For the past ten minutes, Louisa had droned on about her weekend in St. Moritz with some Hollywood celebrity. Taking a large bite of his ravioli so he wouldn't have to respond verbally, he chewed, nodded, and did his best to put on an interested expression, wishing like hell he'd never made this date.

"And then Maurice said the funniest thing. He—"

The abrupt ringing of his cellphone was a welcome distraction. Holding his hand up to stop her chatter, Nick answered, "Gallagher."

"Nick, it's Lewis Grimes."

Before he could wonder why the captain of the Narcotics Division was calling, the man continued, "There's been a shooting."

The fine hairs on the back of his neck rose. The instant he heard the victim's name, he went to his feet. "I'll be right there."

He threw a wad of cash on the table. "I gotta go. That should pay for dinner and a cab home."

Before she could open her mouth to answer, Nick was already running toward the door, his date forgotten. His mind screamed a denial, but Grimes's stark words reverberated in his head, refusing to allow him to deny the truth. "Thomas O'Connell has been shot."

WHATEVER IT TAKES
A GREY JUSTICE NOVEL

To Save His Family, She May Be His Only Hope

A Strong-willed Woman

Working for the shadowy division of the Grey Justice Group is the perfect job for Kathleen Callahan. Compartmentalizing and staying detached is her specialty. Get in, do the job, get out, her motto. Wealthy businessman Eli Slater is the only man to penetrate her implacable defenses and she fights to resist him at every turn.

A Tenacious Man

Eli Slater has worked hard to overcome his family's past and repair the damage they caused. A new light comes into his life in the form of security specialist Kathleen Callahan. Even though she rejects him and everything he makes her feel, Eli is relentless in his pursuit, determined to make her his own.

An Evil No One Saw Coming

Darkness has a way of finding and destroying light and Eli learns his family's troubles are far from over. Dealing with threats and attempts on his own life is one thing but when those he loves are threatened, it's a whole new game. And he'll stop at nothing to win.

But evil has a familiar face, along with an unimaginable goal of destruction, putting both Eli and Kathleen in the crosshairs and threatening the happiness they never believed they'd find.

CHAPTER ONE

Slater House Hotel

Chicago

"Did you sleep well last night, Sophia?"

"Yes, Daddy," Sophia said with an emphatic nod. "I went to sleep right after story time. Slept all night long."

Not to be outdone, four-year-old Violet chimed in, "Me, too, Daddy. I slept-ed all night long, too."

"Good for you both. I know Miss Teresa appreciates what good girls you're being while Daddy's away."

"What are you eating for breakfast, Daddy?" Sophia moved closer to the screen to see what was on Eli's table. "We're eating strawberry pancakes."

"I wish I could have something that yummy. I'm just eating plain old boring cereal."

"When are you coming home?"

"Soon, I promise, Violet."

"Miss you, Daddy."

Eli's heart clutched, as it always did at the sheer sweetness of his daughters. There was no artifice, no hiding. Talking to them after a day of negotiating, dealing with fake smiles and hidden agendas was as refreshing as diving into a pool of cool water on a hot Texas day. This was the reason he continued despite all the worries and problems he had taken on. If not for Violet and Sophia, he wasn't sure he would have retained his sanity.

"It's time to get ready for school, girls," Teresa said. "Say good-bye to your daddy."

In between smooching sounds and "I love you's," he watched his daughters leave the kitchen table.

As soon as they'd left the room, Teresa Longview, nanny, housekeeper, cook, and all-around lifesaver, came on the screen. "They miss you, Mr. Eli, but they're doing just fine."

"Thank you for taking such good care of them."

"They're a pleasure, sir. You know that."

"Anything I need to know about?"

"No, sir. It's been amazingly quiet. Seems like everything is settling into place...finally getting back to normal."

Eli hoped that was true but didn't count on anything these days. "No odd incidents? Phone calls?"

"No, sir. I've been very careful with everything, just like you warned me."

That was a relief. It'd taken almost a year, but the Slaters were finally back on the right track. But just because he'd worked his ass off to clean up the mess didn't mean everyone was happy. No doubt there were still plenty of people who would love to see the Slaters completely decimated.

"Thanks for being vigilant, Teresa. I don't expect any problems but can't let my guard down."

"I understand, Mr. Eli."

"I'll call back tonight at bedtime."

"We'll look forward to it. Have a good day."

"You, too, Teresa."

Eli closed his laptop, now ready to start his day. A few minutes spent with his daughters were better than any vitamin ever created.

So far, having Slater as a last name hadn't impacted his children. The girls were just babies, much too young to comprehend. They still believed they lived in a safe, sane world. His daughters had no idea that it was all a lie—a lie he would willingly tell for as long as he could get away with it. He would do whatever he had to do to protect them from the family they'd had the misfortune to be born into and the world they would eventually have to face.

He had learned that hell the hard way. In one seemingly endless nightmare, his life had imploded. It had begun with the murder of his wife, Shelley—although he hadn't known it was a murder at the time. Eli had believed, as he was meant to, that she had taken her own life. Unintentionally, yes. Mixing booze and drugs was always a bad idea. And for Shelley, who'd been both an alcoholic and a drug addict, it had been a lethal combination.

After Shelley's death, he'd been hanging on, barely, but he'd been surviving. Then the clouds had gathered above them, the storm had settled in, and the shit had come down in torrents.

All of that was behind them now, but not without loss…not without major consequences.

Mathias, his father, was dead. And after an excruciatingly long and painful trial, his brother Adam was in prison, where the bastard would spend the rest of his miserable life.

Eli had worked like a demon to repair the damage the two had created. He had bartered, badgered, apologized, and pleaded, then scrubbed and scoured, doing everything he could to erase what Mathias had spent a lifetime creating. Businesses had been sold, stocks and bonds liquidated and contracts demolished. All the records found, in both Adam's and Mathias's offices, had been examined with a fine-tooth comb with one intent—to remove the scourge his father and brother had perpetrated.

Eli had succeeded. And while the Slater name still had a black cloud hanging over it, and the family's wealth had been cut in half, at least they could all sleep at night. Perhaps by the time his daughters were grown, being a Slater would be something to be proud of again.

His mother and sister were in France, as far away from this mess as he could get them. And Jonah, his youngest brother, understandably bitter, was on a personal mission of vengeance. Eli worried for him but understood. Jonah had yet to come to terms with everything that had happened…everything he had lost.

He and Jonah were like two survivors of the same catastrophe. So far neither of them had been able to discuss that night, or the events that had led up to it.

Eli leaned back in his chair, wishing once again that he hadn't had to come to Chicago. He didn't like being away from home, but traveling was sometimes an unavoidable burden. Whenever he did travel, he had breakfast via webcam with the girls each morning, and each night at bedtime, he called and read them a story. It wasn't as good as being there in person, but the girls seemed to enjoy the uniqueness of talking to their daddy via video.

Standing, Eli went to the bedroom and started dressing for the day. He clicked on the television, more for noise than to listen to the news. His mind on the myriad items he needed to accomplish, he didn't catch the beginning of the news story that was now on. It wasn't until he heard a husky, feminine voice thick with emotion that he paid attention. He turned to see the owner of that voice and froze in place, mesmerized.

"I have nothing to say to you people. You've gotten all you're getting from my family."

"Miss Callahan, do you feel shame for your sister? Not only for being a prostitute but for being accused of so cold-bloodedly killing Frank Braden?"

Fire burned in extraordinary eyes of aqua blue. "Do you feel shame for your stupid questions?" she sneered.

Undeterred, the reporter continued, "You're testifying today. What will you tell the court?"

Shoulders straight, expression resolute, she said fiercely, "That my sister was taken advantage of. She was not a prostitute. And that she most definitely did not kill Frank Braden."

She turned her back to the camera and strode rapidly away.

A smug smile tugged at the reporter's mouth. "To recap, the trial of Alice Callahan, who is accused of murdering local businessman Frank Braden, will resume this morning at ten o'clock. And as we just heard, today's testimony will include Kathleen Callahan, the accused's sister. Considering what we've learned so far, one can only speculate what today's revelations will be. Reporting from Cook County Courthouse, this is April Majune."

Eli clicked off the television, but it didn't matter. The image of Kathleen Callahan's captivating face stayed etched in his mind. The husky, musical tone of her voice was a sound he knew he'd never forget.

Returning to the kitchen table where he'd left his laptop, Eli opened it and entered the names Callahan and Braden into a search engine. He had heard nothing about the trial. Dallas and Chicago were hundreds of miles from each other. And having no love for the media and their shenanigans, he usually avoided the news, local and national, as much as possible.

A lengthy list of hits appeared. Eli clicked on one and skimmed the information. The more he read, the more intrigued he became. Exiting out of one site, he scrolled down until he came to the name Kathleen Callahan. Clicking on that one, Eli stared hard at the photograph of one of the most striking women he'd ever seen. This shot had been taken at a happier time in Kathleen's life. Though still not smiling, there were no tension lines around her mouth, no shadows beneath her eyes.

His gaze moved to the text, and once again he became immersed, unaccountably fascinated, so deeply engrossed that when his cellphone rang, it took him several seconds to identify the sound.

He headed back to the bedroom and grabbed his phone. When he saw the caller's name on the screen, and then the time, he winced. Dammit, he was never late.

"Hugh?"

"Eli, everything okay?"

"Yes. Sorry. I know we were supposed to meet downstairs. I—" Making a split decision, Eli said, "Listen, there's been a change of plans. Come up to my room and let's talk. I need to move some appointments around."

Thankful that his assistant wasn't one to ask needless questions, Eli ended the call and then immediately pressed a speed-dial number to one of his most trusted friends.

"Justice. Eli. You have any information on a case in Chicago involving the murder of a Frank Braden?"

Grey Justice wasn't often taken by surprise, but Eli could hear it in the man's voice—his British accent always became a little crisper. "Frank Braden? Chicago? Not that I recall. Is it something I should check out?"

"Yes. I'd—" He'd what? What was he going to say? That he'd seen a beautiful woman on television, looked her up on the Internet, and was now obsessed with knowing more? Hell.

"The case sounds like something you'd be interested in." Eli winced at the lameness of his answer.

"Is that right?" The slight amusement in Justice's tone told Eli that he hadn't fooled his friend in the least.

Eli relayed the basic facts. Grey Justice and his people could find out everything about the case within a matter of a few clicks. And even though Eli's interest in Kathleen was definitely personal, what he'd told Justice was true. This case sounded perfect for the Grey Justice Group.

"Let me look into it," Justice said. "I'll get back to you."

Eli returned the phone to the desk and stared out at the Chicago skyline. He had no explanation for what he was about to do. Impulsiveness had been beaten out of him long ago, and damned if he could begin to formulate a reason for his actions. Never in his life had he had such a visceral reaction to a woman. Something about Kathleen Callahan called to him, compelled him to know more. Despite all the scheduling problems, the headaches he was about to cause, Eli refused to not see this out.

Made in the USA
San Bernardino, CA
10 July 2016